The
Long
Search
for Home

Ray Wenck

This novel is dedicated to the men and women of the 180th Fighter Wing of the Ohio Air National Guard

Part One

One

THE CHILL THAT RAN down her spine was all the warning Becca needed. They were getting closer. Her breaths came in deep painful gulps, but to quit would be the end. Knowing what they'd do if they caught her, she raced on, ignoring the pain. But the outcome was inevitable. They were bigger, stronger, and more numerous.

Sprinting hard over the open high grass of what had once been a golf course, she reached down and found the handle of the long survival knife her father had given her many years before. A knife she never believed she'd ever have a need for. In mid-stride, she yanked it free of the sheath strapped along her thigh. With the blade now rising and falling in her hand like a relay racer's baton, her father flashed through her mind. He was the reason for this journey. If she was going down, she would make him proud.

The pain in her side was almost unbearable, like a knife being pushed deeper with each stride. The thundering footsteps of her pursuers echoed behind her in time with the pounding in her chest. Becca would have to make her stand soon. The potential safety of the trees ahead were not in reach.

As she readied for the battle, she thought of her

brother. *Where the hell was Bobby*? He had gone ahead while she rested, before the men found her and gave chase. If she survived this attack and found he was watching her from a distance, with one swipe of her knife, Becca would make him her sister.

Her pursuers grunted as they pushed harder to overtake her. It was time to face them, before they took her down. She was determined to cause as much pain as possible. These fools had picked the wrong fair maiden.

Stopping took three hard steps to slow and turn. With a savage scream, she whipped the blade in a high arcing backhand swing. The honed edge tore through the first assailant's throat. The man clutched at his neck as blood spurted into the air in a crimson fountain.

The dying man's body bumped her as he fell. The second man launched at her. Becca just managed to face him when he struck her high on the chest. The blade impaled the man's large bare gut, but his momentum drove her over backward. They rolled in a heap, coming to a stop with her hand still clutching the blade, but the man's body pinned them both to the ground.

The third and fourth men arrived together, hooting at their captured prize. With a huge evil smile, the first man reached for her. She raised a foot to kick him away, but he grabbed it and laughed. That was when the third eye appeared on his forehead wiping the smile off his face. His body stood for a second as if to say, "Damn, so close," before collapsing.

Bobby!

As the body fell, the fourth man stood gaping. He stopped unfastening his pants, a frantic, almost deranged look on his bearded face. Given the brief gift of time, Becca threw a shoulder into the corpse that still trapped her knife. The body slid and started to roll.

Another shot snapped the man's attention from Becca, causing him to duck. After a third, he screamed, yet still

4

he stood, unharmed, frozen in place, his manhood clutched tightly in his hand.

He looked behind him. Becca watched him as she freed one leg, pressed her foot against the weight, and pushed. He snarled, focused his wild eyes back on Becca, and pulled his knife. "Bitch," he spat.

With the blade forward like a spear, he lunged to skewer her. Becca slid free from the body, emitting her own growl. Yanking her blade free, she rolled. Rather than immobilize her, as her fear would've done just weeks before, she used the angst to spur movement. The knife wielder was unable to stop his thrust as Becca moved. The downward jab threw his weight forward and off balance. Heart racing, Becca spun on her bottom. Before her assailant could right himself and turn for a second attack, she screamed and dived at his leg, slicing clean through his Achilles tendon.

The man screamed and hobbled on one leg. Becca rolled clear as the wounded man dropped the knife and fell to the ground, clutching his injured foot. Becca stood and glared down at him. She ignored the sweat burning her eyes. Her breaths came in short, harsh gulps, exploding from her. Her victim rolled from side to side. Two more bodies lay a few yards back. *I should've known. Bobby never missed.*

The wounded man whimpered. She stood over him, void of emotion. The man pleaded, first for his life, and then for help with his wound.

Steps thundered from behind. Becca spun and crouched, ready again to do battle.

"Becca." A concerned young man, rifle in hand stopped ten feet from her. "Are you all right?"

All Becca saw was another enemy. With great effort, she sucked in a deep breath and blew it out. She relaxed and lowered the knife. Bobby came closer, and then she nailed her brother with a punch to the chest that rocked him back a step.

"Ow!"

"That's for taking your time shooting those assholes."

"I wasn't taking my time. I was in those woods scouting on the other side. I didn't even know those hounds had picked up your scent."

She snorted at the appropriate use of terms. She shuddered at the thought of what they would have done to her had they managed to take her down.

Bobby stepped forward to put an arm around Becca's shoulders. "Hey, Sis, I'm sorry. You know I wouldn't play games with your safety. Are you all right?"

Becca cringed. She hated being comforted by him. She wanted to shake him off to show she didn't need his sympathy, but in truth she did need him. She wanted to cry and bury her head in his chest, but this new world had stolen any real emotion from her weeks ago. Everyone she had ever cared about was dead – everyone but Bobby and, hopefully, her father, mother, and little brother.

She was so different now and struggled with the conflict within her as if she were two separate people inhabiting one body. Gone was the spoiled, self-absorbed young woman, leaving a shell driven by some strange wild creature. Confused and angry, with each passing day Becca seemed to lose more of her previous identity.

No, she didn't want to be coddled by her brother, but the small part of her old self that still existed craved the simple comfort.

Bobby held his sister, but not too close. He was well aware of the knife still hanging at her side. Becca was capable of instant and violent reactions. He feared he was losing her, and the thought scared him. When he had seen that pack of animals closing in on her, the fear of failing made keeping his hands steady difficult. He had to stop once, take two quick calming breaths to chase away any emotion, before acquiring his target. He was almost too late. He fought off his own shudder for fear Becca might feel it too.

Pressing ahead of his sister to scout their path had been stupid. That decision had almost cost Becca her life. He vowed never to make that mistake again. Twice today his poor judgment had cost them. They were lucky to be alive. This new world did not allow too many second chances.

With a sigh, Bobby gave his sister a squeeze and whispered, "I'm sorry, Sis, but we need to get away from here before someone else finds us."

Becca moved away from him and wiped her face. "You can't go wandering off like that anymore. You hear me?"

Bobby nodded. "I know. I'm sorry." To change the subject and avoid her accusing eyes, he added, "Let's see if they have anything of value and get moving."

Ignoring the wounded man, they went through the nearest bodies finding very little that was useful. Four handguns, four knives, and two granola bars. The two dead men farther back yielded another handgun and a shotgun.

"Ready?" Bobby asked.

"Yep." Becca started back the way they had come.

"Wait! Where you going?"

"Back to get our stuff."

"No, wait." Bobby ran to catch up with her. "We'll be walking right back into trouble."

His sister continued walking.

"I don't care. I want our things."

"Becca, listen. By now those scavengers have taken everything of value."

"No, they haven't. They've taken all the food and

7

water, but not what was valuable."

"Food and water are the most valuable commodities now. They're long gone. It's not worth the risk to go back there. You're only asking to attract more trouble."

"No, Bobby, they're the ones who asked for trouble when they tried to carjack us." She whirled on him.

He stopped abruptly to avoid running into her.

"And for your information, the pictures and scrapbooks are the most valuable things we brought with us. They are the only things we have to remind us of our past, of our family. They are important to me. I will not lose them."

"But, Sis —"

"No!" she screamed, turning on him. Her nostrils flared and eyes narrowed. "I need them. I need them to remind me of better times. I need them because they give me hope that perhaps one day life can be as good again as they were in those pictures. They may be all that's left of what our family was once like. I can't leave them, Bobby. I won't."

She spun around, walking briskly again.

Behind them the injured man yelled, "Please, you can't leave me here."

In an instant, Becca pivoted, let out a war cry, and sprinted toward the lone survivor.

Fearing the carnage, Bobby tried to stop her, but she busted through his arms driving an elbow into his chest. When she reached the man she kicked him twice. He cried out in pain. Then, as Bobby watched in shock, she lifted her foot and stomped on the man's head. He no longer cried.

"Bastard!" She spat on him and stormed back toward Bobby.

As she passed him, her face appeared unlined and calm. She smiled. "Come on, baby brother, let's go get our stuff." She laughed, pushed an arm in the air and released a triumphant shout.

Bobby followed. He marveled at the changes in his sister but those changes frightened him, too. She had always been beautiful, smart, and popular, but she had been so lost in herself she seldom noticed others. Now her beautiful face had sunken cheeks, dark-circled eyes, and she had lost the extra pounds her sedentary lifestyle had gathered. She was a hardened, lean woman who had killed several times to survive. Bobby liked this new version of Becca much better, but he was also afraid of and for her. Volatile and often unpredictable, she was strong now and he could rely on her in dangerous situations. But he was never sure of how she'd react.

He jogged to catch up to her. "Becca, did you forget they also have control of our arsenal as well? We didn't get a good look at how many of them there were. But if they got their hands on the weapons we stashed, it's gonna be real hard getting your pictures back."

Again she turned on him, this time advancing. "Our pictures, Bobby. They're *our* pictures, of *our* family. How are you going to feel if we get home and find" – she choked – "that they're all dead?"

"Don't say that, Becca. Don't even think it." Bobby swallowed hard and looked away. He didn't want to think about that possibility. Pushing her words from his mind, he softened his voice, "Becca, we have to hope."

"Dead. Dead. Dead. What if this entire trip is for nothing? Won't you wish you had those scrapbooks then to remind you of who they were and what they looked like?"

Crying, she turned and stormed off. "Well, I'm going even if I have to go alone."

Bobby stood while she lengthened the distance between them. She really pissed him off sometimes. But her words had struck home. What if their parents were dead? His throat constricted, but just as fast he said

9

aloud, "No! I won't think about this now." A quick backhand across his eyes removed any potential tears. Frowning, he ran after her. Without a word he pulled up in stride next to her.

"Okay, but follow my lead when we get there."

"Dream on, dumb jock."

"God, you can really be annoying."

"And you can really be a pain in the ass."

"Bitch."

"Prick."

Within three steps, they were both laughing.

"Let's do this, Sis."

"You know it, little brother. And I better not find anyone wearing my new shoes or I'm really going to have to hurt someone."

Bobby smiled. That was the old Becca.

Two

THE SKY HAD DARKENED by the time they made it back to the car. A party appeared to be in progress, the celebration in full swing. Women were trying on Becca's salvaged wardrobe of expensive designer clothes. They were perhaps the last remnants of the woman she used to be. They screeched and laughed as they swirled in front of each other as though they were in some bizarre fashion show.

The men were firing off their new weapons as if they had an unending supply of bullets. The cases of food were torn apart, and empty cans and containers lay strewn across a wide area.

Somewhere to the right, a man and woman were getting busy. The woman had one of Becca's tight skirts lifted up around her neck as the man grunted with each push.

"Ew!" Becca whispered from behind a row of pine trees along the side of the road. "That skirt cost a lot of money."

"Seriously! That's what you're thinking about?"

"Oh, shut up."

Bobby scanned left to right, trying to get an accurate count of armed men. Six men and four women. The three women not involved in sex stood at the side of the car, rummaging through boxes.

Becca tensed when one of the women looked through a

scrapbook and pitched it aside like worthless garbage. Bobby grabbed her arm and held her in place. A low animalistic growl poured from her throat.

"Easy, Sis. Give me a chance to form a plan."

She relaxed, but her gaze never left the woman.

The car was right where they had left it when they'd been forced to flee for their lives. Fortunately, the attacking mob was not well organized. They also were not very good shots.

Bobby and Becca had been driving down a country road not twenty miles from their destination – home – when a car shot out of the driveway of a farmhouse and broadsided them. The impacting car continued plowing forward until the siblings' car was sideways in a shallow drainage ditch. Bobby's shooting kept the attackers at bay while Becca climbed up and out through her window. She then laid down covering fire, allowing Bobby to get clear. A brief gun battle ensued until Bobby saw they were being flanked. Time to run.

When the pursuers seemed to have given up, Bobby told his sister to take a breather while he scouted ahead. Soon Becca had attracted the six men they had put down on the golf course.

The men were on the far side of the car drinking the warm beer Bobby had hidden inside the trunk. Becca wouldn't have approved of the use of space. If they could sneak up on the women on the near side of the car, they might be able to gather the things Becca wanted and get away before the men knew they were there. Of course, they would have to subdue and secure the women first.

"I've got a plan," Becca said. "I'm going to take care of the lovers to balance out the odds a bit." Her knife slid cleanly from the sheath.

Bobby stared at his sister. He had seen Becca kill but never relish it as she appeared to now. He touched her arm. "Sis, remember these people are only trying to survive just as we are. We don't necessarily need to kill them all."

"Listen, little brother," she spat with venom. "You see what that man is doing to that woman? Their friends wanted to do that to me before they killed me. Don't preach to me about killing. We didn't attack them. They attacked us. There was no talk, just violence. We didn't ask for this new world, but we have to live in it. Killing seems to be an acceptable part of it now."

When Becca had been forced to kill someone for the first time, she had cried, vomited, and cried some more. Now she had no qualms about taking another's life. She seemed to take pleasure in killing. That was what frightened Bobby most.

"Just remember, we need to survive too. Don't go crazy and draw the others' attention."

"Don't worry. You just keep the others off me." Becca slithered away like a ninja.

Bobby loved his sister, but she was scaring him. Her body wasn't the only thing that had hardened over the past month. The scars of the new world were leaving a permanent personality change on her. He needed to watch her closely.

As Becca disappeared into the long grass, Bobby moved left to have a shot at the men. If he timed it right with their target shooting he could drop two of them before they knew what was happening. The rest he'd keep pinned down until Becca made her move. He wished his sister had been more reasonable and willing to develop a real plan. She often reacted without thinking. Even if she retrieved the boxes she wanted, they had no way of hauling them out of there. They had no means of escape other than on foot. He had to plan on the fly.

The pickup truck that rammed them into the ditch was now sitting in the middle of the street crossways. What were the odds the keys were inside? He looked back at the men. Unless they were all totally drunk or stupid, they weren't going to stand still and let him shoot them. He and Becca would have to run through open ground to get to a ride.

Glancing to his right, Bobby's breath caught. One of the women headed for the copulating couple. The other two were watching and laughing. The approaching woman was swirling the dress she had donned and hiking it higher. He hadn't been able to persuade his sister to leave her wardrobe. The abuse of one of her dresses wouldn't go over well with Becca. The woman was either taunting the two or lining up to be next. Whatever her intentions, she had no idea she was heading toward certain death.

A nervous sensation spread throughout his gut as he moved. *Dammit, Becca.* They should have waited. At least until after dark. Now it was going to get bloody.

Bobby looked back at the woman. She had the dress hiked up to her chest, attempting to squat down over the other woman's face. The volume of laughter increased as the other two women joined in.

"Stop!" the woman on the bottom shouted, but she also seemed to be laughing.

"If you don't want it, I'll take it," the man said.

He pushed his face toward the woman's body. She dropped the dress over the man's head and squealed. The laughter grew louder. Some of the men turned to look.

"Don't do it, Becca. Don't do it," Bobby whispered, as he hurried to find a good shooting spot.

Becca rose from behind the squatting woman. She was in full view of everyone except the threesome.

Shit!

Bobby swung back to the men. They had yet to understand what they were seeing, but they were no longer target shooting. After his first shot, they'd know his location. He had to shoot fast which increased his chances of missing. He took a deep breath and lined up his first shot.

Three

BECCA CREPT CLOSER. Once the bitch who was wearing her dress – her favorite dress – squatted her nasty body down and covered the man and woman's faces, she moved.

She pushed the laughing and body slapping and gurgling sounds from her mind and concentrated on her target. The man was first, then she'd take care of the bitch in the dress. The woman had ruined it already by putting it on her skanky body.

Becca rose behind the woman, knife held high. She plunged the knife into the man's back. His legs and head arced upward, his scream muffled. Becca repeated the process, cutting his pain short.

The woman on top started to scream. Becca backhanded her across the face, knocking her backward off the other woman and sent her rolling down the ditch. *Damn, I wanted to cut her.* Becca pulled out her gun, and as the other woman pushed clear of the man's body, she brought the gun down on her head twice. The woman ceased to move.

Becca moved toward the car. Bullets whizzed around her as she refocused on her surroundings. Another shot rang out, and for the moment no more shots came her way. *Bobby.* She bolted for the car where the remaining two women huddled.

BOBBY FOUND THE MAN shooting at Becca, sighted, and fired. The first man dropped. The other men became instant motion. Some ducked, two ran, and one stood there shooting at Becca. The two running fired in Bobby's direction. The bullets were closer than he'd have liked, but with one of them taking shots at his sister, he couldn't move or take cover. He aimed and fired again. The shooter went down.

Bobby moved, wanting to stay away from the car. He wanted to keep some distance so they weren't trapped together in the same area. Ducking, he ran back then to the left. Twenty feet later, he stopped and sighted through the rifle's scope. Several seconds later he acquired another target. One man ran toward the car, keeping low, an immediate threat to Becca.

He made some adjustments to account for the moving target, thankful for the training his father had given him years before when deer hunting. Bobby released his breath and squeezed the trigger. The man pitched sideways, but the way he fell led Bobby to believe he had either missed or only wounded him. He couldn't dwell on it, he searched for another target.

BECCA DUCKED BEHIND THE car. She waited while she caught her breath from the dash. For one instant she worried about confronting the two women, but then she remembered she wouldn't be there at all if they hadn't crashed into Bobby and her and stole their things. Anger reared up again and she moved. The two women huddled together, covering each other. Becca crawled to them.

"Hey, you stupid bitches, where's my stuff?"

The women jumped and let out screams, clutching at each other for support.

Becca pushed the gun into the taller of the frightened women. Her eyes rolled up and she fainted. Becca turned to the shorter woman. "I need an answer."

"We didn't know it was important stuff. Honest."

Becca felt a chill. Her stomach did a flip, threatening a revolt. Her voice hardened. "What. Did. You. Do?"

"The men took the boxes. They said something about using them to start a fire." She ducked and covered her head. "Please, don't shoot me."

"Fire!" Panic set in. The bile rose. She lowered the gun as the first retch hit. "No!" Becca took rapid quick breaths then allowed the anger to take over. That quick her stomach settled. She reached up and opened the rear door. The back seat was empty save for a few loose clothes. Becca slapped the woman, grabbed her hair, and yanked her head up. She let out a scream.

"Where is it?" Becca moved within inches of the woman's face.

"I-I don't know," she cried. "They took everything with them."

Becca was a second from banging the woman's head against the car when a noise drew her attention. Someone was on the other side of the car. She doubted Bobby was there. He would know enough to keep his distance to avoid having two targets in the same place.

A quick flick of the woman's eyes looking past Becca told her a lot. She jumped past the woman, turned, and fired. Repeated shots exploded from both directions. The woman let out several screams, and then the firing stopped. Becca was sure she'd hit the man, but couldn't tell how bad. The woman lay in a bloody heap in front of her.

Becca backed to the front of the car while watching near the trunk. She risked a peek around the front bumper. It was clear. She hugged the bumper and looked in both directions. Nothing moved. Everything had gone still.

Four

BOBBY MOVED. He was afraid to lose sight of his sister, especially now that shots had been fired from her area, but to stay in one spot allowed his opponents to pin him down and flank his position.

He crawled faster than intended, farther to his left until he came to a tree. Shots were fired near the car. Bobby had to find Becca. Staying prone, he scanned the car through the scope. No air escaped his lungs until he found her. Nothing. Anxiety built. Bobby swung the rifle toward the other side of the car. He almost jumped to his feet as she came into view. Becca was at the front bumper. Her gun pointed down the driver's side, but her face and knife were facing the other way.

Bobby let the crosshairs play down the length of the car. Maybe he could take the threat away from Becca. Movement off to the side made his heart jump. He swung toward it. One of the women ran away. By the time he moved back to Becca, Bobby almost missed the action.

Men popped out from both sides of the car, trying to catch Becca in their crossfire. Becca's gun bucked in her hand. The bullet flew wild. She dived to the ground facing the passenger side. Bobby watched as she stretched her body to see around the tire.

Bobby fired in haste and missed. The man at the rear bumper flinched and ducked. *Where was the second man?*

In a panic, Bobby moved his sights. The second shooter peeked around the front bumper. He was behind Becca. Bobby shifted the rifle, sighted, then a bullet struck the tree inches from his face. His chest tightened: he was too late. Without taking aim, he fired a hasty shot hoping to distract the shooter. The bullet pinged off the hood two feet in front of the gunman, but had the desired effect. He shrugged downward, ducking any further shots, his own shot forgotten.

Bobby took the chance to line up a better shot. The shooter at the rear of the car exchanged shots with Becca. To his left, someone was running, perhaps looking for a better angle from which to shoot Bobby. To protect Becca, Bobby pushed the danger aside. As the gunman behind Becca lined up a shot, Bobby pulled the trigger. The shot was not fatal. Bobby had little to target. The impact threw the would-be assassin forward. He hung over the fender.

More shots drew Bobby's attention. Becca was on the ground firing. Using both hands now, she pulled the trigger in a steady cadence, one after the other, until the second shooter fell back on his butt. He looked from his bloody hands to Becca. Seconds later, his face erupted as Becca's next shot tore through it.

More movement to his left forced Bobby to focus his attention there, Becca was safe for the moment. He snapped the rifle in that direction. Running figures headed away from the battle. Bobby let them go. He would not kill if there was no threat. This new, more violent, world had not corrupted him that badly, yet. Besides, so few people were left in the world now, how many more had to die before they neared extinction?

Becca crawled around the car, but Bobby stayed on vigil in case another threat appeared. He waited until Becca called to him.

"Bobby. I need your help here. They're all gone. Give me a hand, would ya?"

Bobby waited a few more minutes to make sure her calls hadn't attracted a hidden assassin. In a crouch, he made his way to the car.

"Most of it's still here, but those bastards scattered a bunch." Becca gathered the spilled family mementos and replaced them in the boxes. Then she found the smoldering remains of the fire. Small whimpers came from her as she clawed at the ashes. "Aw, no!" Becca wailed. "No! No! No! No!" Becca wrapped her arms around her torso and cried.

Bobby's heart ached, but for his sister's agony, not the loss of the pictures. His eyes moistened. How much more could his sister endure? Using a sleeve he wiped his eyes.

"Don't just stand there. Help me collect the rest of it."

Once more, he worried about his sister's state of mind. "Becca," he said, his voice soft, "we need to go before others arrive."

"I'm not leaving these things here. If you help me, we can get away faster."

Bobby scanned the area through the scope to make sure no one was lurking, waiting for them to let their guard down. He squatted next to his sister. "Becca. Becca!"

She finally looked up. A brief flicker of red ignited her eyes. Bobby flinched. The devil? He let out a breath. Only a reflection of the setting sun behind him.

"You keep gathering whatever you want to take with us. I'm going to see if I can get the truck started."

Her smile was suddenly angelic. "Okay." She dropped her head and continued crawling around, picking up her belongings.

Bobby prayed they found their parents alive. He feared for Becca's sanity if they were … not.

He walked to the truck.

Five

No one else arrived to take shots at them. Becca collected the majority of her precious things. The rest they found in the fire pit, blackened corners of photos and ash all that remained. The keys were still in the truck's ignition. They packed up the truck and gathered whatever weapons and ammunition they could from their attackers. Becca cried to entire time. When she came to the wounded man in front of the car, emotions filled and erupted in rage. She fell on the man plunging her knife repeatedly into him long after he was dead.

Bobby watched in shock, unable to move and pull her away. When she reached the truck, blood soaked her shirt and coated her face. She flashed a smile through the red mask reminding him of many horror movies he'd seen. She climbed in and in a calm voice said, "I'm hungry," as if nothing had happened.

Fighting off a shudder and praying he never made her that angry, Bobby drove off without headlights, away from the ambush site.

Darkness had fallen by the time they left. Driving on the unlit country roads was difficult. Unable to see for any distance, the driving was slow.

Less than an hour later, Bobby pulled into a long driveway that wound through trees. He stopped in front of a large house that appeared deserted. He got out, checked the area, and decided to stop there for the night.

"Let's get some sleep. If we don't have any more delays, we should be there early tomorrow."

"Okay." Becca's voice was that of a child. She crawled between the seats and spread out in the extend-a-cab back seat. She had brought a pillow from her dorm. One side was smudged with grass stains now. She fluffed it a few times, snuggled her head into it and said, "Goodnight, Bobby. I love you."

"Goodnight, Sis. Love you, too."

Bobby lifted his legs and stretched them across the front seat. He replaced the missing bullets and slid the magazine back in place. He set the rifle, stock first, on the floor so it stood next to him. He placed his handgun on the dashboard. Sleep for him was not in the plans. Bobby could not shut his mind off. Too many thoughts. So much had happened in such a short time.

He let out a deep breath and allowed the now familiar pictures to play past his eyes like some bizarre drive-in movie theater. For Bobby, sleep wouldn't come until the movie ran out. Each day created a new chapter. It had become a nightly routine, a pre-sleep nightmare. Bobby kept the movie playing in his head. Maybe somewhere in there were answers to their current situation.

Less than a month ago people started dying. With no explanation and no help, the local population dropped in massive numbers. Panic spread as answers never came from those in positions of power. The survivors went crazy. Looting and violence took over as people struggled to survive, the battle for food and water fiercer than the oil wars ever were. The cities were to be avoided unless desperate.

Before the TV stations shut down, reports spoke of

possible terrorist action involving some deadly virus. Flu-like symptoms occurred first, followed by painful cramping and vomiting. Within two to five days, the victim succumbed. Whatever happened the powers-that-be were caught unprepared with no way of stopping the germ's progress. The disease struck too swiftly. Health care providers were overwhelmed and not immune to the virus's effects. With their numbers dwindling, no one was left to treat the patients or do the research needed to combat the disease.

Bobby had been a second-year engineering student at the University of Cincinnati. Becca was a senior in the musical theater department at Ohio Northern. A smile tugged at the corner of his lips. She had been such a snobbish diva.

Talented, Becca might have had a career in the theater or movies. Now she was a hard-assed killer with a confused, embattled mind. She looked nothing like his sister anymore. Again, Bobby prayed his parents were still alive. He feared she might be lost forever if they finished their journey only to find they had died.

With the world around him crumbling and becoming more deadly, Bobby left Cincinnati in hopes of finding Becca. Why did some die and others were spared? If genes played a part, maybe Becca was alive.

The trip that normally took an hour and a half at best had taken three days. The highways were clogged with crashed and stalled vehicles. People had tried to flee the city. Many perished along the way, their bodies still behind the wheels of the wall of cars.

Several times, Bobby was forced to leave his current ride and hike to the front of a traffic jam to find another. He dragged the bodies to the side of the road, said a silent prayer over them, and drove off.

Twice along the way, he had been attacked. The first had been only ten miles from the city when he had just cleared a massive traffic jam.

THE STENCH OF THE bodies was enough to make him walk a wide berth from the road until he reached the front. He hopped in a newer Cadillac and was still in rearview mirror sight of the cars when a man stepped out from behind a metal guardrail and waved him down.

"Hey, Bud, am I glad to see you. How 'bout giving a fellow survivor a ride?"

The man wore a big smile and a baggy shirt that covered the gun behind his back. Relieved at first to see another living person, something in the man's demeanor set off Bobby's internal alarms. Confusion slowed his reactions. Before Bobby could answer, movement from the opposite side of the road caught his eye.

Two more men, guns in hand, emerged from the drainage ditch and ran to the car. The passenger side door was already being opened by the time he moved. A fist seemed to grip his heart and squeeze. Turning back he caught a glimpse of a gun moving toward his head. Without freezing in panic, he floored the accelerator, throwing the man off balance. The shot that would have ended his life blew through the roof. The man tried to hold onto the door, but as the heavy Cadillac lurched forward, he was dragged a few feet before falling along the roadside.

The other two men opened fire and drilled numerous holes in the car's frame. Unfortunately, several had a fatal effect. Less than a mile farther the car slowed, sputtered, and died. Bobby leaped out of the driver's seat. He grabbed the backpack he had brought with him, keenly aware that the men were giving pursuit. He slipped his hand inside, wrapped it around the revolver that only held six rounds, and pulled it free.

Hesitating a few seconds, he wondered whether he should he use the car for cover and try to pick off his assailants. He wasn't sure he could kill another person.

24

Perhaps if he fired a few warning shots, they'd see he was armed and back away. In the end, as they drew nearer, he turned and fled.

Two of the men continued the chase. The only things he had in his pack were some clothes, a few bags of snack foods, and several bottles of water. The monetary system had changed. Food and water were the new currency.

Bobby considered shrugging out of the backpack and letting them have it. The granola bars and water bottles weren't enough to die for. Inner anger triggered within him. A snarl grew deep inside and rose to his throat. They'd have to kill him to take what was his.

Now he was willing to kill to keep what was his.

As he passed a short bridge over a small creek, Bobby ducked behind the far cement guardrail. Trying to force his breathing under control, he placed his hand on the rail for support and leveled the gun at the oncoming men. They were either unaware he held a gun or didn't care, because they kept coming.

The distance grew shorter and the men screamed like attacking barbarian warriors from long ago. Bobby had to let them get closer for the handgun to be effective. The seconds dragged. As the men advanced, they began shooting. Even with bullets flying around him, Bobby still hesitated. These were living men. But when a bullet threw stone chips between his feet, Bobby pulled the trigger.

His first two shots missed. He had snapped them off too quickly, panicked by the shots landing around him. He hesitated, fear mounting, allowing the men to get within twenty feet, before exhaling slowly and squeezing off his next two rounds. The man on the right stood straight up with a jerk as if he had run face-first into an invisible barrier. He took two more steps before falling over.

The second man screamed again and leveled his gun, now only ten feet from Bobby. Bobby fired his last two shots. The man kept running, hitting the cement rail inches from Bobby and flipped over to the bank below.

Bobby couldn't move. The hammering in his chest made him think he'd been shot – it became difficult to breathe. A full minute later, his breaths were not as ragged or pained. He chanced a body scan but was unharmed. He sat on the railing, sweat pouring down his face, and tried to recover from the fear. He slapped his hands to his face. He should be overwhelmed with emotion, having just taken two human lives, but no tears came. The two men were no longer human. They had attacked like berserkers, unconcerned that they faced death. Bobby was now living in a war zone. Kill or be killed was the new law.

Bobby jumped down from the rail and went through both men's belongings. Other than the weapons, he found precious little. But the guns would be of real value as he continued his journey.

The encounter changed him. Twenty miles later, in his new car, he came upon a woman's body stretched across the highway, her arms reaching out beckoning for him to stop, he barely slowed as he drove around her.

SOMEWHERE HE WOULD FIND others like him who still valued life and wanted to rebuild rather than destroy. He looked back at Becca's sleeping form, her face so serene now, and wondered which side of the rebuild or destroy equation she lined up on.

Six

BECCA STRETCHED AND YAWNED. If she'd dreamed, she had no memory. She sat up and looked around. A second yawn woke Bobby. They crawled out of the truck.

"Morning, baby brother. How'd you sleep?"

Bobby did a neck rotation. "Let's just say I slept, but it doesn't feel like it."

"That's too bad. I feel really good. Shall we check out the house?"

He noticed she had changed her blood-soaked shirt for a wrinkled designer blouse. "Lead the way."

The house, a large two-story, was surrounded by woods. A three-car garage stood behind the truck. After verifying its vacancy by knocking and looking through the windows, Bobby broke in through the rear patio door. With his gun ready, he stepped back and listened for any sounds of life. A few seconds later, Becca moved forward and sniffed the air inside. Musty and warm, but no smell of decaying bodies.

Becca reached through the broken glass, unlocked the door, and pushed it open. She drew her gun and the two went from room to room clearing the house. No sign of life existed. A thin layer of dust had settled over everything. In several corners, cobwebs had formed.

"Nothing?" Bobby asked.

His sister shook her head. She sniffed the air, lifted her arms, and sniffed again. "Oh. My. God. I frigging reek. What I wouldn't give for a shower." Specks of blood still dotted her face.

"I'm with you there. We'll have to see if we can rig something up. Maybe use some rainwater or stop at a pond or something."

Becca went through the cupboards. "Yeah, that'd be good." She pulled out a box of crackers and a jar of peanut butter. "Oh!" She spun and showed Bobby a can of soup, holding it almost reverently. "Do you know how long it's been since I had hot food?"

"Yeah, I know, but the gas won't work."

Becca pointed past him.

He turned. A gas grill sat on the patio. She made her eyebrows go up and down and smiled.

Bobby laughed. "Get a pot."

"Really?"

"Yeah, let's do this."

Becca ran to the stove and snatched up a pot. Bobby went outside and said a silent prayer that there was gas in the tank so his sister wouldn't be disappointed. The way her mood swings ran she would immediately get depressed. She might even shoot the tank.

He turned the valve on the canister and pushed the button for the automatic igniter, but nothing happened. After several failed attempts, he studied the igniter and found it was corroded. His heart sank.

Suddenly, a small flame in front of his face made him jump back.

Becca laughed. "Look what I found." She handed him the eight-inch lighter.

Bobby slid it between the grates and pulled back on the trigger. The flame sparked to life. He lowered the fire slightly and took the pot. Becca had poured several

28

different kinds of soup into the same pot. He looked at her.

"What? I couldn't make up my mind, so I put one of each in."

Bobby laughed and shook his head. "No problem, Sis. It will be like having a soup buffet."

Becca returned to the kitchen and came back out with bowls and spoons and the box of crackers. She spread some of the peanut butter on them and laid them on a platter. She picked one up and brought it to her brother.

"Appetizer," she said proudly.

Bobby smiled and took it, enjoying the crunch as he chewed.

When the soup was hot, he poured some into each bowl. Becca found cans of warm pop and poured them into glasses. She set the patio table with napkins and even brought out salt and pepper.

They ate with great appetites. Near the end, Becca picked up her bowl and slurped down the remaining broth. She held it out in both hands and said, "More, please."

Bobby laughed. Becca wore a reddish soup smile on her face. He took the bowl and stood to refill it as she belched loudly. His sister really had changed.

When she finished, Becca slapped the table, making the bowls jump, and leaped to her feet. "I almost forgot." She disappeared inside and returned seconds later. "Dessert." She held out a bag of chocolate chip cookies.

"Oh, yeah, now we're talking." Bobby dug his hand inside the package and withdrew a handful of small cookies.

They munched in silence.

"It's a beautiful morning," Becca said.

The sun climbed through a cloudless sky. A warm, light breeze blew through the trees and bushes. Above them birds sang. For a moment, Bobby forgot the world had changed so drastically. He tipped his face upward and enjoyed the sun's caress.

Bobby said, "You know, we should start stocking up on food and water. We can't be sure we'll be able to find them whenever we want."

"If I know Mom, she'll have the whole house stocked up by now."

Bobby stopped feeding cookies into his mouth and studied his sister. He swallowed his words, and then choked them back out. "Becca, what if—"

"Stop it, Bobby," Becca snapped. "Don't you dare say it. They'll be there. They have to be there."

"I know, Sis. But we should still be prepared. It's certainly not going to hurt to store some food. Besides, Mom will appreciate it if we show up with gifts."

"Yeah, that's true." Her mood was light again. She popped another cookie into her mouth then talked through the chewing. "That's a good idea. Let's see what else they have here we can take with us."

Becca disappeared inside. Bobby saddened. The talk of his parents had reawakened his fears, but he didn't want Becca to see. Fixing on a false smile, he hopped up and followed Becca through the patio door.

Seven

ALMOST AN HOUR LATER, they were back on the road with an old cooler and two cardboard boxes packed with packaged and canned food. They also grabbed the canned and bottled drinks and some first aid supplies. Becca found a used paperback, a title she'd always wanted to read. Her mood had improved by the time they left. As they drove away, she had her bare feet propped up on the dashboard and the novel open.

With Becca occupied, Bobby let his mind wander. They were only twenty miles from their parents' home. In normal times, the drive would take less than thirty minutes. Now, especially after yesterday's ambush, they went slower and more cautious. Pockets of humanity existed, but in these hard times people became very unpredictable. Some were good, others not. But they all had one thing in common: survival.

Bobby checked the gas gauge and decided he could afford to turn on the air for the remainder of the trip. He glanced at his sister. She smiled as the cooled air blew across her face.

She'd come a long way since the day he found her cowering in her dorm room. Bobby remembered driving onto the desolate Ohio Northern campus. Bodies lay everywhere. Nothing moved. He had swallowed hard, the fear climbing his chest and clutching at his throat.

INSIDE BECCA'S DORM HE could hear pounding and a male voice screaming. As he turned down Becca's hall, there was a crash and a female scream. Running and closing on his sister's room Bobby heard, "I've got you now, bitch. You're gonna pay now."

Bobby rounded the door without breaking stride. The enraged man was punching down at his sister, who lay on the floor kicking her legs. The large sliding window stood open. Evidently Becca had planned to jump the three stories to escape the madman.

Without much thought, other than an overwhelming desire to protect his sister, Bobby launched himself at the man. He hit the unsuspecting assailant in the back and drove them both over the ledge and through the window. The only thing that saved Bobby was spreading his legs wide enough to catch the window on one side and crossbar on the other. Even so, the maneuver only stopped him for a moment.

The weight of his body dragged him slowly downward. Below him he could see the other man's body slam to the ground. Pressing his legs outward with all his might and using his hands, Bobby attempted to push back up the outer brick wall. It was no good. His legs were losing the battle with gravity.

It was then he saw the bedsheets pour down past him.

"Grab the sheet," his sister called to him. "I've got it tied off."

Even hanging upside down, Bobby hesitated. Did he give up the tenuous hold he had to trust that his sister knew how to securely tie sheets well enough to support his weight? If his body fell, the snap of his weight against the sheet would be a tremendous force against the slim material. But when he felt his legs weaken and his hold slipping, there was no choice. Even with his sister holding his feet, Bobby had seconds to react. He reached out, wrapped the sheet around his left hand several times, and then grabbed it firmly with his right. Taking a deep breath, he pulled and turned his body back up toward the window.

It was at that moment Bobby's right foot slipped from its precarious hold. He felt his stomach leap to his throat. He clutched the sheet close to his chest.

"Oh God!" Becca screamed.

But to his surprise he did not fall. He looked up and saw his sister leaning out the window staring down at him. Her arms were wrapped around his left leg, her torso pressing down, pinning it in place.

"I've got you, little brother."

With his body now turned toward the building it was easy to climb hand-over-hand until he could grab hold of the ledge. Becca helped Bobby get both legs inside then pulled him through. Brother and sister tumbled to the floor in a tangled heap. They lay there for several seconds before both broke into uncontrolled nervous laughter.

"You saved my life, Sis."

"Just returning the favor, Bro."

THEY'D COME A LONG way since. And for the moment, the underlying tension of what they might find when they arrived home was pushed aside.

Eight

BOBBY SLOWED THE TRUCK as they approached what was left of their childhood home. He hit the brakes, stopped two houses away and stared at the half-burned structure. His jaw slackened. His stomach knotted hard. He was unable to swallow.

The garage and the front wall of the house still stood, with much of the roof missing or badly charred. Black soot stained the white brick. Most of the upstairs windows were broken. It was a nightmare version of the beautiful house that had once stood there.

Bobby heard the door open before he realized his sister was moving. It snapped him from his shock. "Becca, wait!"

Bobby opened his door and hopped out to give chase. He changed his mind, climbed back in, and drove forward, stopping in front of the house. He grabbed the keys and his gun and ran after his sister. Becca had disappeared around the side of the house.

"Becca!"

No reply. The air still smelled of burned wood. He rounded the rear corner and froze. The back of the house had been consumed by fire. Portions of the second floor hung suspended with little to hold them in place. It resembled a Hollywood stage set with only the façade complete, or an oversize dollhouse open from the back. The entire structure looked unsafe. Bobby moved closer, trying to locate Becca. What had prevented the entire house from burning?

A cry from inside the house spurred Bobby into action. He ran up on the deck, gun ready. He stopped outside where the patio door had once stood and peered in. A jagged hole replaced where the kitchen table had been.

Two charred bodies littered the floor around it. An instant stabbing of cold fear pierced his heart.

"Becca!"

With a cautious step, he placed a foot on a suspect section of floor. It held. He moved one step at a time farther inside the room.

Soft jogging steps sounded from the stairs. Becca appeared, and Bobby sighed with relief. Panic showed in her eyes.

"Becca, slow down before you get hurt. This floor isn't safe."

"They're not here, Bobby." She stopped on the far side of the hole and pointed at the charred remains. "But who are these guys?" She clutched her face with both hands. "Where are they, Bobby?"

"I don't know." He edged closer to the hole and looked down. Remnants of the table lay smashed below in a pile of black ash. "That's where the fire started. By the size of that pile, it looks like it might have been set on purpose."

"Why would somebody do that? None of the other houses are burned."

Bobby looked around. He discovered a third body in the family room. To the right, in the kitchen, the refrigerator had been upended and wedged between the basement door and the island in the middle of the kitchen. Bullet holes riddled the door, and the upper half had been torn open and hung above the refrigerator.

"There was obviously some sort of battle here." He pointed toward the door. "Somebody had to do that. They tried to trap someone in the basement."

"So what ... they started the fire to burn their way out? That doesn't make any sense. They would have suffocated from the smoke."

"The bigger questions are, who were they and who locked them down there?"

"Help me, Bobby. I have to go down there."

Becca sat at the edge of the hole, her legs dangling over the edge. She had already placed her palms on the loose sagging floor and turned her body so she hung halfway down the opening.

"Becca, damn it! Wait for me before you get hurt."

He squatted next to her, setting the gun on the floor. Grabbing her wrists, he supported her as she lowered. For a moment, panic surged through him as Becca's weight threatened to pull him down after her. He lay down for added balance and swung her to avoid landing in the ashes.

On the third swing, he let go. Becca landed, hit something, and rolled. "Shit!"

"Are you all right?"

Bobby leaned his head over the edge. With only the sunlight through the hole for illumination, a lot of area in the basement was still in shadows. *Flashlights.* They needed to add flashlights to their list of things.

"Sis, before you go exploring, take a good look around. Make sure you're the only one down there. And take out your gun."

He reached for his, glanced nervously at the dead men, and then outside.

"Aw, yuck."

"What?"

"There's another dead body down here. This one is

well done."

"It's not …" He choked on the words.

"No … and don't you even think that." She pointed an angry finger up at him. Becca spun in a circle. "I don't see anyone else. I'm going to look around."

Bobby tried to follow her movements but lost her behind a pile of melted slag he realized was the furnace. A heavy smoke smell hung in the air like a lead weight.

Becca came back into view. Her movements became more frantic. "Two more burnt bodies but not them."

"Becca, they're not here. We'll have to keep looking for them."

A sob escaped her, and his heart sank. She buried her head in her hands and sagged to the floor. A low growl escaped between her fingers. Her hands flew from her face and she slapped and kicked the floor in a full-blown tantrum. Becca flung her head from side to side, screaming as loud as she could.

She had been banking on finding their parents. He feared her sanity depended on finding them alive. Sadness weighed heavily upon Bobby's heart. Closing his eyes, he hoped to lose the image, but it would be with him forever. He tried to mentally block the screams as tears fought to escape his eyes.

Then suddenly, the screaming stopped.

Panic raced through him. Bobby opened his eyes. Below him, Becca held one of her old dolls in both hands and stared at it. The doll was blackened. Half of its lower body had melted, now misshapen. Most of the once long brown hair was singed or gone.

She stroked the side of the doll's face. Then her entire body began to shake. She hugged the doll tight to her chest and cried loudly.

Bobby could no longer hold back his emotions.

He sobbed.

Nine

AFTER BECCA CAME BACK upstairs, the siblings went through the house trying to find mementos of their family history. Becca found a pillowcase that survived the fire and filled it with the treasures, including the doll.

Hour later, the sun was beginning to set as they stepped out onto the deck and turned toward the house, possibly for the last time. Bobby draped an arm over her shoulder. She laid her head down on his.

"I told you, Artie, didn't I?"

Becca ducked and spun around, knife pulled. Bobby reached for his rifle but was too slow. They stood facing the two armed men. One was skinny to the point of being anorexic, the other short and round.

"I told you they'd come back," the skinny man squealed. "Now we'll make them pay for what they done."

"Where's the old guy who was with you?" Artie asked.

"Careful, Artie, he might be hiding in the house."

"Put them guns down, or we'll have to shoot you. I'm a damn good shot. I'll take out your knees first."

Becca looked at Bobby, trying to read his thoughts. She stayed in her crouch, the knife hidden behind her leg.

Bobby shrugged. "Okay, easy. Don't shoot." He lifted the handgun from the holster on his hip. He bent at the knees to place the gun on the deck. As he did, he leaned forward in front of Becca. He was giving her cover to make whatever move she could. As he crossed in front of her, she drew her gun. Becca turned her body sideways to the men, ready to spring.

"I don't like that look, Artie. Shoot one of them. Shoot the guy. We don't want to waste the girl … yet."

Becca shivered with revulsion. She looked past the men to the two small crosses stuck in the ground in front of the trees that lined the back of the property. Her shiver turned ice cold. A painful dread clutched at her heart.

"Oh no, Bobby!" She stood, entranced. Her body swayed. Her vision clouded. For a moment she felt faint. Without a thought, Becca dropped her gun and walked in a zombie-like path toward the graves.

BOBBY FOLLOWED BECCA'S GAZE and saw the crosses. His shoulders sagged. There was only one purpose for the crosses to be in their yard. Blurred vision registered Becca's movement.

"Hey, you stop right there," the skinny man said. His body twitched with nervous energy. "What's she looking at?"

"Don't look, it's a ploy to distract us." He backed up a step and shot a quick glance behind him. "There's no one there, but there might be someone in the trees."

"Artie, I think the old guy is in the trees."

Artie turned and pointed his weapon at the trees. Becca kept advancing toward the graves.

"Stop or I'll shoot you." Artie's voice crept up an octave.

Intentional or not, Becca's path crossed the line of sight between Bobby and skinny man. With Artie's attention drawn to the trees, Bobby made his move. Dropping to one knee, he scooped up his handgun. As soon as Becca passed the nervous man, Bobby fired.

Becca never flinched at the sound of the shot, but Artie did. He jumped and turned as his partner fell to the ground. Two rounds flew from Artie's gun, striking the house to Bobby's right.

In a flash, Becca brought up her knife. In one large step and a wild animalistic howl that froze Bobby in his steps, his sister ripped an upward slice through Artie's gut, ending near his left shoulder. The gun discharged again, into the ground, before falling from his grip. Becca grabbed the man by his shoulder, pulling him in close as she thrust the blade deep into his flesh.

She screamed again, a long eerie wail. Bobby watched in horror. Her arm was like a piston, firing time after time into the bloody body. Her eyes never left the two crosses. Artie died long before Becca was through plunging the knife. She kept his body upright until she could move her arm no more.

Bobby stepped cautiously to his sister's side and put a gentle hand on her knife arm. It took a moment for her to break her stare with the graves. She turned her head to him. There was pain in her eyes, but something more, too – an emptiness, like a deep black void. Her green eyes watered, yet looked dead, like her soul had been torn from her body.

He had to look away. The pain of losing his parents was one thing. He had been preparing for this moment. But the anguish his sister now endured overwhelmed him beyond his preparation. His hands fell to his side. The gun hung from limp fingers, as if refusing to let go.

Ten

"OH, BOBBY, no," she cried and released the body.

Stepping on and over the corpse, Becca dropped to her knees between the two crosses. Bobby followed. Through teary eyes he could make out the words etched into the crossbars.

In loving memory, Ben.

In loving memory, Sandra.

Down the shaft of each cross was the phrase, *In my heart forever.*

These were the graves of their mother and youngest brother.

Becca tore at the long grass, threw her head back, and keened at the setting sun. For the first time, the end of the world felt like the end of the world. His grief too complete to allow thought, he walked past his sister to the nearest tree and clutched it to keep from collapsing.

Unaware of how much time had passed, Bobby didn't even know how long his sister's screeching had failed to fill the dusk sky. He turned at the grunt. Despite everything that had happened to them over the past few weeks, he was still shocked to see his sister straddling Artie's body and tearing into him with her knife.

Whatever was left of his sister was now long gone.

Blood drenched her like some nightmare vision. He half expected her to sink her teeth into the body and drink his blood. Becca had gone over the edge. She was more monster now, than human.

He looked at the gun still in his hand, hanging at his side. A strange calm descended over him. He looked to his sister in her crazed grief-stricken rage and thought of her as a wounded animal. Tears fell anew and he advanced on his sister.

Becca seemed unaware of his approach, not that she would have cared at this point had she known his intent. To be put out of her tortured misery would certainly be a blessing. There was little left of the body below her to recognize it as human, but then there was little of the gore-covered, blood-soaked body of his sister to suggest she was human. Wherever Becca's mind had gone, she no longer existed in this body.

Bobby raised his gun as he walked between the graves of his mother and brother. His eyes blurred with the tears. Turning his head, he wiped his eyes clear and saw the etching on the back of the crosses. Comprehension took a moment. *Wait! What?* In the dusk the engraving was difficult to decipher. He bent to take a closer look, and then dropped to the ground. "He's alive. Becca, he's alive." Becca stopped and looked over her shoulder to where Bobby knelt. He motioned to her.

"Becca, can you hear me?"

She looked at him, but Bobby wasn't sure if she even saw him. His hand traced the crosses. She wiped at her blood-streaked face, but only managed to cover her face more completely.

"Sis, Dad's still alive."

"Wh-what?"

"Dad. He's still alive. Who do you think dug these graves? It had to be Dad. And come here. Look." He motioned with an excited hand gesture. "Come on, Sis, please."

Becca looked at the destroyed body, at the knife embedded in the neck. She pulled it free and studied the blade.

"Sis, you can't kill him any more than he is. Please, come here and look at what Dad wrote."

Becca pushed herself slowly to her feet and spat on the corpse. She took a staggered route to Bobby. Blood dripped from her hand. He pushed to his feet and backed up to allow his sister to see. She turned her back on him and bent to look.

"'There, on the cross pieces. Read from one to the other."

She looked closer.

As she did, Bobby once more became aware of the gun in his hand and thought about what he had been about to do. Had the discovery he made altered anything? He made up his mind then that the face that turned around and looked at him would determine whether he pulled the trigger.

BECCA TRACED EACH LETTER as she read aloud.

B and B, come find me. She moved to her brother's grave. *I'm close. 5m. 5/14.* Five miles, May fourteenth. From deep inside her chest, convulsions grew. She collapsed to the ground racked by full body sobs. Moments later, she lay exhausted. "Daddy's alive," she whispered to Ben's grave. A sudden unnatural chill ran down her spine, causing her to stiffen in alarm. Unsure of the source, she listened with hard intent. The only sound was the forced staccato breathing from Bobby. The icy chill bit in deeper. Her hair stood on end.

Still on her knees, she straightened her torso erect. Bobby emitted a nervous sound. He was crying.

"Do you fear me, brother? Or do I need to be put

43

down like some rabid dog? I might not be myself, but I would never hurt you." Her voice was detached and matter of fact.

She stood suddenly, as if daring him to shoot. He gasped and stepped back.

"At least wait until we find Dad. If we find he is dead too, I will welcome death and the relief it brings."

She turned her head and caught Bobby's eyes. "Is that okay with you, Bobo?"

He smiled and lowered his gun. She expected her old nickname for him to work. She smiled, hoping the expression appeared as false and sickeningly sweet as intended. Before he could react, Becca was on him. The glare in her eyes pierced him deeper than the knife ever could. The point of the blade pricked his neck.

"You're my brother, Bobby, and I love you. But don't ever point a gun at me again ... at least not until it's time." She winked at him and planted a kiss on his forehead. "Okay, Bobo?"

She stepped away as quickly as she had arrived and turned back to the graves. There she knelt, pruning away the long grass and humming softly.

BOBBY FOUGHT TO CONTROL his body shakes. He touched his throat. One small drop of blood dotted his fingertip. He looked down at the gun in his hand and swallowed. Sliding the gun into his holster took several attempts. When he was calm enough, he walked past his sister and retrieved the bags.

He turned. Becca was watching him. Bobby handed her a bag and they stood looking at each other.

"Don't give up on me yet, Bobby. I'm not completely gone."

"I'm worried about you, Sis. I hate seeing you like this. I don't want you to suffer."

"So, you wanted to ease my pain? That's nice, Dr. Death. But I'll be all right."

They stood in an awkward silence.

Bobby broke the silence. "He was here a little more than two weeks ago."

"Yeah. What's your guess as to where he might be?"

Bobby looked in several directions. "West. He wouldn't have gone toward the city."

The silence fell again as they stared at the graves.

"I hope it was the disease that got them," Becca said. "And not," she motioned toward the bodies, "you know."

"Yeah." Bobby's throat constricted and he wiped tears from his eyes.

Tears fell on Becca's blood-streaked cheeks. "Are we good?" she asked.

"Yeah, we're good."

"Then let's go find Dad."

"Absolutely."

They hoisted their gear and walked off side-by-side around the burned shell of their childhood home.

"By the way, welcome back, Sis."

"I love you, Bobby."

"Love you too, Becca."

The last sliver of sunlight descended over the trees behind them. They tossed their belongings in the back and sat inside the truck.

"So, Boy Wonder, any idea where we're going?"

"Other than west, not a clue, Wonder Woman."

"Huh, typical male."

"Hey, it's not like there's a gas station for me to stop and ask directions."

"Maybe Boy Blunder is a more fitting name."

"Yeah, well you're still Wonder Woman to me."

"Aw, that's so sweet."

"No, I meant, I wonder if you're really a woman."

"Oh."
He started the engine.
"Prick."
"Bitch."
They laughed.

Part Two

Eleven

THE BOWSTRING WAS TAUT next to his face. The prey he'd stalked had stopped. The deer must have sensed something was wrong. Its head turned to the left. The doe would make a good meal, a good many meals. The hunter's hands began to shake. He relaxed his breath and the string, lowering the bow. He justified not shooting by telling himself he had no way of storing that much meat or anywhere to keep it. His fear of killing a living thing had nothing to do with the decision. The hunter would not sacrifice the life of the deer and waste the meat. Since the world had gone primitive, he had submerged his thoughts and actions in his Indian ancestry. They would have frowned on a wasted kill.

He stood, and the doe buckled its knees, ready to bolt.

"Go, my sister. Be safe."

The deer darted off. There might come a day when he could not afford to allow the deer to live, but for now, food was still easily found. He turned his back and went to find another smaller target.

Myron Golden had taken advantage of recent events to live out his childhood fantasy. His mother had told him they were descendants of a Sioux chief, but he was forbidden to ever talk about his heritage because of his father, a wealthy politician, who wanted nothing to tarnish his image. He supported the two of them, but was no longer married to his mother, though he came around when he wanted a screw.

Strange, but only a month before the plague hit, his parents had been together. Now they were both dead.

He stalked through the woods in search of dinner. He was patient. Something would come up; it always did. But usually in the form of canned or packaged food he found in a house. Myron enjoyed his new freedom. He smiled as a rabbit scampered from its hiding spot. He crouched and attempted to follow, his bow and arrow ready.

Myron had fantasies as a boy about being a mighty Sioux warrior. Now he was living that fantasy. He referred to himself as Golden Feather. His father's name had been Golden. When Myron found a lone somewhat golden feather from an unknown bird, he wore it hanging from a small braid in his hair.

Two days prior, Myron had broken into a Western outfitter store. There he found the leather britches he now wore, as well as the moccasins. He added the expensive wooden longbow, a quiver, and hunting arrows at a sporting goods store. Taking a backpack, he filled it with survival items, which included the long knife he wore in a leather sheath strapped to his leg.

Since discovering his parents dead, Myron had been alone. Trekking to the big city looking for help or anyone else alive, he was sickened at the death toll. Shots in the distance dissuaded him from going farther. Myron retreated to his house, gathered what belongings he might need, and fled to the wooded areas west of the city.

Golden Feather crouched low, drawing the

50

bowstring back midway. He froze and listened, his gaze never leaving the spot where he had last seen his prey. He didn't move at all, other than to draw in slow breaths. The rabbit had either escaped or had as much patience as Golden Feather.

In truth, he had never even shot at an animal, let alone killed one. He wasn't sure he could kill. Soon he might have to find out. He wouldn't be able to find food in houses forever.

Ever so slowly, Myron bent. Holding the arrow with his left finger wrapped around it and the bow, he released the string and let his fingers scrape across the ground until he found a pinecone. He arced the cone just beyond where he believed the rabbit to be, quickly grabbed the string, and drew back before the cone landed.

The rabbit bolted straight toward him. Myron lined up the shot.

"Stop!" A voice yelled from beyond the trees.

Myron dropped to the ground, his heart pounding. The rabbit scampered to safety while Myron looked for his own. Panic set in. *Was the voice calling to him?*

"Stop! Don't make me shoot."

Fear gripped Myron. He turned his head in a slow arc. With his senses heightened, he crawled toward the voice. An engine raced somewhere in front of him. He crept to the edge of the tree line and lay flat.

Before him a man and woman, both young, sprinted across an open field for the trees. Forty yards behind them on the road was an Army jeep with a mounted machine gun. A man stood behind the gun dressed in military garb. The driver and another man standing in the front seat were dressed the same way. Flanking the couple, two more uniformed men ran. They carried rifles and wore camo. To Myron's eye, the pursuers would overtake the couple before they reached the trees.

The fleeing man turned and fired a handgun in the direction of the jeep. A futile effort at that distance, let alone while running. However, the two chasers dropped to the ground, giving the couple a little more lead. The couple was still ten yards from the trees. They would enter the woods about five yards to Myron's left. His mind raced as he tried to decide what to do. He wanted to help the man and woman escape but feared exposing his presence and location to the armed men.

The soldiers in the jeep were talking to each other. The two men giving chase gained ground but more cautiously. They would overcome the man and woman in the woods and would have them in a crossfire. *What would my ancestors do?* Steeling his nerves, Myron rose to one knee. Drawing back the string, he lined up a shot at the pursuer on the right.

Five yards from the woods, the escapee turned, firing two shots at each man on foot. Myron flinched at the gunshots. A distant voice shouted, "Down!" Almost before the two chasers hit the ground, the machine gun opened up. The gunner walked the rounds through the field until they climbed the couple's backs, tearing them apart. Their destroyed bodies fell into the woods.

Twelve

Myron dived for cover as the bullets began to fly, his cry of anguish lost in the explosive chattering of the gun. He covered his ears and curled into a ball, tears rolling freely. The noise stopped, and for seconds, the quiet was as complete as death.

"Are they dead?" the voice shouted.

Someone close to Myron let out a harsh laugh. "I sure as shit hope so after that."

Myron covered his mouth to keep from screaming.

"Well, check to make sure. You know the general's gonna ask."

Myron froze. He feared his pounding heart was loud enough to be heard by the soldiers. Any movement would give away his presence and seal his fate. His head throbbed. Warmth spread between his legs. He didn't want to be brave anymore. He wanted to run home and hide like he used to when the neighborhood kids chased him after school.

Despite the fear paralyzing him, he turned to see what was happening. He picked up movement in his peripheral field. The two soldiers were ripping clothes and stripping the bodies of anything useful.

"Man, what the hell are you doing?" the second soldier said. "You ain't gonna have sex with a corpse are you? You can't be that desperate."

"Shut up, fool. Look." He pointed at the half-naked body.

The other man stood and approached. He stopped suddenly. "Ah, shit!"

"Yeah, she was pregnant. I felt the roundness of her belly when I was searching her. From the looks of her she was seven to nine months."

"That's a shame, man. Dude's gotta stop being so trigger-happy."

The two men looked back at the jeep.

"Yeah, I agree. How we ever gonna grow if he keeps killing everyone we find?"

The first man glanced into the woods. For an instant, Myron thought they had locked eyes. He screamed inside. *Run,* he urged, but could not make his body respond.

A second later, the man looked away, deeper into the woods. He sighed, picked up his bounty and said, "Let's head back." He turned and walked away.

The second soldier took one more look at the dead woman. He shook his head and said, "It's a damn shame," and then followed his partner.

To Myron, an eternity passed before the jeep drove off. Even then his brain took several minutes to convince his body to move. He stood on shaky legs staring in the direction of the bodies. Tears dripped from his face as his legs struggled to keep him erect. They moved, as if of their own accord, toward the carnage.

At first sight of the blood Myron stopped, unable to move closer. He'd seen dead people before – lots of them – but he'd never witnessed anyone actually die, especially in such a violent and bloody way. The man's head was almost gone. The woman's torso was covered in red. Myron dropped to his knees and vomited.

How could anyone do that to another human being? After all mankind had been through over the past few weeks, how could anyone take life so callously – so easily? Why was this new world so cruel? Hadn't there been enough death?

His stomach lurched and he retched again.

Thirteen

IN A MORE SOUTHWESTERN corner of the woods, Mason Armstrong had watched with an almost orgasmic excitement as the two people were gunned down. He wanted to howl, but was able to control his need to celebrate death.

He crouched and watched the two men in uniforms search the bodies. A snarl escaped his lips. He hated men in uniform. He hated anyone in any uniform. Most of his life had been dealing with people in uniforms – usually white. But sometimes blue, like when the police came for him.

The doctors, nurses, and orderlies were always yelling at him. Making him do things he didn't want to – forcing their poison down his throat. But no more. He showed them. When that stupid guard had come to let him out of his locked and padded room, Mason had used his cunning to escape.

He remembered the man's words.

"It figures that all the good people are dying and a homicidal maniac like you lives. That's just not right." He motioned for Mason to move, but left his hands and legs shackled. They moved down the hall toward the door that led to the common room.

Mason smiled. He wasn't allowed there often. He wanted to hurt the other loonies. They needed to die. They weren't as smart as he was. In fact, few people were as smart as Mason Armstrong. The only hindrance to a normal and very successful life was that he liked hurting people.

When the guard reached the door, he said, "You probably haven't noticed, but people are dying. There won't be anyone to take care of you anymore. I'm leaving after I let you out of here. You'll have to fend for yourself."

When he turned to unlock the door, Mason looped his cuffed hands over the guard's head and strangled him. While the guard fought, Mason cackled. He had seen an old John Wayne movie once, with a hobbling old man who laughed funny. Ever since then, whenever Mason got real happy he copied that sound.

The guard reached for a Taser on his hip, but as he pulled it free, Armstrong gave a quick jerk and snapped the man's neck. The body fell to the floor, and Mason grabbed the keys and the Taser. First he opened the cuffs on his hands and feet, and then he opened the door. The common room was empty. It was always empty of other residents when he was allowed in there, but now it was also vacant of any staff, as well.

Feeling bolder, Mason explored the entire facility. He found one other patient wandering the halls. Mason stabbed him repeatedly with a pair of scissors.

When he got outside, he shouted and danced. He was free. Over the past few weeks, he had wandered the city. He hid from any mobs, fearing they would put him back inside the institution. The two occasions he found people alone, he killed them. The fewer people around, the less chance of being locked up again. He liked this new world.

Now Mason saw men in uniform and wanted to kill

56

them too. But there were too many of them, and their weapons were more powerful than his knife. He held up the knife he had found in a house. It was a stainless-steel chef's knife with an eight-inch blade. Killing them would take some planning. Mason directed his attention farther into the woods to the man he had been stalking before the army guys arrived. The boy who thought he was an Indian.

He could wait until the soldiers left and then continue hunting his prey. The uniforms hadn't seen the other man yet. Mason felt the excitement building inside him. The soldiers went back to the jeep. Mason hated them. Anger grew into rage. Those men threatened his freedom. He snarled louder this time. One of the men turned around and looked in his direction. Mason froze. *Come on, soldier boy, come find me.* But the man climbed in with the others and the jeep drove off.

Mason glanced to where the easy kill hid. He wanted that kill, but the sound of the jeep accelerating drew his attention. He could find the boy anytime. But with the soldiers alive, he'd never feel safe. They had to die.

Mason ran through the woods and crossed the street. He'd follow the jeep, and when he got the men alone, they would die.

Fourteen

MYRON CRAWLED AWAY FROM the death scene. *I should bury them.* Animals will be at the remains within hours. But as the distance increased between him and the victims, the desire to do so faded. He couldn't face the corpses. Killing for food was one thing, but killing for no reason, especially a person, Myron couldn't accept.

He walked back the way he'd come, to the far edge of the woods. To the right, the tree line stretched for a long way. Fifty yards to the left, a road ran east and west. For the moment, it was clear of any traffic. A cornfield stood twenty yards in front of him, reaching from the road to the extent of the woods. The partially grown stalks would offer some cover, but Myron had trouble getting up enough nerve to dart across the open space between the field and woods.

The sound of the machine gun amplified in his head. Fear immobilized him. *Why had they run?* Perhaps they were criminals. No. The man looked like he was protecting his wife and unborn child. Regardless of whom they were or what they did, they didn't deserve to die like that.

With another look at the road, Myron moved. He crawled across the open space until he was several rows into the two to three-foot-high stalks. There, he stopped and sat on the ground, knees bent, head between them, until he stopped shaking.

The sun was setting. He feared being outside in the dark alone. Picking up his pace, he reached the end of the corn. The open space before him was too far to brave crossing. A gravel driveway ran from the street back to an old two-story farmhouse. With only a sliver of light stretching over the horizon, Myron studied the structure. A barn and another long outbuilding stood behind the house. The buildings looked uninhabited. *What if this was where the killers lived? If not, what if the soldiers came in the middle of the night and caught him there? Will they kill me too?* He shuddered.

As he stood trying to decide, a cool breeze blew, reminding him of his wet pants. He glanced down, ashamed of his cowardice. He choked back a sob. He hated this world – hated that he was not brave enough to function better within it.

Sucking in several deep breaths, Myron tried to harden his resolve by getting angry with himself. "Come on, you chicken shit, move." He stepped from cover, faltered, and stepped back. He was too afraid to be in the open. Flopping to the ground, he covered his face and cried. *Those poor people. Why did they have to die?* How was he supposed to survive if he had to constantly watch for two-footed predators?

When he was cried out, he stood, wiped his face, and walked toward the farmhouse. It was now dark enough to cover his approach. He went around back and looked down the drive at the road. There was no sign of lights or life. Myron climbed the back porch and tried the door. It was locked.

Reaching behind him, he withdrew the handgun he carried. It might have come in handy, but he was afraid to fire it. He hated the noise. Still, it had its purposes.

Holding it by the barrel, he smashed the door's window and scraped any remaining glass from the frame. Once inside, he stood holding the gun in a shaky hand.

He had only fired it once. The gun had pitched backward, the barrel almost hitting his face. He wasn't strong enough to control the weapon. When he stole it from the house he'd broken into two days ago, he'd been excited. It was a .45. All his favorite heroes on TV used one just like it. When his breath rushed out, he realized he'd been holding it. With caution, he advanced through the house, afraid at any second someone or something might jump out at him. He set his pack down on the floor making too much noise. His heart pounded and a muffled cry escaped his lips. Seconds later, when no one came to challenge his presence, Myron moved from room to room ensuring he was alone. He held the gun in both hands in front of him. When he cleared the house, he sat on a bed upstairs and stared at his feet. A moment later a putrid smell rose to his nostrils. The acrid odor came from him.

The tears welled up again. The horror of the gruesome bodies and the shame he felt for his cowardice was too much for him to bear. He brought the gun up under his chin and began pulling back on the trigger. *A little more. Just a little more.* He pleaded with himself, but his finger wouldn't budge. He placed it at his temple and imagined the bullet ripping through the flesh. Still, he was unable to end his anguish. Next, he rammed the gun into his mouth, chipping a tooth and gagging on the barrel. It wasn't going to happen. Myron threw the gun on the bed and cried again. *I'm too chicken to live and too afraid to die.*

Myron stood and searched the closets until he found clean clothes that fit. Then he went into the kitchen where he found a few bottles of water in the refrigerator. They were warm, but that didn't matter. He drank one and carried the other bottles upstairs to the bathroom. There, he stripped off his clothes. Pouring some of the precious liquid onto a face cloth, he scrubbed away the dirt and embarrassment from his body. Myron toweled off and dressed in his new clothes. That complete, he went in search of anything edible.

The pantry held many staples, including canned soups and veggies, but he opted for peanut butter and crackers. While he ate, the memory of the murder ran through his mind once more. He had to get much tougher. Perhaps if he'd been able to help the man and woman survive, he'd have had some friends.

If he had helped them escape, would they be alive now, or would he be dead too? In his mind-numbing fear, he had left his bow and arrows behind. Myron reached over and ripped the feather out of his hair. "You're no Indian Chief, you coward. You don't deserve to wear this feather." He tossed it on the table.

Myron placed the unused food in his pack then removed his shoes and slid under the covers of a bed. He stared at the ceiling. *What horrors would tomorrow bring?*

Fifteen

MYRON WOKE WITH A start. He scanned the room in a panic, not remembering where he was. As the memory streamed back, he relaxed. He gave his face a vigorous rub and scooted out of bed. He stretched and put on his shoes.

He walked out of the room and down the hall to a front window. The sky was dark, announcing the threat of rain. No other people moved. He studied the outside for a while without seeing it.

Myron used the bathroom and went down stairs. He rummaged through the kitchen drawers until he found a can opener. Pulling cans of chicken noodle soup and pears from the pantry Myron opened them. Grabbing a spoon and a two-liter bottle of cola, he went to the table and sat down. He dug into the cold meal with a hearty appetite.

After eating his fill, Myron stared at the feather on the table. Letting out a long slow breath, he slapped the table and stood. It was time to earn that feather back. He slid it into his pack. He vowed not to wear it again until he deserved to.

Myron cleaned up, placing the empty cans in a plastic bag. The pop was too big to carry so he poured what he could into an empty water bottle and put it in the netting attached to his backpack. The peanut butter and crackers went into the pack.

Outside, he deposited the garbage in the trash can and went into the garage. There he found a shovel. Shouldering his pack and with a new resolve, Myron retraced his steps until he found where the bodies lay. He angrily fought back the urge to vomit. He swallowed hard and set about digging a large hole. Unused to manual labor, his arms and back hurt. Blisters formed on his fingers and hands. But Myron dug on, pushing the pain and discomfort from his mind.

Several hours later, the irregular hole was deep enough for both bodies. Myron hoped it was also deep enough to keep the animals from digging them up. He steeled himself and before he lost his nerve, grabbed the man's legs and dragged him to the hole. Myron rolled the body in. The man didn't lie flat. One leg was up on the side, but Myron wasn't about to jump into the hole to fix him.

He returned for the woman, her accusing eyes still open. Flies had begun their work on them, giving her a demonic look. He closed his eyes and said a prayer for forgiveness. "I'm sorry," he said, before pushing her to join her man. She landed face down, her weight causing the man's leg to drop flat. The bodies were face-to-face, perhaps as they should be. The hollowness of loss filled him, even though he had never met them.

Myron moved away from the grave, refusing to allow the tears welling in his eyes to fall. He let out a low growl and took up the shovel. Thirty minutes later, the job was done. He stood over the mound, tried to think of a eulogy, but gave up. Leaving the shovel, he picked up his pack and bow and arrows and walked out into the open field the couple had run across. Five steps out, he stopped. Brave was one thing, stupid something else. He backed up and used the trees to move away from the road.

Sixteen

HOURS LATER, MYRON stopped when his stomach told him it was time to eat. He pulled out the peanut butter and crackers and a chocolate chip granola bar. He polished off the remaining pop and stowed the empty bottle with the remains of the food. Emitting a moan as he stood, Myron clutched at the complaining muscles of his back.

How far had he come? The day's journey had taken him across quite a few country roads. Crossing them had caused many anxious moments. At any second, he envisioned the jeep barreling straight at him with its deadly machine gun spitting massive rounds at him. Each road became easier to cross, but still that chill passed through him.

Myron had no idea where he was. He had never been this far away from the city before. Traveling west was the best direction to find other people. However, from what he'd seen so far, he wasn't sure he ever wanted to meet anyone else.

With his muscles loosened somewhat, Myron started out again. The woods he traveled curved toward the east-west road. He approached a north-south unpaved lane. Five minutes later, knee-locking fear struck him. Motors reverberated across the open spaces and bounced around the trees. Myron couldn't tell from which direction the sound came, but it was loud and there was more than one.

He threw himself to the ground and crawled to the tree line. There he waited as the engine sounds grew. Every fiber of his being screamed for him to run, but whether from fear or curiosity, perhaps both, Myron stayed. Less than a minute later, a convoy appeared. The number of vehicles took him by surprise. They were all military. A Jeep led the way, followed by several canvas-covered trucks. Two more open-backed trucks came next. But the next vehicle caused his jaw to drop.

The tank rumbled loudly as its treads slapped against the concrete. A man sat in the hatch on the turret. He held binoculars to his face and scanned the area. Myron ducked and held his breath. Two more trucks and four more jeeps appeared behind the tank. If Myron hadn't seen the men in the jeep gun down the couple, he would've been happy to see so many living people in one place. Shouldn't the army protect the people? He planned to stay far away from the soldiers. Was it wise to continue heading west since the convoy was traveled that direction too?

Myron lay for ten minutes trying to decide what to do. He pushed from the ground and wiped the leaves and dirt from his clothes. He wouldn't go back, but that didn't mean he had to continue west either. If he moved north, he'd have to cross the road the convoy had taken. That appeared to be more traveled than any of the cross streets he had passed. That only left one direction. Myron turned and began walking south.

He kept to the side of the road, but there wasn't as much cover in that direction. There were also more farmhouses. Not wanting a confrontation if anyone was alive to challenge his trespassing, Myron detoured behind the houses.

By late afternoon, he needed a rest. He wasn't used to this much exercise. Yet something about the outdoors made him feel good. Much of the pudginess he carried most of his life was now gone. The extra energy he had exhilarated him in an unfamiliar way.

At the back of a large brick ranch-style house was a pond. A small shed stood at one end. A picnic table sat on a small paved covered patio next to the shed. Myron stopped there and set his pack on the table. The shed was windowless and the door unlocked. The room inside was about eight-by-ten feet and held a variety of pool equipment. A small bench and cupboard lined one side. Myron found towels and some bathing suits.

He went back outside and watched the house for nearly a half hour before deciding to take a chance and rest there. He pulled out whatever food was left and took inventory. Six assorted granola bars, two packs of string cheese, two apples he'd found on a tree, his peanut butter, and a few crackers. He needed more food if he was to continue his trek.

Two bottles of water remained. He took out the empty and deposited it in a blue plastic barrel just off the patio. He might be one of the few people left in the world, but he still couldn't bring himself to litter.

Myron put the peanut butter away and tore open a granola bar. The pond rippled in the light warm breeze. The sun was on its descent and reflected off the surface. He sank his teeth into an apple and turned his attention to the house. Nothing had moved there since he arrived. When he finished eating, he would investigate. He needed to replenish his meager supplies. He left his pack and bow and arrows, pulled out the gun, and advanced toward the house. There was no place to seek cover, so it was straight ahead or not at all.

Seventeen

GLANCING AT THE GUN as he walked, Myron reasoned there was no sense having the weapon if he didn't have the courage to pull the trigger. *Could I take another person's life?* He created anger to shake off the anxiety and increased the pace of his approach. Windows lined the house. Anyone inside could easily see him.

No shots or shouts of alarm sounded as he reached the door. The storm door was open, but the wooden door was locked. He pressed his face to the glass and peered inside. The house remained quiet. Using the gun as before, he broke the glass and reached through to unlock the door. He wasn't inside for more than a few seconds before his eyes watered.

Myron gagged. He sucked in a short breath and held it as he raced back through the door to gulp in fresh air. When the nausea passed, he stared at the house. By the strength of the stench, probably more than one body was in there. Myron had no choice. If there was food and drink inside, he had to go in.

He ran back to the hut and grabbed a towel. He poured some chlorine on the ends and wrapped it around his head, covering his nose. The chlorine soaked ends were at the back of his head, but the fumes were strong. Not sure how long he could stand inhaling the chlorine or how safe it was, Myron ran back to the house and right through the door. The kitchen was to the left.

As fast as he could, Myron rifled through the cupboards. He filled a large garbage bag with whatever he found, not caring for the moment what it was. The refrigerator yielded some diet pops and flavored mineral waters. Not his favorite, but he'd learn to adjust his tastes.

When the cupboards had been stripped, Myron retreated to the shed, ripping off the towel and dropping it next to the pond. He gasped for clean air.

Myron opened the bag and pawed through the contents. He pulled out a can of beef stew. His mouth watered. He could eat it cold, but his taste buds cried for hot stew. Wasn't there a bag of charcoal in the shed? He spun around. *Yes!* There, next to the patio, was a grill.

He ran inside and snagged the bag.

Myron had a lighter in his pack. He tore through the pack finding it at the very bottom. A search of the shed came up empty for lighter fluid. Flicking the lighter through the hole at the bottom of the grill he tried to light the charcoal dry.

Minutes later, with no progress he grunted and swore. His desire for a hot meal bordered on desperation. There was a thin line of pine trees running from the shed toward the house. In the fading light Myron scrounged for old twigs, pinecones or needles that might burn. "Yes!" he shouted when the charcoal lit.

While he waited for his food to heat, Myron set about making his bed for the night. He spread a tarp he found on the floor of the shed. On top of that he laid two towels. Two more towels would be used for his pillow. From his pack he pulled a small blanket.

As he ate, he looked over the pond. A slim moon cast a dim light upon it. *Maybe I can stay here a while.* It will be too difficult to carry the amount of food he found. He finished the stew and threw the can in the barrel. It was time for bed.

Part Three

Eighteen

"Pull, Caleb."

"I am."

"Well, pull harder."

A large burly man with wild black hair covering his face and head slid along the peak of the roof and grabbed onto the rope Caleb struggled with. With one pull, they lifted the solar panel over the edge of the eaves, almost knocking the man who was guiding the panel from the ladder he stood on.

"Whoa! Easy up there. You trying to kill me?" Mark shouted.

The big man pulled again. "Well, make up your mind. You want it pulled or not?"

"Just pull it up, Jarrod," Mark said from the ladder.

"Uh-huh, that's what I thought."

The panel slid along the shingles and stopped at the feet of the large man.

The tall boy said, "Thanks, Jarrod."

"No problem, Caleb. Now help me move this thing over to the frame."

The two men lifted the approximately three-by-five-foot panel toward the end of the roof.

Mark watched from the extension ladder as Jarrod and

Caleb set the panel and attached it to the framework. He nodded as they worked. *This just might work.* The idea of putting solar panels on the house had been a very ambitious one. But with the need for electricity and the winter coming in a few months, Mark wanted to give the family every chance of staying warm.

He descended the ladder and stood next to Jarrod's flatbed truck where more panels were stacked. He looked across the yard. Lynn and Ruth were busy hanging laundry. Alyssa and Zac were in the cornfield, harvesting whatever they could even though the corn was far from ripe. They learned early the difference between the corn they were used to and feed corn. Darren and Mallory were taking care of the livestock in the makeshift pen. A more permanent one was next on the list after the solar panels.

His new family had come a long way from the days trying to survive the Horde. They had been at peace for a month now. They still had a long way to go. The physical and mental scars of that final battle might never heal, but given time, they'd at least scab over.

Mark looked into the rising sun, shielding his eyes with a hand. He looked toward the east several times a day. The hope never died that one day Becca and Bobby would appear on the horizon. But with each day that passed, Mark was forced to accept the fact they may have succumbed to whatever illness had killed off most of mankind. The hard part was not knowing, perhaps never knowing.

The rope dropped on the truck and made Mark jump.

"One down and a whole lot to go," Jarrod shouted from his unseen perch above.

Mark smiled as he grabbed the rope and tied it to the next panel. The big man had come a long way since being shot in the shoulder, thanks to Maggie and the nurses they had rescued. Jarrod still didn't have full range of motion, but his strength was returning. And Jarrod would never let the injury or the pain it must still cause stop him from helping his friends.

Mark lifted each corner of the forty-pound panel and slid the rope around it. He then tied the end to the hanging portion creating a rope basket. The process was slow, but there was no hurry.

"Okay, lift," he yelled, and then climbed the ladder guiding the rope. There was a two-foot overhang where the eaves were attached. Mark lifted the panel, swinging it away from the house. The panel wasn't that heavy, but the awkward angle at which Mark had to lean so the panel cleared the gutters, made the task more difficult, if not somewhat dangerous. That was why he chose this job rather than be on the roof. Jarrod would try, but his shoulder would hinder him, and Mark wasn't going to risk Caleb's safety.

"It's clear. Pull." The panels were rated at 190 watts. Each one held seventy-two solar cells. However, he couldn't find enough of them to cover the roof, so he grabbed whatever panels he could find. They'd go on last.

Mark had filled the front closet with a stack of batteries. An electric panel was hooked up there that controlled where the electricity was directed. According to the research Mark had done in the small town library, the panels should generate more than enough electricity to run the refrigerator and chest freezer full time, the lights and outlets when needed, and the electric heaters in the winter. Coupled with the windmills they erected a month ago and the two generators, they should have enough electricity to handle their basic needs. They even ran a live to the garage since Caleb, Darren and, Zac slept on the second floor.

Their house was the test house. If the panels worked, they'd start hunting for enough panels to do Jarrod's house. It would be a long process, but it was only mid-July – they still had time.

When Jarrod and Caleb had grabbed the panel, Mark started down the ladder.

"Just stay there, Mark," a voice came from below. "No sense going up and down all day. I'll feed them to you."

Looking up at him was Lincoln Colston. He had moved into the house across the street to the west a week ago with a young blonde who didn't leave the house much. Lincoln had been a pro football player with the Indianapolis Colts before the apocalypse. He had been a star. People wore his jersey, picked him for their fantasy teams, and wanted to be him. Now he was trying to survive like everyone else.

The couple had appeared one day on foot. The young woman, Jenny, collapsed on the street. Lynn rushed to their aid. Jenny, who looked to be no more than sixteen, was dehydrated and suffered from malnutrition.

Lincoln had been very protective at first, not allowing anyone near Jenny. He brandished a gun and threatened to use it if anyone came close. Mark joined Lynn and pushed her behind him.

"I understand," Mark said. "You want to protect her. I want to protect my friend too. She's a nurse. If you want her to look at your lady, she will. If not, we'll go back to our house and let you be. You decide."

Lincoln looked on the verge of collapse himself. He was exhausted, confused, and scared. In the end, he allowed Lynn to help. The family took them in until they were stronger and rested. Lincoln decided to stay, but space was short, so Mark set them up in the house across the street.

Mark smiled. "That'd be great, Lincoln."

Nineteen

Six hours later, the family sat down together for their evening meal. Four picnic tables had been placed in a line. Jarrod and Lincoln stayed for dinner. The job had taken all day, but was done. Now they had to wait and see whether any energy was produced.

With everyone seated, Jarrod bowed his head and said a quick prayer. Then, in a burst of movement and sound, the food was picked up and passed. These were Mark's favorite moments. He glanced around the table. The smiles, the laughs, the loud happy voices, reminded him of Thanksgiving dinner. Only now, they got to do it every day.

His gaze stopped at Lynn. She was watching him with a warm smile. He smiled back and winked, and then took a plate of corn from Lincoln. When he looked back, Lynn was busy passing food. Mark marveled at her strength and resiliency, especially after all she'd been through.

"Hey, wake up down there," Jarrod's voice boomed. "You got hungry people down here."

Mark laughed and took the bowl of green beans Lincoln had been holding.

"I don't think he likes beans," Lincoln said.

"Well, good," Jarrod replied. "More for the rest of us."

"So, Lincoln," Lynn called from her end of the table, "is Jenny joining us?"

Lincoln paused for a second. His eyes clouded over and then cleared in a flash. "Ah, no, she was taking a nap. If you don't mind, I'll fix her a plate and take it to her later."

Lynn continued, "If she was taking a nap when you came over, she should be awake by now. Should I go over and invite her?"

"No," he said too quickly, "she's very shy. I'll go do it."

Before he could rise, Mark covered his hand. "We're not prying, Lincoln. We're just friends who are concerned."

Lincoln deflated. He put his hands on his face and rubbed as if he could clear away whatever the problem was.

Lynn said, "Is she all right? Is there something I can help with?"

"I-I don't know. I can barely get a response from her. She seldom gets out of bed or eats. I don't know what to do."

"I won't pry or get involved if you don't want me to," Lynn said. "But she obviously needs help. Is she ill?"

"That's what I thought at first, but she doesn't have a fever or any symptoms of, you know. There's just something wrong up here." He pointed to his head.

"She's not vomiting or complaining of cramps?"

"No. She just lies there like she's in a trance."

"Do you want me to look at her?"

Lincoln turned toward Lynn with tears welling. "Would you please? I don't know what else to do."

"Of course." Lynn stood. The entire table had gone quiet during the exchange. "Everyone go back to eating and having fun. I'll be back in a minute."

76

Lynn walked toward the other house. Lincoln jumped up and followed. Mark was a few steps behind him.

"Lynn, wait." He caught up with her.

"I don't want to offend you, Lincoln, but I think I should talk to her alone."

"Ah, yeah, sure."

Lynn glanced past him and met Mark's gaze. "Why don't you finish eating while I see how Jenny is?" Something unsettling lurked in Lynn's eyes. Mark tried to understand what she was trying to convey. Did she think Lincoln was the cause of Jenny's problem?

Perhaps he was abusing her. Maybe he had Jenny restrained inside so she couldn't leave. The man came from a violent world as a football player. Could he have turned physical with Jenny?

"Come on, Lincoln, let's go eat. Let Lynn do her thing."

Lincoln stared at Lynn as if trying to puzzle something out. "Whoa, wait a minute. You're not thinking that I'm the cause of Jenny's problems, are you? 'Cause that shit's messed up."

"Lincoln—" Mark started.

"Uh-uh, man, back off me. I would never hurt that girl. What is this? You thinking because I'm black I grab this young blonde to take advantage of her? Screw that, man. You don't know me, and you don't know shit about what we been through."

"Lincoln, I'm not judging you," Lynn said in a calm voice. "Jenny needs help. That's all I'm concerned about. Okay?"

Lincoln relaxed a bit. "I need to tell you something about how I found Jenny. You know how it was in those early days. It was crazy. People were dying, and other crazy people were killing those who survived. I was wandering around half-crazed myself. My wife and kid were dead, and I couldn't find anyone who could make

77

sense of it all."

He stopped and seemed to drift back to that time. "When I first saw Jenny, she was trying to fight off two men who were … well, they weren't doing nice things to her. I stopped them. My anger, my pain, my confusion all built into a rage that I unleashed on those two men. I don't know if I killed them, but neither of them moved.

"I reached down to Jenny, but her eyes were wide with fear. She had just witnessed me destroy these two men. She must have thought I was just taking their place. I convinced her I wasn't going to hurt her, and to be safe she should come with me. She agreed, but as she stood, she walked to a bundle on the ground and picked it up. She cooed at it, so I thought it was a baby.

"We walked for miles. When I found a place I thought was safe, we stopped for the night. It was then I saw the baby was dead. She was seventeen years old and had given birth to a baby a month before people started dying.

"I finally convinced her to let me bury the baby. That was real hard for her to watch. She's been like this ever since.

"So you see, that poor girl, she's going through some stuff in her head that I can't help with."

Lynn put a hand on Lincoln's arm. "I'm sorry Lincoln. I know you did the best you could. The mind's a tricky thing to figure out. Let me talk with her. Maybe I can help her through the pain."

He nodded. "I'd be obliged, Lynn."

She smiled and left. Mark put an arm around Lincoln's shoulders and walked him back to the table. The long day was turning into an interesting night.

Twenty

MORNING CAME EARLY. In truth, they all came early. The family adjusted their day to match the sunlight. Although they now had some stored energy from the three windmills erected a month ago, they only used electric lights for an hour after sunset.

Mark stretched and rose from the couch he slept on and went to the kitchen to make coffee. Lynn sat at the kitchen table sipping her own cup. She looked up and smiled.

"Good morning."

"Morning," she replied.

Mark poured a cup of coffee and sat down across from her. "Rough night?"

"Yeah, Jenny's really messed up."

"You been to sleep yet?"

"I tried, but gave up." She shrugged.

"Why don't you try now? We'll handle things."

"No, that's all right. I'll take a nap later if I need to."

"You want to talk about it?"

Lynn sighed. She set down her cup and leaned forward. "She's just seventeen. She was sixteen when she got pregnant. The baby died in her arms while she walked to find help. Then two men tried to rape her.

They tossed her baby aside and knocked her to the ground. That's when Lincoln stepped in. Jenny saw him pummel her attackers and thought she'd be next. Instead, he helped her. He convinced Jenny that the baby was dead and buried her. She can't get past that. Says she still hears the baby cry." Lynn stared into her mug.

"Jenny did say that Lincoln never touched her or tried anything improper. He's looked after her. I think she sees him more as a father figure."

"Well, that's good to know. You had me worried last night."

She sipped her coffee and stared past Mark.

"So she gonna be all right?"

"I don't know. Time will tell, I suppose. We have to get her out of the house, if only to have meals with us. She needs to have tasks to do to keep her mind off the baby." She stood and poured the remains in her cup down the sink. "That's all I got. I'm not a psychiatrist."

"Well, you're the closest we have to one, and Lord knows you've been called on enough to have earned an honorary degree."

That made her smile.

"And in case no one's said it lately, thanks for all you do for us."

"Aw, thanks." After a slightly awkward silence, she said, "I'm going to wash up. Then I have to start breakfast." She left the kitchen.

Mark knew better than to push her to get some sleep. She was a strong woman and felt a great responsibility to the family.

He finished his coffee, rinsed out the cup and went outside. The air was crisp – a little surprising for July. He walked away from the house to observe the solar panels on the roof. They were constructed to withstand fifty pounds of weight from snow or wind. He'd test the system later after it had a full day's charge.

Mark turned toward the garage to wake Caleb and Zac, and then froze. A car engine raced somewhere to the south. The rumble grew louder.

Memories of the battle they had gone through a month ago resurfaced. He grabbed for the gun at the small of his back, only to find he was not carrying it. With no new threats on the horizon, Mark had got out of the habit of having a weapon near.

Mark raced for the house just as a white SUV turned sharply up the driveway and hurtled toward him. He reached the porch and leaped three steps up. By the time his hand touched the doorknob, a man was leaning out of the driver's window.

"Mark! Mark, wait!"

Mark stopped and turned. Juan Perez, one of his neighbors, who lived a half mile south, leaped from the SUV and rushed toward him.

"Mark, we got trouble coming. There's a whole shitload of soldiers heading this way. And sweet Jesus, they got a tank. A really big tank."

"Slow down, Juan. What's going on?"

"I'm trying to tell you there's an army coming this way, man. Is that a good thing or a bad thing?"

That was a good question.

"I remember those stories you told us about fighting that army of hoarders. Is this them coming back for revenge? Or is this the U.S. Army here to save us?"

"How long before they get here?"

"I'm not sure. I saw them running down Airport Highway in this long —"

"Hold it – wait a minute. They were on Airport?"

"Yeah, heading west." Perez lifted his arm and pointed.

"I thought you said they were coming here."

Perez stopped. "Well, I thought they were. Hey, if they're in the area they could stumble on us at any minute. We have to know what to do. Do we fight, or do we greet them like saviors?"

"Until we know for sure what they're doing, I think we try to avoid them. You don't want to greet them in case they're bad, and you don't want to fight them in case they're good. The best thing to do if you see them coming is to run or hide. We need to get everyone together and go over plans."

"Yes, that's a good idea." Perez scrambled back into the SUV.

"Wait," Mark said, moving to the passenger door.

Perez lowered the window.

"If any of the community is missing or in trouble, you come back for me immediately. Understand?"

Perez nodded and backed out the driveway.

God, don't let it start again. Pure ice raced down his spine.

Twenty-One

WHEN MARK TURNED AROUND, Lynn was on the steps, her brow furrowed.

"What?"

Mark didn't want to cause stress, but Lynn would see through any evasive answer. "I don't know for sure."

"What *do* you know?"

"Juan saw a troop convoy to the south, heading west. It may be nothing, but I asked him to check on everyone. I need, uh, we should send runners to our neighbors and to Jarrod and Maggie."

Lynn sat down as if punched in the stomach.

Mark rushed to her. "Lynn, are you all right?"

When she lifted her head, tears had formed. "I can't do this again, Mark. I'm not like you. I can't deal with the pain and the death."

Mark placed a hand behind her head and stroked her hair. "Lynn, we don't know if there's anything to be worried about yet. Let's not stress until we know what we're dealing with."

She leaned her head forward, pressing it against his hip, wrapping her arms around his legs. They had not touched since the ordeal had ended a month ago. He understood she needed time. He'd be there for her whenever she was ready. Now she held him tight.

"We'll be all right, Lynn. And for the record, you're the bravest woman I have ever known."

Lynn lifted her tear-streaked face toward Mark and smiled. "I don't feel very brave."

"We all have a weak moment now and then. That's why we have each other, to help us through those moments. The people we've drawn around us, that we call family, all look up to you. They need you. It's not a fair burden to place on your shoulders, but you have to be strong for all of us."

She lowered her head and squeezed Mark's legs tighter. His heart tightened. This wonderful woman could never replace his dead wife, but he did love her. He'd die protecting her.

"I'm sorry, Mark."

"You have nothing to be sorry for."

"Yes, I do. For this, and for not being what you want me to be."

Mark squatted to be face-to-face with her. He brushed a loose strand of hair from her face. "You're everything I could ever want."

"I'm sorry I can't be what you want, but it doesn't mean I don't have feelings for you."

"I know. I'm not worried. I'll be here for you when you're ready."

Lynn stood and Mark followed. Very slowly Lynn leaned forward, gave Mark a quick hug, and then stepped back. Their eyes held for a moment, unspoken affection passing between them.

"We better wake everyone," he said.

She nodded.

"I'll need to speak to all of them."

Lynn said, "I'll get the house, you get the rest." She turned and went inside.

Twenty-five minutes later, the entire group gathered

around the picnic tables. Lynn stood a few steps to Mark's side.

"I'm not sure there's a problem, but I would rather be prepared than taken by surprise." Mark panned from end to end.

Most of them stood with blank faces. No one wanted to go to battle again.

"So with that in mind, everyone go back to carrying a weapon. No one goes anywhere off the property alone and without clearing it with me. Keep your eyes open and report anything unusual, which obviously includes any unknown vehicles. Any questions?"

"Are they the same people we fought before?" Alyssa asked.

"No. Like I said, it appears to be a military group. Now whether they're here to help people or to press people to join them is unknown. We're sending teams out to warn the other families. I'll do a scouting expedition. Hopefully that will tell us more."

Caleb slipped an arm around Alyssa. Darren lowered his head. Ruth looked toward the sky, her lips moving in silent prayer.

Mark looked around the semi-circle of concerned faces. "Whatever happens, remember, we're a family. We help each other no matter what.

"I'm going to need two teams to warn the others. Caleb, you and Ruth go see the Grants and the Nelsons and the other families in that direction. Mallory, you take Zac and go see Jarrod and the Szymanskis and the others close to them. Contact every family. Drive with caution. If you see something, you come back here immediately. Do not try to take anyone on. You understand?"

They nodded.

"Darren and Alyssa, go about your normal chores, but stay close to the house. Okay, everyone, let's get moving."

The group broke up.

"Lynn, would you go talk to Lincoln?"

"Sure. It'll give me a chance to check on Jenny, too." She started away, stopped, and turned. "Will you be here when I get back?"

"I'm not sure."

"Well, good luck, and be careful."

"I will."

Without another word, Lynn crossed the street and climbed the porch of Lincoln's house. Mark watched until she disappeared through the door. He went to the garage and lifted the overhead door. Inside, he went to one of the work benches and reached underneath. He withdrew a rifle and placed it on the seat of the pickup truck. On the seat was a nine millimeter with two extra full magazines, a survival knife, and binoculars. They had been there since the last time he had driven the truck, several weeks ago.

Mark checked the rifle and popped the box magazine out. He loaded and replaced it. Taking a deep breath to calm his nerves, he backed out of the garage. He didn't want Lynn to see how armed he was; despite his words to the family, his gut was doing flips. He struggled to drive slowly down the driveway. Stopping at the street, he gave one last look at the house Lynn had gone into, and then drove south.

Twenty-Two

MARK DROVE SOUTH TWO miles and turned west on a parallel path one intersection north of Airport Highway Road. Airport in the old world had been a busy four-lane road connecting the city to the smaller towns and rural communities to the west. And as the name suggested, the airport was located along its path. Businesses, a few small shopping centers, and homes lined the route. As far as Mark knew, they were all vacant.

The road Mark traveled ran through mostly rural areas. The street ended several times, and Mark had to use alternate routes to continue west. The slow pace was fine, because Mark wanted to avoid the main road. If Airport was being used by a convoy, it was likely to be watched. Besides, if he ran into traffic, there would be nowhere to hide. At all costs, Mark wanted to avoid contact until he was sure this group of soldiers was no threat to the peaceful community they had developed.

Mark drove about five miles before turning south toward the main road. He pulled off at an old factory and parked in the lot with several abandoned vehicles. Train tracks ran east and west on a raised mound, blocking him further from anyone traveling Airport.

Mark took his weapons and binoculars and walked

toward the street. He climbed onto the mound and lay down next to the tracks. Lifting the binoculars, he took his time scanning what he could see of the highway a quarter mile in front of him. When nothing moved, he turned and searched behind him before moving forward.

He stayed off the road, advancing to the corner. There he hid behind an old ice-cream store. For ten minutes, Mark aimed the binoculars in both directions. Nothing moved. Mark repeated the routine at the next three cross streets. Still, nothing moved, animal or human. He used the glasses once more to study the buildings on the southern side of the road and stopped his sweep at a newer building with a broken front window. He swore. It was a gun store and from the looks, a large one. Someone was now well armed. *Enough weapons to outfit an army?*

Mark crawled away from the road and went back to the truck. He sat there for a while, trying to decide the smartest course of action. Should he press on or go back and see if he'd missed anything behind? To the west, across the overpass, was the airport. Attached to the airport was an Ohio Air National Guard base. It was large, fenced, and open land – a perfect spot to house an army.

Mark would have to cross the road and check out the airport. If there was nothing there, he'd go home. But his gut was talking to him again, and saying his search was over.

Twenty-Three

MARK RETREATED TWO CROSS streets before risking driving across Airport Highway. He raced to the end of the seemingly endless block and turned the corner. There he sat, glasses to eyes, looking for pursuit. Satisfied he remained unobserved, Mark drove on toward the airport.

A mile short of the National Guard base, Mark parked and proceeded on foot. This was a more residential area and offered more cover than the north side had. Moving from yard to yard, Mark drew closer to his destination.

The sound of a truck's engine froze him. He dropped to the ground and crawled from the open center of a backyard to the cover of the house in front of him. There he wedged himself between the chimney box and the deck. Someone would have to be in the backyard to see him. But if they did, he was an easy target with nowhere to run or hide.

The truck drew closer before beginning to fade. Two minutes later, Mark moved to the corner of the house and peered around it. In front of him, across the street, was an eight-foot fence. Beyond the fence was an airfield. Lowering to the ground, Mark crawled between the two houses and stopped behind a bush. He raised the binoculars. His stomach heaved.

Beyond the gate was an operational army-air force base. Dozens of men and women walked around in uniform. Questions staggered Mark like a blow to the head. He rolled on his back and sucked in air in huge gulps. *How could this be?* Paranoid thoughts of some wild conspiracy theory swept through his mind.

Slowly he calmed his breathing and building panic. Finding the cold persona of the killer he had been such a short time ago, Mark rolled and took up the glasses again. This time he scanned the grounds with a dispassionate eye of a general taking in details before forming a battle plan.

A driveway led to a gate. A section of black steel fencing stood ten feet in front of the standard fence, protecting it from being driven through. Along the drive, past the gate, sat yellow cement barriers. Beyond those, a guard house with two armed men, prevented unwanted entry.

A line of trucks was arrayed on the cement pads in front of two fighter jets. People appeared to be working around the planes. There was a constant unhurried movement about the base, giving it the appearance, at least, of being operational. Unanswered was the question of whether the inhabitants were friends or foes.

The entry gate slid back on an automatic track. The base had power. Mark shifted his gaze to the right and discovered why. A massive solar panel field took up a large portion of land to the right of the gate. Mark wasn't sure how much electricity the field generated, but the panels were larger than the ones now resting on his roof, and there were at least fifty times the amount.

A canvas-covered truck drove through the gate and turned down the road away from Mark. The gate closed and the two guards took up watchful positions just beyond the yellow barriers.

The sign out front read *Home of the 180th Fighter Wing,*

and below were the initials O.A.N.G.: Ohio Air National Guard. Underneath, *Homeland Security Forces.*

The base was in the far southeastern corner of the commercial and passenger airport. The terminal was a long way across the runways. There was no sign of life at that end.

Mark raised the glasses to study the tower rising above the terminal. The runways were clear of any planes, but Mark was sure there were people inside the tower. It would be easy for someone with high power binoculars to see anyone approaching by road. *Had they seen my approach?*

Maybe that's why the truck had been dispatched. He sighed. Or perhaps he was being paranoid again.

Mark backed away from his position and crawled along the other side of the house to get a different angle at the field. Again he focused on the tower. Was it his imagination, or was someone up there turned in his direction? He lowered his glasses. Movement closer drew his attention. A man, an officer by his look, had come out of the first building fifty yards behind the gate. He had a two-way radio to his ear. *Damn, how could they've seen me?*

Mark did a mental head slap. Two-way radios – why didn't he think of that? He'd been in the Marines, for Christ's sake. He should've thought of using them. It would've made things so simple, both in their previous conflict and now to reach the other families.

The officer turned his head abruptly toward the gate. He said something into the radio and then to someone inside the building. Then, to Mark's great dismay, the man began jogging toward the gate. Now was a good time to leave.

Other armed men came out of the building and followed. Mark had seen enough. When he cleared the house, he stood and ran, hurdling fences like a track star.

91

The houses on this street were a distance apart, usually with woods and brush between them. He veered to be farther from the street and deeper into the woods that ran behind the houses.

Several minutes later, a vehicle he could not see from his position passed along the side road. They were out looking for him. They'd be able to cut him off at the next block. Mark forced a calm over his mind contrary to the pounding heart that threatened to explode from his chest. He slowed his breathing. To panic now was to make mistakes that could cost him his life.

Wiping the sweat from his brow, he scanned his surroundings. The panic took hold again. A tightness spread across his chest. He had to move and now.

He was about to be trapped.

Twenty-Four

With a burst of adrenaline-enhanced speed, Mark turned left, running away from the streets and farther into thicker woods. He had to abandon his truck and make it home on foot. He gave no thought to the distance. His lone thought was to make it safely. He had no way of knowing how many men had been sent to track him down, but he did know they would fan out in the woods to cover a greater amount of area. Standard procedure was to stay within eyesight of each other. In these woods five or six men could cover a lot of ground.

Noise to his left caused Mark to duck and hide behind a small tree. He did a quick peek. One man was approaching. The soldier didn't have the same fear of being heard since he had back up with him. But was this man on the end of the line, or were there others on both sides of him?

Mark dared not move. The searcher could hardly miss him, but would he shoot or move to secure him as a prisoner? Mark couldn't afford to be wrong on that guess. He had to chance a move.

In a hurry, he searched the ground for something to throw. Even a brief distraction might help him at this point. He found a small twig and peeked again. The soldier was much closer now. He held his rifle ready for a quick shot. Mark still didn't see anyone else. Perhaps he had been wrong about the search and this man foolishly was alone.

Mark made ready to pitch the twig to the left and bolt. He marked a patch of thick brush fifteen yards away. If he reached it undetected, it might conceal him well enough to avoid discovery.

The twig left his hand and hit leaves with only a slight noise. Mark prayed it was enough. He peeked fast. The man had his weapon pointed in the direction of the twig but was standing still. His head turned side to side in a slow arc. He was too smart to fall for Mark's ploy.

As Mark waited to make a move, the guard looked left and pointed to his eyes and then out to the left, signaling another searcher. Mark's hope sank. These were well-trained men. Survival might depend on fighting his way out.

The partner must have signaled back, because the guard moved forward again, his course only altered slightly. In another ten to twelve steps, Mark's position would be revealed. Thoughts sped through his mind, but none had brakes enough to come to a halt.

A sudden commotion, a rustling of branches and leaves, made Mark freeze. What was happening? Had he been discovered? He was afraid to look. Was his pursuer rushing toward him? Mark could wait no longer. He tensed for battle and spun around the tree, rifle pointed. But no target was there. Confusion morphed into panic. Mark pivoted to the right. Nothing. Behind him? Still no one. The guard had disappeared.

Mark didn't know what was happening, but he wasn't about to stand around and find out. To the far left he could see a body moving through the trees; another soldier in camouflage dress. Mark ducked and moved as silent as his screaming mind allowed. He wanted to run.

He didn't know where his hunter had gone, and he didn't care. For the moment, he was alive and free. He was going to take advantage of the lapse.

A low deranged-sounding cackle came from his left and sent shards of ice throughout his veins. Had the guard played him and brought him into the open? If so, he had lost. With the gun held low so it wouldn't appear threatening, Mark turned very slowly. To his surprise, no one was there. An uncontrolled shiver passed through him and didn't let go for a full minute.

The cackle sounded again farther away. Through the trees, a large, dark, hairy body zigzagged. *Big Foot?* He snapped from his shock when a voice called from behind him.

"Sadler, report."

Mark crouched, and in a much more hurried and desperate pace, left the voice behind. He didn't stop for twenty minutes. The rear of a house appeared to his left. Dropping behind a stack of old discarded tires, he pulled out his binoculars. Nothing moved in pursuit.

He dared not linger. Mark increased his speed while crossing the more open backyard. On the other side he stopped. The property bordered the turnpike. A descending slope led down to the paved lanes. There was a metal center barrier, two more lanes and an upward slope – all in the open. He'd be an easy target. To the left was an overpass, but that road led to the air base. His only option appeared to be the right, following the trees along the top of the turnpike, but there were probably soldiers waiting for him there.

It wouldn't take long for them to realize this was the only direction he could've gone. He was trapped again. Then twigs snapped.

Twenty-Five

AS THE HAIRS STOOD on the back of his neck, Mark, whirled, rifle held waist high, pointing at the woods. The chill descended over him once more – so strange, so eerie, almost supernatural. Unnerved, he darted his gaze from spot-to-spot rather than a full scan. Nothing. He shook the feeling and moved toward the overpass along the edge of the trees.

A truck appeared on a road on the far side of the turnpike. Mark dropped to the ground. The truck reached the bridge and crossed, taking an eternity to cross to the other side and disappear.

He continued to lie there, listening for the sound of doors or running steps. His mind played out a scenario where armed troops were dispersing through the woods to surround him. His angst created a chain reaction within his body; increased heart rate, rapid breathing, profuse sweating, and a desire to flee without caution. What sounded like a muffled scream seeped through the trees. On edge, he jumped. It was time to go.

He crawled to the top of the slope, rose to his feet, and ran crouched downhill until he reached the underside of the bridge. There he looked behind for any pursuit. So far he was alone. But he had been running in the open. If the spotter in the tower had seen him, the soldiers might be on his trail soon.

Mark grabbed the steel I-beam beneath the bridge and craned his neck to see above. No one followed, but he couldn't shake the nagging feeling that someone was watching him. *Could the man in the tower see him?*

Mark slid down the cement slope until he reached the paved road below. Looking left and right, he dashed for the safety of the cement support pillars in the median. Ducking behind them, he sighted through the rifle's scope. Right of the bridge, left of the bridge: no one was in view. Then a dark shadow moved up on the slope. Just a quick flash and it was gone. The vision spooked Mark, and he dashed for the next set of pillars without caring if anyone saw him.

There, he stopped again. This time nothing moved at all through his scope. Perhaps the shadow before had been his imagination. He shuddered like someone was playing his nerves like a banjo. Turning, he sprinted the final distance to the opposite side. Using the bridge to keep him obscured from the tower's line of sight, Mark climbed the slope.

Here was the one danger spot of his escape route. The next source of cover was thirty yards away. In his best days he could run a 4.4 forty, but four seconds was a long time to avoid a sniper's bullet. He searched the brush across the turnpike as well as the road above. Now or never. He hesitated. He feared the never.

With a burst, Mark climbed the final steps to the flat ground above and ran as hard as he could to the trees ahead. No shouts of alarm sounded behind him. No trucks followed nor, more importantly, did any bullets. Mark reached the first tree and blasted straight through the branches until he was four tree trunks deep. There he stopped, bent over, struggling for air.

He was too old to do this stuff again. He'd been too old to do it the first time. Now Mark was just pressing his luck. He took off at a jog heading east and kept under cover until he came to a road. Squatting, Mark slowed his breathing while he studied the open ground left and right. The only sound was his controlled breaths.

Mark was just about to cross the road when he heard the deuce and a half truck. He dived back just as the vehicle rolled to the intersection. It stopped for a moment and then turned, driving right past him. He held his breath. His cover wasn't complete, but he was afraid to move.

To his great relief, the truck continued past. As the army green canvas top disappeared over a rise in the road, Mark bolted for the other side. They had not given up the search for him. The trip home was going to take a long time.

When he reached the road where he had left the truck, Mark toyed with the idea of trying to reach it. Having the truck would make getting home easier, but it also made him easier to spot. There was nothing he really needed inside the truck, and certainly nothing that could lead anyone back to the house, he hoped. In the end, Mark's best choice was to get farther away from any pursuit then find another vehicle to drive home.

He alternated his route east and north, one block at a time. About three miles later, he entered a residential neighborhood that had not been picked over by scavengers. He broke into a house and found bottled sweet teas. Although he hated his tea sweet, Mark drank two bottles and slid a third in the back pocket of his jeans.

He opened a box of peanut butter-filled crackers and munched on them while he went to the garage. A red Cadillac was parked in one space. Mark went back inside to search for the keys. A lone key hung from a series of pegs attached the side of the refrigerator. Bingo! It had the Cadillac emblem on it.

Mark did not start the engine yet. Now that he had a car, he took advantage of the space. He went back inside and rummaged for anything useful. With the car loaded with food and drinks, Mark opened the garage door and backed down the driveway. He put his handgun in the cup holder built into the center console. He practiced grabbing it a few times, and then drove through the subdivision until he found the exit. The road was clear. He drove to the first intersection and turned north.

He took a very circuitous route and only made his way toward the house when he was sure no one was tailing him. His adventure left him with many unanswered questions. If the army unit had moved into the base, they were close.

There was a lot to think about, many plans to make, and much to fear.

Twenty-Six

"DID YOU SEE that?"

"Since it was right in front of us, Sis, it was kinda hard to miss."

"Don't be an ass."

"Hey, I was just saying."

The object of interest was a red Cadillac that had gone by at a high speed. Bobby and Becca were sitting in the pickup in the driveway of a house that sat back off the road a long way. The drive was covered by woods on both sides, making it difficult to see. Which, of course, was the reason Bobby had selected it.

They had stopped for lunch, and to give Becca a chance to wash and change. She looked a whole lot more human now. Bobby stuffed half a canned peach into his mouth. The juice dripped down his chin. Using his sleeve he wiped the trail clean. "Why should we follow?"

"Maybe whoever was driving might know where Dad is."

"He might also be a killer like everyone else we've run into so far."

Becca lowered her head and looked into the half-eaten can of SpaghettiOs in her hands.

"Becca, we'll find him, I promise. You just need to be

patient. There's a lot of area to cover. I know you're anxious. I am too. But it won't do us any good to rush into a situation where we might get killed or captured."

She looked at him. "You promise, right?"

"Absolutely." He crossed his heart, the motion spilling peach juice on his pants. "Shit!" He wiped at the liquid.

Becca laughed.

"Yeah, that's funny, huh? How'd you like it?" He pretended to spill some on her.

In a flash everything changed. Her face scrunched into an evil persona. "Try it," she shouted, but the voice wasn't hers. Before he could blink, she had a knife pointed at his face. His mouth opened in shock. He froze, afraid to move, lest she think his actions were aggressive. But he couldn't slow the pounding of his heart.

They both stared at the point of the blade as she held it perfectly still, inches from Bobby's eye. Becca's face morphed back into her own. She lowered the knife, her cheeks reddened.

"I-I'm sorry, Bobby. I don't know what happened."

"Jesus, Becca, what the hell's wrong with you?" Bobby opened the door and jumped out. He pitched the can of peaches against a tree and walked away.

"Bobby, I'm sorry. Come back. Please."

Bobby ignored her. He needed to calm his nerves. Becca had seemed okay when they left the house, but as each hour passed without finding their father, she reverted to her unstable personality. Her evil self, as Bobby silently named it.

He loved his sister, but in truth, she scared him. They couldn't find their father fast enough. Bobby longed to be able to turn her over to Dad and let him deal with her. After being with her 24-7 these past weeks, he was ready for a break. Besides, he wasn't sure how much longer he'd survive. That knife had come out of nowhere, so fast that Bobby never could have countered her had she decided to plunge the blade into him. He couldn't live this way.

The car door shut. Bobby stiffened, but with great control did not turn to face her. He was taking a huge risk. There was no guarantee which persona came out of the pickup. For all he knew, she was advancing leading with the knife.

Bobby fought the urge to run. Becca's hand on his shoulder caused him to jump. His heart stopped a beat and his bladder threatened to release.

"Geez, Bobby, relax. I'm not going to hurt you. You're my brother. I love you. I could never hurt you. I'm sorry about before. I don't know what came over me."

Bobby looked at her. Her face was so innocent now. Her eyes held sadness. But how long would this personality stay? She stuck out a pouty lip.

"I screwed up. I'm sorry."

More like you are *screwed up.*

She leaned forward to kiss his cheek. Bobby flinched away.

"Come on, Bobby, don't be mad at me. I can't take that. I need your strength."

He held still and let her kiss him. As she went back to the pickup, Bobby resisted an urge to wipe the kiss from his face. He sighed. *Where are you, Dad?*

Twenty-Seven

BACK IN THE DRIVER'S seat, Bobby said, "Ready to go?"

"Yeah, let's find him."

Bobby shifted into gear and edged forward. At the driveway's end, he stopped and looked both ways. Satisfied, he pulled out just as an army truck barreled down the side street half a block away.

The vehicle lurched as the brakes grabbed. The truck swerved but didn't flip over. "Shit!" Bobby spun the wheel hard left and accelerated. The engine growled as it sped forward.

The rearview mirror revealed the truck was turning around. This was not good. How many men were inside the truck? They had a lead and the pickup should be more maneuverable than an army truck. He shot down the road trying to form a plan of evasion. Cross streets were few and far between out in the country, but one was coming up. He glanced in the mirror. The truck was now following.

Bobby turned a hard left and almost couldn't hold the road. The tires spun on the loose gravel on the side of the road before catching. The pickup jumped forward. Up ahead was a major thoroughfare. If he took it, he'd easily outdistance his pursuers, but they'd also be in the open for a long way. He decided to risk it. Behind him the truck had not yet reached the intersection.

Turning right, Bobby headed west. Ahead was a cross street. If he could reach it before the truck reached the main street, the pursuers would have no idea where he was. "Watch behind us, Sis. Tell me if they see us turn."

Becca spun in her seat and looked out the rear window.

Bobby made the turn.

"Nope, we're good."

Bobby began to relax. They should be able to lose them easy now. The pickup rose as it crossed an overpass. Descending the other side showed him a large fenced area to the right and a few houses spaced apart on the left. He toyed with the idea of pulling up a driveway and hiding behind a house, but that would give up his advantage. He continued further and then slammed on the brakes.

Up ahead, a jeep was exiting the fenced area – with a machine gun mounted on the back.

The pickup's tires gripped the road. The tail began swerving sideways, threatening to flip over. Bobby's hands slapped the wheel hard, adjusting in time to keep the wheels grounded, but the move brought him closer to the jeep.

"They're coming." Becca jacked a round into her handgun.

"We have to go back. If they open up with that machine gun, we won't stand a chance." Bobby turned quickly, running across the front lawn of a house, and pushed the pedal to the floor. As they crested the overpass, the canvas-topped truck was driving straight for them. A quick look behind confirmed Bobby's fears – they were about to be trapped on the bridge.

"Hold on," he shouted. He drove straight at the truck. The machine gun wouldn't fire with the truck in their line of sight.

"What are you going to do?" Becca squealed.

"I'm gonna ram the truck. Open your door and get

ready to jump before I hit them."

"Seriously?"

Bobby didn't respond.

She opened the door and stepped on the doorstep.

Bobby slowed for a second. "Now."

He didn't watch, but knew she was gone. He punched the accelerator again. The driver of the truck, evidently thinking Bobby was going to try to drive past him, turned sideways to block the entire road. Too late he saw his mistake. The driver's eyes widened.

The collision lifted the pickup in the air pitching Bobby forward where he met the exploding airbag face-first. Though stunned, Bobby retained enough sense to move. Not waiting to see if the seat belt opened, Bobby used his knife to puncture the bag and slice through the restraining belt. He was out the door in seconds and running to the walkway over the bridge.

Shouting voices came from the back of the truck. Bobby raced past as a hand shot out to grab him. He ducked enough to avoid the grasp and ran for the opposite side of the bridge. He glanced around for his sister but didn't see her. A moment of panic assaulted him, and then he heard the scream. But the scream was not Becca's.

He stopped and turned. Becca jumped down from the truck's running board. The driver was holding his head. Men emerged from the truck's bed.

"Come on," Bobby urged. He started running again. There were woods in front of him. They needed to get there to break up any clear lines of sight shooters might have.

Bobby made the trees safely and stopped to cover Becca. She was ten strides away. Any thought Bobby had of successfully escaping was diminished when he saw the pursuit. Half a dozen soldiers followed, each with a rifle.

Becca blasted past him. "What are you waiting for?"
Indeed.

Bobby ran. There was not enough room to move with

stealth. Brother and sister, side-by-side, crashed through the undergrowth. Bobby looked behind for an instant and was smacked in the face by a branch Becca had pushed through. The blow stunned him for a second, but offered a chance to spy any pursuit. He was surprised to see that no one was following, or at least none that he could see. If these guys were trained soldiers, they could be on him and he might not know until it was too late. The thought spurred him forward. He caught Becca and squeaked out, "Something's wrong."

"What?"

"No one's behind us."

"Maybe they gave up."

"Doubtful. They may have gone around to catch us wherever this comes out."

Becca ran on. A moment later she said, "Well, that would be stupid. We should stop and turn around."

"I don't think so. There's sure to be someone back there. Most likely they're moving forward to pinch us between the two forces. I think we change direction though."

"Okay, what are you thinking?"

"Well, we don't know where this comes out in this direction. We know to the left there's a road."

"And you don't think we can go back?"

"I don't think that'd be smart. To the right is the turnpike. It's so wide open, they may not expect us to go that way."

"So that's your plan? Run into the open?"

Bobby grunted. "You got a better idea?"

"Lead on, brother."

Bobby cut in front of her and went right. Becca followed. A few minutes later they reached the edge of their cover. The turnpike lay below, wide open for miles. There was no one in sight. "Wait to see if I draw fire." Bobby didn't wait for a response. He held his breath and stepped into the open. He slid down the slope. No bullet hit him.

When he reached bottom, Becca began her descent. Bobby started running for the far overpass. It was less than a mile away but seemed a lot farther. He was running so hard to reach cover, he almost didn't hear Becca fall. Ten steps after the sound registered, he turned. Becca was now running with a limp.

Bobby waited for her, scanning the woods above. They'd been lucky so far. As he grabbed her arm to help her, he caught a glimpse of a man standing on the bridge behind, where the truck still sat. Shit! The man was holding his hands to his face like he held binoculars. They'd been found.

Twenty-Eight

MYRON SAT AT THE table and stared out over the water. He had repacked his bag, adding as much food as would fit. But he hated to waste what was left. Back and forth he argued for leaving or staying. It was peaceful here and off the main roads. He might be safe here for a while.

The water looked inviting. If he left, he might not get another opportunity to bathe. The thought of being caught in the water gave him chills, as though someone was already watching him. Despite his apprehension, Myron slipped his T-shirt over his head and looked at the pale skin beneath. "Man, I'm really skinny." He laughed and flexed his muscles, surprised to see the small bulge in his arms. "Where were you when there were girls to impress?" He laughed again, and then covered his mouth when he realized how loud he was.

Inside the shed, Myron looked through the bathing suits. Most were too big or for girls, but he found one he could cinch tight enough not to fall off. He caught a whiff of his pits. "Man, you do need a bath." Grabbing a towel, he peeked out of the shed to make sure the situation hadn't changed.

He walked to the edge of the water and dipped his foot. "Man, that's cold." Myron walked into the water until he was knee deep. There he stood until he said, "Oh, just do it." He ran into the water, gasped, but dived under. He started swimming and was surprised he could reach the other end. He had never been very good, but swimming was one of the few physical activities he enjoyed. His muscles strained as he pulled against the water.

When his feet touched the bottom, he stood crouched below the water. His body adjusted to the cold. Myron leaned forward and pushed off the bottom, gliding across the surface until his momentum stopped and he had to stroke to keep from sinking. He angled across the pond toward the house.

For the next twenty minutes, Myron swam nonstop. When he was tired, he stepped out of the water, shivering at the slight breeze crossing his body. He picked up the towel and dried off. His mind was made up. He was staying at least one more night.

All that activity had made him hungry. He sat under the sun and ate. Soon afterward, he became drowsy. He lay down and closed his eyes. The touch of the sun on his pale skin had a calming and restful effect. It warmed him all the way through his body. He dozed.

Something strange entered his consciousness. His eyes snapped open. He lifted up on his elbows and yawned. *How long have I been sleeping?* If the redness on his chest was any indication it had been a while. He touched his chest leaving a white mark that faded to red. "Oh man!" *I wonder if they have any sunscreen or lotion in the house.*

Then, almost as an afterthought, he remembered that something had woken him. He sat up and looked around. Was it just a dream? Myron stood and walked back to the shed. He dressed in a hurry. Then the sound came again. A car was coming and sounded close.

Myron grabbed his pack and the bag of food and hid behind the shed. He glanced around the corner in time to see a jeep pass. Fear struck him hard, freezing him to the spot. His stomach churned, sending sour and acidic gas up his esophagus. He swallowed hard, hoping to keep his lunch down.

The haunting sight of the man and woman's body dancing to the machine gun's tune flooded his memory. Myron squeezed tight to avoid wetting his pants. He glanced back, but the horror machine was no longer in sight. The path he'd chosen for escape seemed much farther now. Myron might not reach the trees behind the pond in time. He didn't want to die like the couple did. He sobbed. He didn't want die at all. Myron sneaked another peek. Someone was in the yard. It was too late. His legs buckled and he sank to the ground. A tremor rose through his body.

The voice from his nightmares called out again, "Stop! Don't run."

Myron covered his face.

Grunts, groans, and slaps filled the yard. There was a fight going on. That gave Myron a second's hope. If they were after someone else, maybe they wouldn't see him. He risked a look. There were another man and woman fighting with a group of soldiers. One soldier was on the ground, another was holding his knee.

The man and woman each had two attackers on them. As Myron watched, transfixed by the battle, the woman went down, her opponent crawled on top, pinning her to the ground. A punch landed, yet still she fought on.

The man called out, "Becca!" and rushed to her rescue. He leaped at the two soldiers in a flying tackle and rolled both men off the woman. "Run," he shouted.

The woman kicked one of her attackers in the face and scrambled to her feet. She sprinted toward the shed.

Fearing discovery, Myron pulled back. Something crashed into the picnic table. He flinched and closed his eyes. His fingers touched the gun in his bag. As if working independently of his brain, his hand wrapped around the butt and he withdrew it. He was staring at the gun when the woman's head appeared beyond the edge of the shed. He was so startled he almost shot himself. A wave of panic assailed him leaving him unable to move. His throat constricted like he'd swallowed a golf ball. Myron could barely breathe.

An unseen force caught her from behind and began dragging her away. She turned her head and saw Myron. For a moment, Myron thought he saw hope in her eyes. Then, just as fast, she shook her head at Myron and said, "No." But was she talking to him or her attacker?

She looked behind her and must have kicked someone. "Bitch."

The woman grabbed on to the end of the shed. Her face was not more than a yard away.

"Help us," she pleaded.

Myron pushed to his feet and tried to raise his courage. Another look of hope reached her eyes.

A gunshot ripped into the ground near her. They both jumped. Myron dropped the gun and slapped his hands over his mouth to keep from crying out.

"The next one goes in your head," a man warned.

"Save yourself," the woman whispered, before she was dragged from sight.

Twenty-Nine

NOW, MYRON TOLD HIMSELF. He pictured what he wanted to do. Jump out from his hiding place, gun raised. He would pull the trigger and shoot all the soldiers. He could do it. He'd seen the entire scene play out like a TV show. He was ready. Now, he repeated in his mind. Yet still he remained frozen to the ground.

He thought of the woman. She needed his help, but just like the last time, he stood by and did nothing. In his mind's eye this woman's face morphed into the dead woman. She looked at him and said, "You killed her too."

"No," he said. The guilt hit him like a hammer. The weight of his ancestors' judgment sat heavy upon his shoulders. "No, not this time."

Taking a deep breath, Myron jumped out from the shed and readied to fire. However, he had taken so long to work up his courage, the backyard was no longer occupied. He wiped his eyes clear of tears and looked again.

"Oh God." He broke into a run toward the house. Stopping at the corner he pressed into the bricks. A quick peek. No one was there. Myron slid along the side wall until he reached the front. The jeep was just leaving. A man was climbing into the back of the truck, and it began to move. Myron was too late.

"No, not this time," he repeated and went after the jeep. Along the front of the houses he ran, giving chase.

The jeep turned right at the first intersection. The truck followed. It was easy to keep pace with the truck. It was in no hurry. When it turned at the corner too, Myron was only one house back. He crossed the street and ducked behind a tree, waiting until no one in the rear of the truck could see him.

The truck picked up speed. Myron had never been an athlete, so running was not something he could endure for long. He cried out when the pain in his side forced him to stop. No, he couldn't fail again.

Bent over, sucking in air, Myron found a new determination. That woman could have given him up, and he'd be captured too. She gave him his freedom, even knowing she was losing hers. He wouldn't turn his back on her.

Myron straightened up and looked in the distance. The truck's brake lights were two red pinholes in a backdrop of green. Then the small image turned broadside to the right. A second later it was gone, the woman with it.

He saw her face before him, so clear he could almost touch it. She was beautiful. He blinked, and she was gone. *But not for long.* He wasn't sure how, but he would find her. Mentally, Myron marked the spot where the truck turned.

He would start his search from there. Myron retraced his steps to the shed where he gathered his things. He dug through his pack until he found the golden feather. His ancestors were giving him another chance to earn their respect – a second chance at redemption. He would not fail them or the woman, whose green eyes still pierced his mind.

Thirty

MARK STOOD IN THE center of what he called the community. Representatives of eleven households were there.

"I'm sorry to call you together like this, but I thought it was important for you to be aware of a new group of people who have moved into the area."

Mark held up his hand to halt the murmuring. "I don't know whether they're a threat or not, so let me explain first. Juan came to me this morning after seeing a convoy of soldiers drive along Airport Highway. He was concerned and rightly so.

"I sent runners to bring you all here. Earlier I went to scout out this new group. I have to admit, I had mixed feelings when I heard about them. Most of you are aware of the fight we had a short while back with a group I called the Horde. So when I heard another army of men had moved in, I was fearful. None of us wants to go through that again.

"On the other hand, if they actually were American soldiers, they might be here to help us. I wanted to be sure. So I set out to find them, and did."

The buzz in the crowd grew as everyone spoke at once.

"They're staying at the old Air National Guard base at

the airport. I'm not sure how many of them there are. My guess would be fifty. I did see some women and they were in uniform too, like the men.

"I watched for a while and then got spotted. They sent armed men after me. Now maybe they were just being protective of their base and nothing would've happened to me, but I was only going to get that one chance to be wrong, so I ran. They chased me for quite a time before I eluded them."

"About gave us all a heart attack too," Caleb said. "He drove up the driveway fast in a car we didn't recognize."

"Yeah," Mallory said. "He almost got his ass shot."

Tim Grant said, "So, what do we do now?"

"I'm not sure," Mark replied.

Mr. Szymanski asked, "Well, should we send a delegation to speak to them?"

Mark said, "That's certainly an option. I think we need to make contact somehow, if only to determine what their intentions are. I don't suggest we send someone into the hornets' nest though."

"Why?" Szymanski said. "If we show up in peace with no weapons, how can they see us as a threat?"

"I'm not saying you're wrong, Bill. My concern is if they're not friendly and get their hands on one of us, they could easily make that person give up the location of the other families."

"I think Mark's got the right thought there," Jarrod offered. "We need to be alert and watch each other's backs. We stand together, and then it will be easier to fend off any interlopers."

Lincoln said, "Still, we need to know whether this army means to cause people trouble or not. There has to be a way, without anyone getting hurt."

"I agree with everything everyone has said," Mark said. "I'm just saying we need more information before we make a decision. I'll go back and scout them out again and see if I can determine patrol routines. It might be a lot safer stopping one of the vehicles than going to their base."

"That's a good idea," Lincoln said. "I can go with you or take a turn watching. Whatever you want to do."

"That's fine. Now listen, I had an idea about how we can better stay in touch. I sent Lynn and some of the kids to the shopping center down the road a few miles in search of two-way radios."

"Walkie-talkies?" Bill said.

"Absolutely. It will help us communicate with each other. The radios may not have the range to reach each house, but we can pass messages from house to house if necessary. That way, if we see trouble, we can call for help or send a warning. You just have to make sure you have enough batteries on hand. Don't let them run down."

"We should set up a series of signals too, in case we can't talk," Adam Brandford said.

"Yep," Mark replied. "Easy enough to do. I just wish we were all located a little closer together. We may have to find one central area to come to if and when we need to join forces."

"Why not here?" Jarrod said. "It's pretty much centrally located."

"That's fine by me. There's plenty of room. Anyone got another place in mind?"

After a little discussion, they agreed on Mark's property as the meeting place.

Before Mark could move on to other business, the sound of a racing car engine reached them. Seconds later, a car flew up the driveway. Everyone scattered. Mark, Jarrod, and Caleb pointed guns at the car.

Juan's wife, Maria, exited and ran toward the group. There were two young children in the back seat. "Juan. Juan, are you here?" The panicked woman searched the group for her husband.

"Maria," Mark said. "Juan's not here. I was wondering where he was."

"He never came home. He went off to warn everyone about the soldiers, but I never saw him again. He was going to come back and get us. He was so worried about leaving us alone. I was to pack some things and he would come here. He never came back." Fat tears rolled down Maria's face.

Mark put an arm around her. "We'll find him, Maria." Then to Lincoln, "How quick can you be ready to move? We can't wait for night."

"Two minutes." Lincoln darted off across the street.

"What should we do, Mark?" Mr. Szymanski asked.

As Maria continued to cry against his chest, Mark looked around at the tense faces and prayed a new battle wasn't about to begin.

Part Four

Thirty-One

THE ROAD MYRON TRAVELED dead-ended into another street, making the decision to go right an easy one. A quarter mile farther, he ran for cover. A vehicle was near.

He ducked under some low branches and watched along the road. In front of him, not more than forty yards, a jeep moved at a slow speed. Myron curled into a ball and tried not to shake. *Shit! Those are the same guys who murdered those people.* The men inside turned and looked both ways. Then, with a lurch, the jeep turned toward Myron. He froze, afraid to breathe. He closed his eyes. The Jeep flew past and turned down the street Myron had left.

Maybe this was an entire army. If so, Myron was in over his head. Every bit of common sense shouted at him to turn around and run, but he couldn't erase the woman's eyes from his mind. In some strange way they gave him the courage to continue. With great effort, he slowed his breathing. Though his heart still pounded hard, he calmed enough to at least fake bravery.

He crept forward, keeping to the cover of the trees and brush twenty feet off the road. Up ahead on the left, a wide driveway appeared. Myron continued until he was almost out of cover. He craned his neck.

"Oh my God!"

There, spread out before him, was an entire army base. Myron dug in his pack for the small binoculars and scanned the area. Beyond the chain link fences and the concrete barriers, past the buildings and the parked trucks, were two fighter jets.

Activity bustled around the jets. Someone was inside the cockpit of the jet on the right. *How many soldiers were on the base?* He watched for another minute and then retreated for more cover.

Myron laid his head on his hands and sighed. *Now what do I do?* His heart rate slowed as a sense of doom washed over him. How was he supposed to take on an entire army to rescue that woman? *After all I really don't know her.* There was no way. He needed to get as far away from there as possible, yet something refused to let him go. His stomach cramped.

"Are you kidding me?" he said much too loud. He looked around and lowered his voice, continuing his one person discussion. "Do you care about what some dead guy might think of you? How stupid is that? We're talking about your life here." He paused as if waiting for a response. "I mean, I do want to help her, but if it's me against an army, there's just no way. What can I do?"

From some place deep inside, anger surfaced and voiced its opinion. *At least scout the area and gather information before you quit like you always do.* He didn't move. The decision was too hard. *Come on, Myron, at least try.*

Myron used the glasses to scan the opposite side of the street moving away from the base. About fifty yards to the left of the base was a house. He studied the house for a while. There was no movement, but that didn't mean the house was vacant. Maybe one of the officers lived there.

Another ten minutes and Myron crawled backward,

away from the road. From there he traversed sideways until he was across from the house. Checking the house and the road once more, he gathered whatever courage he possessed and dashed for the house, running all the way into the backyard. Woods dominated the land behind the house. Where Myron thought the base's fence might be stood a barrier of large trees. At least there was cover for his reconnaissance. The trees, however, stopped six feet from the fence.

Stepping through the trees, Myron reached the eight-foot high chain link fence. He used a branch to determine if it was electrified. Maybe the army had electricity. For that matter, maybe they were the ones responsible for the epidemic that killed everyone. Though that thought frightened him he continued walking along the fence.

Twenty more steps brought him behind a large two-story metal-roofed brick building. Another smaller one-story building stood twenty feet past the first. Both backed to the woods, ten feet inside the surrounding fence.

Myron continued past the two buildings until he could see the entire base. There were a lot of people, but none of them were close to the buildings. Uniformed bodies bustled around the jets and the larger buildings on the far side of the base. To the far left of the buildings, runways stretched off in the distance. Assorted size hangars were offset on either side of the runways. A large glass-enclosed tower rose from the terminal, A second set of runways, off to his left, ran north and south.

Myron took in the details, but he didn't need to be an analyst to understand that if the woman was being held inside the base, a snowball had a better chance in hell than he did at a successful rescue.

Turning his attention to the jets, Myron stared in awe. These were actual fighter jets like he'd seen in movies. When he could break his eyes away from the jets, Myron made a mental map of the grounds. Behind the jets were two large buildings with a massive door in the center of each that Myron thought must be the hangars. Next to them were other smaller structures.

Farther down the fence to the left were two rectangular cement block buildings. They were twenty yards beyond the first two buildings he passed. Myron scampered past the space between the buildings and stopped behind the last building in line. It was also the smallest structure. The ground was wide open beyond the buildings.

Myron continued in that direction until he could look back at the base. It offered him a view of the area in front of the near buildings. The sight made him drop to the ground. Covering his head, he held his breath. Any second, bullets might rip into him. His heart hammered in his chest like a drum leading the enemy to him. After several long moments he released his breath and risked a peek. Slick with sweat Myron had to wipe his eyes to see. The last building was a flat top brick building perhaps twenty by thirty. What made this building different though, wasn't the design or the construction, it was the two armed guards standing in front of the door.

Thirty-Two

MYRON MOVED BEHIND THE small building, keeping it between him and the guards. Why would there be guards? To keep someone out or to keep someone in. Perhaps this was where they kept their weapons and ammunition.

Two small, darkened windows sat high in the rear wall.

Myron studied the building and the fence, which was thirty feet from the rear wall. That was a lot of open ground to cover without being seen. It was too far to risk without knowing what was inside.

Myron set his pack on the ground. A sudden adrenaline-laced fear raced through him. He had to do something. He fought back the rushing panic and focused his glasses on the base.

Before he changed his mind, he slipped his shoe inside a link, grabbed higher up, and pulled. He rose slowly. With each step, his body shook and the fence rattled. He grabbed tight and closed his eyes. With all his concentration Myron willed his body still. With a deep breath he opened his eyes and ascended again. When he was high enough to have an angle to see inside the building, he pulled the glasses from his mouth and pressed them to his eyes.

Myron looked into the window. A wall came into view. He turned his head sideways in both directions, but saw nothing. He tried to look down and again saw – wait. He tried to lift higher, but had no angle. Something was there. It looked like hair.

Putting the binoculars back in his mouth, Myron scaled higher. His hand was at the top crossbar now. He worked an arm over the top, hung there, and searched through the glasses again. A head. No, two heads. He straightened his legs and rose above the top of the fence. Multiple heads. The people must be sitting on the floor.

He scanned left and stopped. His heart missed a beat and he almost lost his grip on the fence. There she was, her head leaning against the wall, her face looking upward, her eyes closed.

Myron studied her. She was beautiful. He couldn't take his eyes from her. Then, as if she knew he was there, her green eyes opened and seemed to be looking right at him. He did lose his grip then and slipped painfully down the fence.

When Myron hit the ground, his ankle twinged. Fear of discovery pushed the pain aside, and he snapped up the pack as he scampered into the woods, making entirely too much noise as he went.

Myron exited the trees on the other side, into the backyard, and turned right. From there he sprinted away from the house and deeper into the woods. A few minutes later, he dropped his pack. From there he crawled back toward the fence. When he reached a position where he could look down the fence line, he used the glasses to see if anyone was looking for him.

By some miracle Myron hadn't seemed to draw any attention. He crawled to his pack, rested his head on top, and stared up at the treetops. *Well, I found her. Now what the hell am I going to do?*

Thirty-Three

MARK EASED TO A stop. He looked around, swinging his head in a fast arc from left to right. Cornfields that were being overrun by weeds lined both sides of the road.

"What's the matter?" Lincoln asked.

Mark didn't respond. Turning, he grabbed the back of Lincoln's seat and studied the area behind them. He saw nothing, but the hairs on the back of his neck sprung to attention.

Lincoln had his gun in hand. "Mark, you're making me nervous, man. What's going on?"

Mark faced front and pointed. "You see the SUV in that field? I think that's Juan's."

They had been driving more than an hour up and down roads Juan might have used to reach his home.

Up ahead, perhaps seventy yards, the rear end of an SUV protruded from the stalks on the right. The field began twenty feet from the road. Had Juan gone off the road by accident or had he been forced?

"Shit!" Lincoln said. "Maybe he just ran off the road. He could be inside, hurt."

"Yeah, maybe." Mark scanned the surrounding road and fields again. "I'm gonna go out there and check. You get in the driver's seat. Keep watching the roadsides and behind you. Move up if I motion you."

"Shouldn't I go with you, you know, to back you up?"

"No, if this is a trap we'll need a fast getaway. We can't afford to give up our ride."

"But if it is a trap you're gonna need the extra firepower."

"Lincoln, just trust me. This is the best way. If there's someone out there, we don't want to stand and exchange shots with them. We want to get out of here as fast as possible." Mark opened the door and stepped out. With an eye on the SUV, he said, "Listen, if something happens and you see me go down, don't you risk your life to come get me. You turn this thing around and get back to the farm." He looked Lincoln in the eyes and held them with a hard stare.

Lincoln's breathing was rapid and sweat ran down his face.

"This is important, Lincoln. You have to think of everyone else. Do not hesitate. Go back and get them ready. Call all the families together."

"Man, you can't—"

"Hey, can I count on you or not? Tell me you can do this."

Mark's tone was harsh, but it needed to be to get the man to understand the importance of seeing to everyone's safety.

"Yeah, I can do it." Lincoln shifted into the driver's seat. "Just don't get your ass shot."

"That's my intention." Mark pushed the door closed and pulled his gun.

Mark advanced toward the crash site, his gaze constantly sweeping left to right and back.

A gust of wind blew, moving the thigh high stalks. Mark crouched and spun to the right, gun aimed and ready. Nothing. Just the wind. He stood and tried to shake the tension from his body. He searched for the calm he had during the fight with the Horde, but it would not come.

He continued his approach. When he was even with the SUV, he studied the interior for movement. He stepped off the road and angled toward the driver's side where the door stood open. It was Juan's vehicle. The "proud parent of…" sticker adorned the rear bumper. The child in question had died during the first round of deaths. Miraculously, the only loss the family of five had endured. Well, perhaps until now.

Stop it! Believe he's still alive until you know for certain.

He reached the door and looked inside. No body. That was a good sign. Maybe. Maybe the crash was something as simple as an accident.

Mark began to relax. Maybe Juan was trying to walk home. He could be dazed from the impact, which looked to be minimal, and having trouble finding his way. Then he noticed a spot in the passenger door, a small hole. The size a bullet might make. *Damn!*

He walked around the vehicle and found several other holes. Juan had been attacked. Mark went back to the open door and looked inside. No blood there, but small dots of red stood out on the green stalks trampled beneath the tires. Juan had been hurt.

He followed the blood, but the trail stopped after only a few feet. If Juan was dead, where was the body? Juan either escaped or had been taken captive alive. Mark sighed. *Where do we go from here?*

He was afraid he already knew the answer.

Thirty-Four

THE DOOR OPENED AND two men in uniform tossed the small Latino man on the floor.

Bobby and Becca moved to help the beaten man. Bobby looked his body over to see if there was anything broken.

Becca whispered, "Don't worry, you're with friends now. We'll help you. Where does it hurt?"

The man opened one eye and stared at her. His pupil looked dilated, but Becca wasn't sure what that meant.

"I can't see or feel any obvious breaks," Bobby said. The cut above his own eye had scabbed over. The area around the socket was turning colors. He also had a swollen lip. "Let's try to lift him and move him to the wall. Go easy though in case there's something internal."

They each grabbed the man under an arm. Bobby supported his head, which the injured man did not seem able to control, and slid him to the wall.

Becca glanced at the other two people in the room. They cowered there, a tall hairy man who sat with his arm around a skinny and equally unkempt woman. The woman had done nothing but cry since they all arrived. Becca wanted to slap her into silence. The wretched thing had been quiet for a while, but now started up again. The tension rose, and Becca was ready to spring.

A hand touched her arm. Bobby shook his head at her. She held his gaze for a moment and then relaxed. How could her brother remain so calm?

THE LATINO MAN TRIED to speak. "Did you ...?"

"What?" Bobby said. He leaned closer.

"Did you do it?"

"Do what?"

The man swallowed hard. Then he coughed. Before he could speak again the door opened.

The two soldiers entered first, followed by what Bobby thought were two officers. Behind them were two more guards. The first officer walked to the far end of the room. The building was just the one room, and seemed to be on a military base. The walls were bare and there was no furniture. The room appeared to be a holding cell.

The second officer stopped and took a long look at each of his prisoners.

"My name is General Edward West. I am in charge of this National Guard post."

General West was a medium-sized man who had hard eyes and the look of a real officer. His voice was high-pitched and resonated with controlled anger.

"You have been brought here for two reasons. First, to be new recruits of the 180th division of the new American army. The second reason, however, is more important. Two of my men have been murdered. I want the killer. If that person is in this room, I will find you. That person will be executed."

He pointed to the injured man. "I deplore using

131

that kind of force against American citizens, but as you are aware, these are not normal times. We are here to protect America from being overrun by enemies of this country. When these men, who are putting their lives on the line, are brutally murdered, I will go to endless lengths to find and punish the person or persons responsible.

"Spare yourself and your fellow Americans the pain of interrogation and speak now. Which of you killed my men?" He started pacing toward the other officer. "Perhaps you thought it was in self-defense. Maybe you thought the soldiers were there to harm you, and you panicked. If any of this is true or you have some other explanation, tell me, I'll listen. Sometimes mistakes are made. I understand that."

West turned and waited. The skinny woman cried harder.

Becca sprang to her feet. Every man in the room except the general pointed a weapon at her.

"We didn't kill any of your men. Although I'm sure some of them have some injuries from when they attacked us, for no reason. We did nothing to you or your men. As far as I'm concerned, the only guilty people here are you and your army, for kidnapping us." She pointed at the injured man. "You claim to want to protect Americans and look what you've done. Tortured one of your people."

The general let a humorless smile touch his lips. He motioned for the men to lower their weapons. "Well, as I said, these are unusual times. If you are innocent, as you claim, you have nothing to worry about. You will be inducted into the guard to help protect this great country."

He walked closer, stopping a foot away from Becca. "Tell me, was that your knife my men brought to me? The survival knife in the sheath?"

"Yeah, and I want it back."

"What's her knife have to do with anything?" Bobby asked.

The General shifted his gaze to Bobby. "That's an interesting question. You see, both of my men were killed with a large knife, like the one she has admitted carrying. The killer sneaked up behind my men, like the coward he or she, is and stuck them in the back. They were stabbed repeatedly as if the killer were in a frenzy."

He looked at Becca.

"Tell me, why would those men have made you so angry?"

"I didn't kill your men." Becca poked him in the chest. "But I'll give serious thought to killing you if you don't release us."

Before she could say anything else, the soldiers were upon her. Bobby sprang to his feet. He grabbed one man across the chest and kicked his legs out from under him. Ripping the rifle from the man's hands as he fell, Bobby pointed it at the general.

The general didn't move. The only sign of tension in the man was a twitch in his jaw line.

"I think you should give up the weapon or your sister will die first."

Thirty-Five

BOBBY NARROWED HIS EYES. "Then you'll be the second to die."

"And you will be third. If you're innocent as you claim, are you willing to sacrifice your lives? If you don't put your weapon down, you will have no opportunity to prove your innocence."

"I have no desire to be interrogated like you did this man. Nor do I have any interest in joining your band of merry men."

The general smiled. "Put the gun down and cooperate, and you'll have nothing to worry about."

"We didn't kill your men. We don't hurt people who aren't trying to hurt us. The first I saw of your men was when they began chasing us. That's all there is to it."

"Well, if that's all there is, you have nothing to worry about."

"That very statement makes me worry. Just let us go and you'll never see us again."

"That's not going to happen. There are only three possible outcomes here. You and your sister will die. You will be tried, convicted, and executed as a murderer, or you will be cleared of the crimes and enlisted in our army. There's only one way you get to live."

Bobby's mind raced. He couldn't shoot his way out of there. They were innocent of the crime, but would he get a fair chance to prove it or just automatically be convicted? The only chance of survival was to surrender. With luck, they might get a chance to escape and run for freedom. They couldn't do that if they were dead.

"Just shoot him, Bobby."

Startled, Bobby tightened his finger on the trigger. Becca's voice surprisingly helped make up his mind. He lowered the weapon. The soldier he had taken it from stripped it from his hands. As he was pushed against the wall Bobby noticed the shocked, open-mouthed look on his sister's face. Then a look that hurt more crossed her eyes. It was one of disgust.

Becca was shoved against the wall next to him. "I told you to shoot him." This was killer Becca, not the sane one. There would be no rationalizing with her.

Bobby's hands were secured behind his back and he was yanked roughly away.

THE GENERAL PUT HIS lips next to Becca's ear. "We'll start with him. If he's cleared of the charges, you'll be next. I'd take you now, but I want you to anticipate what my interrogation techniques will be for you."

The general left the room. The guard pressing Becca to the wall bounced her head against it and then backed off. Becca spun on the man. Both he and his partner had their rifles aimed at her.

The man who had pinned her to the wall winked at her. "We'll be back."

They exited and locked the door.

Even hearing the lock engage, Becca still threw herself at the door, banging and kicking until her fury dissolved. She said in a quiet voice, "I told you to shoot him, Bobby. You should've listened." She leaned her head against the

135

door and fought back the tears.

The hairy man said, "You shouldn't antagonize them. You could get us all killed."

She looked at him with contempt. "Yeah, lamb, go to the slaughter without a fight." She walked to the injured man and sat next to him. The woman sobbed loudly. "And tell that bitch to shut up before I shut her up."

The woman became more inconsolable. Becca put her head against the wall and thought about Bobby. *Please let him be all right.*

She lifted the injured man's head and placed it in her lap. Putting a comforting hand on his back, she waited for her turn.

Thirty-Six

MYRON CRAWLED TO THE edge of the trees, his heart beating a cadence that could march an army. No one investigated the noise he made the first time. Myron was determined to sneak back and get another look at the woman. He dashed to the fence and climbed once more. The woman was still there. Her eyes were closed, head tilted back, her face up. She appeared to be a little older than he was.

Myron had been watching and fantasizing about rescuing her and having her fall in love with him, when the door opened and a man was brought in and thrown to the floor. His fantasy girl and another man moved to help the injured man.

Myron watched the man with growing jealousy. Was that her boyfriend? The thought made him angry. He watched the interaction between them and tried to determine the relationship. The man looked tough. Myron wanted to rescue the woman and show her he was better for her than the other guy. Maybe he would leave the guy and just rescue her.

With his arms getting tired of clinging to the fence, Myron lowered silently to the ground and hid in the trees. He wanted to help the people inside escape, but wasn't sure how to do it. Also, he was still waging a war inside battling his paralyzing fear.

Were the small windows even big enough for a person to squeeze through? What was keeping them closed? Maybe they were sealed so they wouldn't open. He'd have to go inside the fence and look. The thought made him sweat.

To bolster his courage, he wanted to look at the woman again. He climbed the fence again and draped an arm over the top bar. The door opened and a group of soldiers entered. One man talked to the prisoners. Myron's heart leaped to his throat when his fantasy girlfriend poked the speaker in the chest.

Then everyone was pointing guns at her. Myron wanted to cry out to her. His arm extended over the fence toward her. His mind was tortured by visions of her death. He saw her doing the bullet dance the woman in the field had done. He didn't want to watch but couldn't turn his head away.

The man sitting next to her jumped up, snatched a gun, and pointed it at the speaker.

For anxious minutes, the standoff continued. Then, to Myron's shock and dismay, her savior lowered his gun.

"No!" he said.

When the soldiers pushed her face-first into the wall, Myron almost jumped the fence. He looked back inside the building in time to see the man who had grabbed the gun be led out the door. Fear gripped him. What if the woman was dragged away next? He couldn't allow that to happen.

Myron jumped to the ground, oblivious to any sound he made. *How can I save her?* He looked at the fence. He could climb it. That part was easy. But what then? The window was too high to reach. He couldn't rush the guards in front.

He began to pace. A good forty feet from the end of the building, Myron stopped, suddenly realizing he could be seen. He ran for the woods. Once under cover he squatted and tried to relax. *What would a real hero do?*

Myron looked at the building again. Once inside the fence how would he get up to the window? He looked around for anything that might help. His gaze stopped on a stack of logs to the left of the building, cut for use in a fireplace or pit. An idea came to him.

He glanced toward the sun. At least two more hours of daylight remained. The smart thing to do would be to wait for nightfall, but by then, it might be too late to save her. He had to go now.

He forced his legs to move and was surprised when they did.

Thirty-Seven

MYRON WORKED HIS WAY back to a point where he was concealed by the building. He left his pack and bow and arrows, but carried the knife and gun with him. Stopping at the base of the fence, he fought fear for control of his body. With a sudden move he scaled the fence to the top.

There he swung his leg over the crossbar, trying not to think about what he was doing. Myron attempted to sink his foot into a link but missed. His body fell, his back leg catching on one of the prongs. He stopped his plummet, but felt the metal pierce his thigh.

Myron bit back the scream. The pain was severe, but then, his endurance was never that great. He pushed up on the top bar, controlling the sharp bite as best he could, and lifted the trailing leg over the top. He hung suspended by his hands for a moment before finding a link with his toes. Supported now, Myron descended to the ground.

As soon as his feet touched down, he limped to the wall. There he crouched and felt the hole in his leg. His hand came away red. His stomach threatened to revolt. He swallowed the rising bile and took in short rapid breaths.

Now was not the time to panic. Myron pushed up against the wall as if using it for balance. He looked from the fence to the window overhead. His breathing began to slow.

Myron reached for the window. If he stretched, he could touch the ledge. Maybe he could jump and grab the brickwork, but then he had to pull himself up to see inside. There was no way he could hang there long enough to get the window open. He had to have something to stand on.

Myron slid to the end of the building and peeked around the corner. Then he turned toward the woodpile and tried to judge how long it would take to get there. He'd be in the open. Anyone could see him. But there was no getting inside without the added height a log would give.

Okay, be brave. You can do this.

What was the best approach? If he ran he'd get there quicker, but that might draw the most attention? If he walked, the amount of time he was exposed was longer, but maybe if he was seen no one would react. *Aw!* He grabbed his head as if it were about to explode. *Just do something!*

He took one unsure step away from the building, and then another. When he was far enough away from the corner to see the hangars and jets, his legs began to shake. People moved around the planes. They were a long way from him, but if they sounded the alarm, the guards at the door could be on him in a second.

Myron tried to remain calm as he took one step after another. When he'd gone more than halfway to the pile, he looked over his shoulder. No one had seen him yet. Unable to control his fear anymore, he broke into a run and dived headfirst behind the wood pile. He grunted from the contact, banging his arm on a log.

He rolled around, holding his arm and tried to swallow his cries. Forcing himself to look, he stopped his contortions and lifted his head above the logs. Myron fully expected to see armed men racing toward him. He was shocked to see he had gone unnoticed.

Minutes went by before Myron thought about moving.

Several peeks later confirmed he had so far gone undetected. Getting back, however, especially carrying a log, would be much more difficult.

Myron looked through the pile until he found one he thought would give him enough height to reach the window and a large enough base to keep him from toppling over. He reached up and rolled it behind the pile. Myron hefted it to make sure it was something he could handle.

Rolling the wood to the end of the pile, Myron readied to make his dash. An explosive roar rent the air and his heart nearly exploded from his chest. He dropped to the ground and covered his head. The deafening noise continued. Fearing he had been discovered, Myron forced a quick look.

To his great relief, no one was coming for him. The source of the noise was one of the jet's engines igniting. Myron lifted the log and took off running. In his haste, he tripped and fell, and the log flew from his grip. He rolled, came to his feet in a crouch, and looked toward the jet. Just then, the engine died.

Myron eyed the log and sprinted for it. He scooped it up, almost fell again, and then regained his balance and made it to the building. He set the log down under the window and sat on it. He couldn't stop his body from shaking. He had never been so scared. His mind threatened to shut down. Tears mingled with the sweat pouring freely down his face. His breaths became labored.

At any moment, he expected armed men to come around the corners and shoot him. Myron lowered his head to his knees and covered it with his arms. No amount of inward anger could get him to rise from the ground. The rescue was going to have to wait until his panic attack was over.

Thirty-Eight

AFTER EXPLAINING WHAT HE'D discovered, Mark said, "I think I have an idea where he might be. I hope I'm wrong though 'cause getting him back will be difficult."

"But that's a good thing though, right?" Lincoln said. "Not finding his body. If they wanted to kill him his body'd still be there, wouldn't it? I mean why take a body?"

"Yeah, there's that. My concern is why they took him at all? And if they interrogate him, what information will he give up?"

"Ah man, I hadn't thought about that. He could tell them everything."

"That's why we need to hurry. Hopefully they haven't started on him yet."

Mark crossed the main road and headed farther south than he had gone before. Afraid someone might be waiting for him if he showed up in the same place, Mark drove well past the airport, and then cut across until he was a mile from the runways on the far side of the airport.

He parked behind a house. They checked to make sure the house was vacant and then proceeded into the woods. The height and density of the trees were sufficient to keep the sun out, making it much cooler and darker under the canopy.

Mark set a quick pace, not worrying at this distance about making noise. Every minute Juan was in enemy hands was another minute his captors got closer to finding the other families. When he judged they were within a quarter mile of the base, Mark slowed.

Several times Mark stopped to listen. He couldn't shake the feeling they were being followed, but there was never anyone in sight. The standing hairs on the back of his neck set his nerves on end. He crouched without warning Lincoln. The football star bumped into Mark and then ducked, making too much noise. Mark opened and closed his finger around the trigger. *What was out there that had him so jumpy?* Closing his eyes, he focused on his hearing, but the only thing he could pick up was Lincoln's rapid breathing.

"What?" Lincoln whispered.

Mark shook his head. "We must be close to the base. We do not want to engage these people if possible. Try to avoid being seen. Only shoot if we have no choice. Understood?"

"Uh, yeah, as long as they understand the same rules."

"Slow and quiet from here on."

Fifteen minutes later, Mark held up a fist and knelt on one knee. He grabbed the binoculars from a belt pouch and scanned the field. They were at a corner section of fencing. The western fence ended and turned on a southwestern heading. Two runways went off in that direction.

Straight across, the tower stood. The main terminal was underneath. Several other buildings and hangars flanked the terminal. No people were on the ground. However, a man stood inside the tower as before. Mark watched him, hoping to find a pattern he could use.

Mark backed up until he was next to Lincoln. "There's

a guy in the tower watching for any intruders. That's how I was spotted the first time. If we approach from this direction, he can spot us from the south or east window. If he spends about the same time at each window, we'll have six to eight minutes to get in and find cover."

Lincoln frowned. "We don't even know if Juan's in there. This could be a real bad decision."

"I understand, but I have to go in. I have to know if he's there. You stay out here and watch my back."

"What are you gonna do if you find him?"

"I'll try to sneak him out, but if I can't, I'll try to bargain with them. If they see us and start shooting, it's up to you to keep their heads down. Can you do that?"

"Yeah, but now I wish I brought more bullets."

Mark handed Lincoln the rifle and his spare magazine. "Hopefully, I won't need it. If I get in a gunfight inside, I'll be dead anyway. Take good shots and make them count. Oh, and stay out of sight of the guy up there."

Mark left Lincoln and moved through the trees toward the first building inside the fence. It was a one-story brick building. He'd use the building to shield his entry onto the base.

Mark had gone no more than thirty feet when a noise came from the woods to his right. He froze. Someone was there. He lowered to a prone position and waited. Someone was moving toward him, stealthily, as if with a purpose.

Mark slid the gun forward just above the ground. He angled it up. If the intruder kept coming, they'd stumble right over him. Mark slowed his breathing and waited.

Then the sound stopped. Whoever was out there was being as cautious as Mark. *Are they aware of me? Is someone tracking me?*

He was in a deadly game, and whoever moved first lost.

Thirty-Nine

BECCA COULD BARELY STAND the waiting any longer. She released one agitated sigh after the other and tapped the back of her head against the wall. She would have screamed if she wasn't cradling the injured man in her lap. It was more than an hour since General Dickhead had taken her brother. She couldn't sit still another second.

The injured man had fallen asleep. As gently as she could, Becca lifted his head and set it down. He shifted, but did not wake. She was certain the man had a concussion. At some point she recalled learning that sleep wasn't good for head trauma, but she didn't remember the details, and besides, there wasn't much else she could do.

The couple across from her huddled so close together they looked like they'd melded into one being. Her eyes were closed, but the man watched Becca.

Becca stood and stretched her aching muscles. She studied the windows as she did. They were small, but she thought she could squeeze through. The problem was getting up to them. She stepped to the wall under one window and extended her arm upward. She was more than a foot away.

Becca backed up from the wall took a couple of steps and jumped. She smacked into the wall and fell back, landing on her butt. She was eye level with the man and saw the smirk on his face. "Let's see you do any better. For that matter, let's see you try to do anything at all."

"No way. I'm not gonna piss them off. Look what it got your brother."

"At least he had guts enough to stand up to them."

"And they're probably beating him to a pulp now."

Becca took a menacing step toward him. "Shut up before I beat you to a pulp."

The woman woke up. "Vince, what's going on?"

"Nothing, babe, just Miss Super Bitch flexing her muscles."

"Why don't you leave us alone?" the girl squeaked.

"Why don't you make yourself useful and give me a hand up to the window?"

The man's mouth dropped open. "Are you crazy? What if they walk in? Uh-uh, don't get me caught up in your stupid schemes."

"No problem, chicken shit."

"Here, miss, I'll help you."

The voice behind startled her. The injured man had woken. He looked better, his eyes more focused. Well, eye – the other one was swollen shut.

He pushed to his feet and swayed like he might fall over. Becca leaped forward and snatched his arm, keeping him upright.

"Dizzy. Just give me a minute."

"Look, maybe you should sit down. I think you have a concussion."

"No-no-no, if you can get away, you have to go. I have friends who will come for us. I'll tell you where to go. You bring them back. Will you do that?"

"Of course I will. I have to come back for my brother anyway."

The man nodded. "Okay, let's do this." He held onto Becca's arm as she guided him across the floor. He leaned against the opposite wall and held his head. "I'm sorry, I must rest."

"Okay, don't push yourself."

Something scratched at the window above her. She looked up. Was someone out there watching and listening to them, or was it a branch brushing against the glass? The sound came again, and then louder before stopping. Becca wasn't so sure of her plan now. Maybe one of the soldiers was sealing the windows so they wouldn't open.

"I think it's best if I get down."

Becca gave him a smile. She understood. There was no way his head injury would allow him to stand. But then he surprised her. He got on hands and knees and crawled under the window.

"Okay, this is better."

This man was tougher than he looked. Becca put one foot on his lower back and tested it.

"Vince, stop her. She's gonna get us all killed."

Becca glared at Vince. "Yeah, Vincey, come stop me. Keep your mouth shut, and if I get out of here I'll rescue you too. What's it gonna hurt? I may be your best chance."

Vince nodded his concession.

Becca pushed up on the kneeling man and heard him grunt. She rose slowly so as not to lose balance on her unsteady plank. Before she reached the window, the scraping sound came again. She froze. What or who was out there? She had to find out. What difference did it make? If there was someone out there preventing her escape, she wasn't any worse off than she was now. Besides, her lift was only going to last so long.

Placing her fingers on the ledge, she pulled, rising to her full height. In the window was a face. She let out an unintended scream and fell backward to the floor. The injured man collapsed in pain. He rolled, holding his head.

Someone outside was using a key to open the door. By the time the guards came in, Becca was back in her original place. Both men had their weapons up.

"What's going on here?" guard number one said.

The couple cowered together. The woman started to point her finger at Becca, but Vince covered it with his hand and pulled her arm down.

Becca said, "It's him. He needs a doctor. You guys went too far with him."

Guard one stared at her.

Guard two, however, had more compassion. "Watch her," he said, and knelt next to the man and tried to take some vitals. When he lifted the eyelids, the guard shook his head.

"He does need a doctor," he said to his partner.

"All right, report it to the lieutenant. Let him deal with it."

"No, I'm going to take him now. It may take too long for the doctor to get here."

Becca stood, her hands above her head. "I'll help you lift him."

The soldier nodded to his partner who motioned her to move using the barrel of his rifle. Becca knelt next to the injured man and slid an arm under his head.

"Put the other one under his arm," the soldier suggested. He looked at her. "We're not the enemy here. We're here to help people."

"Yeah, I can see that."

His face reddened. "I'm sorry about this. They're a little angry right now. Someone killed two of our men, our friends. They're trying to find the killer."

"Well, it's not us."

"I hope not, for your sake."

149

They lifted the Latino man, and the guard put him in a fireman's carry. Probably not the best thing for a head injury, Becca thought, but at least he'd get medical attention, if he survived the trip. As the soldier walked toward the door, Becca said, "Thanks."

He looked her in the eyes and said, "In spite of what you might think, we're not monsters."

"I guess I'll find out soon enough, huh?"

He looked like he was about to say something else, but changed his mind. He left.

The other guard backed out of the room, saying, "Don't worry, honey, you're next. One of the men who died was a friend of mine. If we find you were the one who killed him, I'm going to volunteer for the firing squad."

"Awesome," Becca shot back. "I'll have a good chance of surviving then."

The man's face darkened. "Bitch." He closed the door.

"Yeah, good comeback!" she shouted.

Forty

BECCA REPLAYED THE ENCOUNTER at the window. Something about that face had struck a memory chord. She had only had a fraction of a second's look, but she could still see the image.

If she tried again she'd have to do it on her own. She doubted her roommates would be much help.

Something tapped at the window. The skinny bitch began to cry again. Becca shushed her.

"Quiet. I need to hear this."

The tapping came again.

Becca stepped back and ran at the wall. Leaping with all her strength, she managed to get her fingertips over the ledge. She hung there for a moment, and then slowly, digging her feet into the wall, rose toward the window.

Her head was almost at window height when her grip failed and she began to slip back. However, with a sudden rush she was moving upward again. Below her the hairy man stood with one of her boots in each hand.

"Thanks," Becca whispered.

Outside the window was the face again. It was a round white face of a teenaged boy. Highlighted against the sunlight beyond, he had an ethereal look as if his head was floating. With a start the memory came to her.

He was the boy she saw when she'd been captured. The boy she had pleaded to help her, and then told to run and save himself. But he had come for her. Her heart leaped. She could not contain the smile.

He tapped the window and pointed at the latch. Becca tried to move the metal, but it was rusted in place. Using both hands and straining with all her might, she broke the latch free. The release threw her off balance and she almost fell again.

"How much longer?" the man below asked.

"Place my feet on your shoulders and hold them from behind."

He did, and Becca was secure for the moment.

The unknown boy outside was working a knife into the seam where the window closed. Someone had painted the frame closed. The tip of the knife pushed through. Using both hands, the boy worked the blade sideways. It slid ever so slowly to the end of the window. He pulled it out and did the same thing toward the other end.

Becca grabbed the latch and pulled down, but the window still held secure. The downward seams were more difficult to get to. It was a long and tedious process. When the knife wielder had gotten halfway down on each side, Becca tried to pull the window open again. With the boy pushing on the frame from the outside, the window broke free with a groan.

For a second, all eyes turned toward the door. A collective release of air filled the room when none of the guards entered.

"Hi," she said.

"Uh, hi."

They broke eye contact for a second while Becca examined the window. The frame opened from the top downward, but did not lie flat. Instead, it angled upward toward the ceiling, making the opening smaller. To get through, Becca would have to get above the glass and slide down from the top. Even if she got that high, there might not be enough room for her to fit through the opening.

"Can you push me up as high as you can? If I put too much pressure on the window, it will break and the guards will come in."

"I'll try. Hold on."

With a grunt, Vince lifted Becca. She touched the ceiling with her hands for balance. Taking a moment to study the best approach, she lifted one leg and slid it through the opening. A hand grabbed her ankle.

A whispered voice said, "It's going to be a very tight fit."

Becca didn't bother with a reply. Her legs would fit, but how was she going to get her body through without putting her weight on the glass?

"Turn around," she told Vince.

When he did, Becca bent over and placed her hands on Vince's head. She lifted the second leg and placed it on the window ledge. The balance was precarious. She moved a hand to the now empty shoulder for a wider base of support and then lifted the leg. Becca was upside down now. Her leg banged against the glass and slid back inside the room. She held her breath, fearing she had broken the pane, but no glass hit the floor.

She looked down into the hairy man's face. He was struggling trying to hold her. Whatever she was going to do, it had to be now. She slid one leg through the opening at a time, and her mysterious rescuer grabbed them and guided her out the narrow opening.

Vince said, "Don't forget us."

"I won't."

Becca grabbed and closed the window.

Forty-One

WHOEVER WAS HOLDING HER outside had a grip on her hips. Hands slid up her body, holding her tight. Unable to hold her as she descended, Becca toppled to the ground landing on top of the boy.

Dazed from the impact, Becca shook her head and took a quick inventory of her body and any registered pain. She hurt, but nothing seemed too major.

Becca got to the boy's face and covered his mouth to stop his pained moans. Holding a finger to her mouth she looked him in the eyes.

"We have to hurry," she whispered and was up, running toward the fence.

It took all her willpower not to leap at the fence and scamper over to escape. But to do that would make too much noise. This close to freedom, she didn't want to get recaptured. Her rescuer joined her at the fence as she began to ascend.

At the top, she swung her legs over the top. She was now face to face with her hero. There was a brief pause, and she climbed down. She ran for the trees and waited for him to join her.

When he arrived she threw a big hug around him. "Thank you," she whispered. She was already forming a plan on how to save her brother.

It was darker within the trees. Despite her desire to get as far away as possible, she reined in her adrenaline and slowed her pace. She needed to implement a plan before any pursuit began.

She stopped. "Do you have a car someplace?"

He shook his head. "Ah, no."

Becca frowned. He sounded nervous. "Okay, we'll have to find one. I don't think we'll get too far on foot."

In the black-haired boy's hands was a backpack and a bow and arrows. She nodded. She started walking again. They'd only been free for a few minutes when a commotion began behind them. Her escape had been discovered.

She reached back and snatched the boy's hand. "We have to hurry. They'll be coming."

She kept from running, but only barely. They were making way too much noise. Then a sound behind her froze her in place. The sudden stop caused her new friend to bump into her.

She placed her lips next to his ear. "Someone's coming." She crouched and moved at a snail's pace.

All Becca's adrenaline-soaked nerves screamed at her to run. Her body shook from the effort to fight off the desire. In agonizing stillness, they waited for a sound that told them where their pursuers were. After what felt like an eternity of silence, Becca motioned to move.

They went twenty to thirty feet at a time and then stopped to listen. With each move, Becca began to think they might be safer. No sound of pursuit had followed over the last three moves. She gave the signal to move again.

They hadn't gone two steps before the branches parted and a dark form pounced. Her partner let out a scream and was no longer standing next to her. She spun and kicked the assailant making solid contact. Following that with a straight punch to the face, Becca gained space enough to run.

No longer worried about noise, she crashed through the trees like a rampaging moose. With the cacophony she made, there was no way of hearing if the assailant was after her, but she wasn't about to slow down to find out.

Then pain struck her back, and before she could react she was driven to the ground. The resulting crash caused her tackler to lose his grip on her for a second. Animalistic sounds escaped her as she clawed, kicked, and punched. A fist landed a glancing blow on her cheek. She snarled and dived for the arm, digging her teeth in as deep as they would go through the material of his shirt.

He slapped her mouth free and used his superior weight and strength to roll on top of her. Becca was pinned, and when she ceased thrashing her head from side to side, her attacker stuck a gun in her face. Her eyes sighted back up the barrel to the face of her attacker: the nice guard who had taken the injured man away. His face was not very friendly now.

Her only defense against the bullet was to close her eyes.

Forty-Two

MARK WAS SURPRISED BY the sudden sound not ten feet from where he hid. Whoever had been stalking him was apparently now in a fight. It wasn't his fight and he had more important things to do than get involved, but one of the combatants sounded like a woman. He knew what happened to unprotected women.

He crawled forward. The thrashing was just beyond a fallen tree that blocked his vision. Mark peeked above the trunk. A man and woman wrestled on the ground. The woman fought hard, but the man used his heavier body to leverage her under him where he straddled her, pinning her helpless.

Crouching, Mark walked the length of the trunk. Once around the tree Mark made a slow approach behind the assailant.

The woman fought on, even though her efforts appeared hopeless. Then a gun was pointed inches from her face, and the battle was over.

Whatever the man's purpose, Mark was going to stop him.

"STOP! DON'T make me shoot you," the uniformed man said to Becca.

Movement over the guard's shoulder drew Becca's attention. At first she thought it was another soldier, then she dared hope it was her rescuer coming once more to save her. But when the image came into focus her eyes went wide, and despite her predicament and the welling tears, a broad smile spread across her face.

"Hi, Daddy."

The guard stiffened at Becca's statement, but didn't turn. "I'm not falling for that."

Then the gun barrel touched the man's head. "I think it'd be a good idea for you to get off my daughter."

The soldier dropped the gun and put his hands behind his head as Mark instructed. He climbed off Becca, but remained on his knees.

"Becca, take his weapons, but stay out of my line of sight."

Becca patted the man down and took away his gun and knife.

"Take off your boots." The man hesitated, but as Mark's eyes narrowed, he complied. "Take the laces out and tie his hands and feet."

"Okay, Daddy, but don't hurt him. He was the nice one."

"Well, beating on my daughter is a strange way of showing that." He paused. "Is Bobby …?"

Becca finished her task and walked to her father. "The last I saw him he was all right. But they took him away to torture him for information. That was a long time ago." She wrapped her arms around him.

Her father gave her a hard one-armed hug.

"Why were they torturing him?"

"I don't know. I think they believe we killed some of their men?"

"Did you?"

"I don't think so. I mean, we killed some people, but none of them was dressed in uniform.

"Why did you kill someone?"

"Because they tried to kill us."

"Is that why you're torturing my son?" he asked the prisoner.

The man didn't respond.

"Answer me," Mark snarled. He cocked the gun and stepped forward.

The man flinched.

"No, Daddy," Becca said. "Don't hurt him. He tried to help one of the other prisoners his superiors went too far with." She walked to the kneeling man and squatted in front of him. "We did not kill your friends. We only kill people who try to hurt us." She walked to her father's side. "They must have discovered I escaped. That might mean they brought Bobby back. He would know. Why don't you ask him? But do it quick, because they're probably searching for me." She turned to leave.

Mark said, "Where you going?"

"I have to find my friend. He was hurt. I can't leave him. He risked his life to rescue me."

MARK WASN'T SURE WHAT to say. There was something very different about his daughter; something very grown up, yet also very scary. It was in her tone and her eyes. When she was gone, Mark focused on his prisoner.

"What do you know about my son?"

"Look, I'm just doing my job. I don't wish harm to you or your family."

"Your actions so far don't support that statement. I also don't wish to harm anyone, but you have my son. I will not hesitate harming you to find him. Do you understand that?"

The man nodded.

"So talk to me."

The man hesitated, and then said, "I just brought him

159

back to the holding cell."

"Is he all right?"

The pause was telling. "Yes, but he was worked over."

The answer flared anger in Mark. A red veil descended over his eyes. He took a step closer and fought against the increasing pressure on the trigger.

"Please, sir ... don't."

The words cut through the rage. Mark let the anger go, but his heart was racing. "How many men are guarding the cell?"

"I will not help you kill my friends."

Mark nodded. He understood loyalty. But this man needed to understand blood.

Forty-Three

MYRON'S EYES FLUTTERED OPEN. His head hurt—his vision fuzzy. As the image in front of his face became clearer a strange warmth spread over him. "Am I dead?"

"No, silly boy."

He stared at the angel hovering over him, losing himself in her eyes.

She smiled. "Can you get up?"

He tried to push up, but his arms didn't want to support his weight.

"Let me help you."

She stood behind him and slid her hands under his arms. "Bend your knees and push."

He did as instructed and was on his feet seconds later. His head thumped. He touched the spot where it hurt. There was a bump and something crusty. His fingers came away sticky.

"Wh-What happened?"

"You got knocked out. Come on, we have to get going. Can you walk?" She put her arm around his waist and helped him move. "Daddy, this is the boy who saved me."

"Honey, we'll do introductions later. Right now I need you to watch our guest. Can you do that?"

MARK HANDED HIS DAUGHTER the soldier's gun. "I'll be right back.

Do not take your eyes off him." Mark backed away from the group and returned a few minutes later with Lincoln.

"Lincoln, this is my daughter, Becca."

Lincoln looked from Mark to the young woman with his mouth open. "Oh my God, she's alive."

He started to laugh, but Mark shushed him.

"From what this man tells me, my son is also alive and held captive inside that building. He may be hurt. I need to get him out, and I need your help. Can you do it?"

"Ah, yeah, sure. What do you need me to do?"

Mark turned to the bound man. "I need your ACU."

The man shrugged. "Yeah, sure."

"Lincoln, untie him and step back. Keep him covered."

Lincoln did.

"Now take off just the shirt."

The man complied and tossed his Army Combat Uniform shirt to Mark. He put it on while Lincoln retied the prisoner.

"Rebecca, I need you and your friend to stay here and watch our guest."

"Okay? What are you going to do?"

"I'm gonna get your brother. Lincoln, I need you to come with me. I'll explain as we go." Mark turned to the soldier, "I promise you will not be hurt. I will let you go when we get back. However, if you try to escape or call for help, my daughter will be forced to shoot you."

"With no hesitation," she said.

Mark and Lincoln started toward the compound. The remaining sunlight was fading fast. Mark threw a hand across Lincoln's chest to stop his progress. "Did you hear that?"

The two men focused their attention on the woods around them. In the distance, what sounded like an animal cried out. A chill ran through Mark's veins. The sound did not come again. Mark motioned for Lincoln to continue, but he couldn't help but glance around him. He had heard that sound before. In the woods when the soldiers had been chasing him. And for some reason he didn't believe it was an animal.

162

The high-pitched cackle was the sound of someone laughing.

Forty-Four

BOBBY LOOKED AT THE guard. The guard glared back. He stood inside the door to make sure no one else escaped. Two more guards were stationed outside.

When news of Becca's escape had reached the lieutenant, he stormed inside and demanded answers from the other couple in the room. The woman cried, but the man stated calmly that Becca had forced the window open and climbed through. It was clear to Bobby that the officer did not entirely believe the story.

He gave orders to his men and left.

Bobby prayed Becca got away, and although he hoped she might be able to find a way to free him, if she didn't come back, he would understand. Although happy for her, Bobby kept his emotion in check. He was unable stop the adrenaline from making his heart beat faster though. His face hurt, but he refused to touch the spot or show any signs of pain in front of the guard. He stood to stretch.

Immediately the guard shouted, "Sit back down."

"Why don't you make me?"

The soldier advanced two steps then stopped, his glare ineffectual. Bobby flexed his torso and touched his toes. Pain danced through his body, but it made him feel alive.

His body protested, but he used the pain to fuel his building anger and his desire for payback.

Bobby told them truthfully what he had been doing the past few weeks. The discussion ground to a halt when the sergeant, who paced menacingly around the chair Bobby had been cuffed to, got in his face and called him a liar.

Bobby said, "I don't care what you think. I didn't kill your men. And I'll be damned if I'll serve in an Army run by fools."

The sergeant backhanded Bobby, rocking him back in the chair, almost toppling over. As the chair bounced back on all four legs, Bobby jumped up, chair still attached, and planted a kick into his assailant's groin. That's when the beating began.

Bobby walked toward the back of the room and did more stretching. On his way he stopped in front of the couple. "What happened to the Latino man?"

"Your sister convinced them he needed medical attention. They took him out, supposedly to get help."

Bobby squatted close to the man and whispered. "Did you help her?"

The wild-haired man shot a nervous glance at the guard and nodded.

"You need to move away from him, and yes, I will make you."

Bobby narrowed his eyes at the guard. "Thanks," he whispered and stood up.

With the guard giving him his best death stare, Bobby sat down across from the couple. *Okay, Sis, I hope you're safe. Everything's up to you now.*

Forty-Five

MASON ARMSTRONG HAD TRACKED the two men into the forest. He stopped and hid a few times when he thought the white guy had heard him. The hunt excited him. He was there primarily to kill the uniforms, which he had done twice already, but there were so many of them, so he'd switched targets.

When his prey stopped and separated, Mason thought he might finally get a chance to take the white man. Mason stalked him, but something spooked the man, so Mason froze and waited. He ached for another kill, but the thought didn't consume him so badly he lost all perspective. He had no intention of being caught.

Now there was a uniform right in front of him, with his hands and feet bound. He was watched by a young man and woman. Mason's mind whirled with the possibilities of making three kills at once. If he was going to take them, he needed to do it before the other two men came back.

He smiled. *Yes, that should work very nicely.* He inched forward toward his goal.

MARK AND LINCOLN DESCENDED the fence with slow deliberate strides and walked to the rear of the building. A log lay on the ground to Mark's right. Perhaps what that kid used to help Rebecca escape.

He motioned to Lincoln that he was moving. Lincoln nodded. They moved in opposite directions to the end of the building. Mark focused the binoculars on the control tower. Some sort of ambient light shone inside. A shadow moved from the front window.

Mark counted off what he hoped was four minutes, looked over his shoulder at Lincoln, and then went around the corner. Would Lincoln be able to do his part? If not, Mark would be caught in the open with no weapon ready. He reached the front corner. One glance told Mark the information the prisoner had offered was accurate, so far.

He shoved the gun behind his back. With head down, but eyes up, Mark stepped around the corner and moved toward the door. He was five steps forward when the closest guard noticed him. Two more steps until that guard informed his partner, and three more steps before they spun toward him.

Their guns were ready, but not aimed, yet. *Any time now, Lincoln.* The guards brought their weapons on target.

Lincoln stepped from around the building and placed his gun against the back of the rear guard's head. The lead guard turned to see what was happening behind him. Pulling his gun, Mark ran the last few steps, got past the barrel of the rifle, and jammed his gun into the man's belly.

These men could not be real Army. He ripped the rifle from the guard's hands. "Open the door."

The man's eyes widened and his jaw sagged open. He fumbled in his pocket for the keys and with a shaking hand tried to line up a key with the doorknob.

"Relax," Mark said. "If you do what I say, no one will get hurt."

The guard nodded and the key slid home.

WHEN BOBBY HEARD THE key enter the lock, he tensed, ready to spring. If the guard turned his head for even an instant Bobby was going to pounce. He'd been thinking about his best chance for escape ever since his return to the cell. Now might be his only opportunity.

He pictured his actions. Hit the guard from behind, blow past whoever was coming in, turn to the right, go around the building, hop the fence, and disappear into the woods. Simple. He just had to outrun the bullets.

When the door opened, Bobby readied to move. As soon as the guard turned his head, Bobby exploded off the floor. His focus was on the inside guard and not whoever entered.

The guard crouched and spun, but Bobby hit him before the rifle could come on target. But the man grabbed Bobby and took him down too.

As the two men landed and rolled, each trying to gain a dominant position, men flooded the room and the door was closed. Bobby's hopes sank. There would be no escape now, but he was determined to at least get in a few licks before they beat him down.

In a desperate effort to rise to the top, Bobby gambled on a move that backfired. His opponent ended up on top, cocked his arm to drive it into Bobby's face. Then Bobby saw a gun touch the side of the guard's head.

Bobby switched his gaze to the right. He opened his eyes wide, his heart skipped a beat, and the smile stretched so far it hurt. A whimper escaped his lips and his vision distorted looking through the watery build up. "Dad!" The word almost stuck in his throat.

"I don't understand why my kids are always on the bottom. Didn't I teach you better than that?" His father nudged the man with the gun. "Would you mind getting off my son?"

Forty-Six

THE MAN COMPLIED. Mark motioned him to join the other two guards at the far end of the room where Lincoln watched them.

Bobby stood next to Mark. The boy wiped a sleeve across his eyes. Mark fought down any emotion. A reunion would have to wait.

"It's really good to see you, Dad. Did you find Becca?"

Mark nodded. "She's waiting for us. We have to move fast. You two take off your shirts. Now!" he shouted. "You too, tough guy."

The guard who had been wrestling with Bobby did not move. He glared with unconcealed hatred.

The couple on the floor moved away from the action. The woman was in a panic. The man tried to comfort her. Mark told Lincoln and Bobby to put on the uniform tops. Then he instructed them to tie up the soldiers using their laces.

When the hard-nosed soldier refused to take off his shoes, Mark advanced on him and placed the gun to his forehead. "I didn't come here to hurt anyone, even though you've hurt my children. But I promise, I'm not afraid to pull the trigger. Do as I say and no one gets hurt."

"Empty promises."

"If I wanted you hurt, you'd be dead already. It would easier for us, and I wouldn't have to worry about you coming after us. Now do it."

The soldier stared at Mark, and then sat down and took off his shoes. Lincoln took out the laces and tied the man's hands and feet. "This fool's making it difficult for me. He's tied, but I don't think it's gonna hold for long."

"That's all right," Mark said. "I expect once they work together they won't be tied for long anyways."

"And you better pray I don't find you," the soldier said.

"Don't take my letting you live for weakness," Mark said. "I'm not a killer. But if you follow us and try to hurt us, I will kill you."

He backed away from the captives. "Let's go."

Mark opened the door a crack and peered out. Lincoln and Bobby stood behind them.

Bobby looked at the couple meeting the man's eyes. "Dad, what about them?"

Mark studied them. "It might be better if they stayed here."

The man started to protest, but Bobby interrupted. "He helped Becca escape."

Mark sighed. "Come if you want, but you have to keep up – and you have to keep her quiet." He moved his attention back to the door. Across the camp the buildings were lit, and a group of soldiers had gathered. All were armed. "We have to hurry," he said. "I think they're organizing pursuit." Mark knew he should check the tower spotter again, but didn't want to stay there any longer. With a little luck by the time word was passed down of their escape, they'd have a good enough lead to avoid capture.

"Okay, we're going to the right and straight to the fence," Mark said.

The woman cried and told her man, "I can't."

Mark stepped aggressively toward her and said, "You damn well will, or you will be the only one still here. He's coming with us, with or without you. Now get it together and follow us."

Mark motioned Lincoln to lead the way. He opened the door and was gone, Bobby on his heels. Mark let the man pull his girlfriend next and followed close behind to keep her from dragging.

He closed the door, locked it, and tossed the keys.

At the fence, he helped push the woman up and guided her over. She whimpered the entire way, but at least kept moving.

At the top of the fence Mark looked back over the base. His heart sank. A group of armed soldiers were running toward them. They weren't going to have the lead he hoped for.

Forty-Seven

MARK JUMPED TO THE ground and ran past the group. "Move," he said without pausing. He didn't bother looking back.

As he neared where he'd left his daughter, a scream followed by two gunshots sent a shockwave of fear though him. Without concern for the noise he made, Mark ran. In the distance, the insane laughter he'd heard before penetrated the woods.

Breaking into the tiny clearing he saw the body, but not Becca or her friend. Mark swung his gun, tracking for targets. Branches parted on the other side of the body and Mark increased the pressure on the trigger. Becca came into view, followed closely by the boy.

Mark stepped forward with his gun still pointed. Becca aimed her gun. Mark ducked.

"Oh God, Daddy, some crazy guy killed that poor man."

Mark quickly sized up the situation as the rest of the group came into the open. He knelt next to the soldier and confirmed his death. "Where were you?" His tone was harsh.

"Ah, Myron lost his pack when he got knocked down. I helped him find it."

As if to confirm this the boy, Myron, held the pack up.

Mark swallowed his next comment. Chain links rattled in the distance. The pursuit had reached the fence. "We have to go. This way." At a run, Mark tore through the branches. They had a long way to go and needed distance first and then stealth. When the soldiers discovered their dead comrade, they'd be out for blood and would shoot on sight.

He slowed his pace, motioning everyone to pass him. He fell in next to Lincoln. Mark didn't doubt Lincoln could easily outrun them all, but he was serving as the rear guard.

"Lincoln, they're gonna catch us before we get to the truck. Lead them about another hundred yards, and then stop and hide. Make them stay quiet."

"Wait, what are you gonna do?"

"Lead them away."

"Aw, man, that's crazy."

"There's no time to discuss it and no other way to save them. Just do what I say. I'll be all right."

Lincoln looked as if he wanted to say more, but instead sprinted to the front of the group. Mark slowed and watched as they disappeared into the darkness. His heart felt heavy. He had just found his children alive, and now might never see them again. But now that he knew they were alive his sacrifice would be worth keeping them that way.

He waited a few more seconds to get separation and then broke to the west, deliberately crashing through underbrush and snapping branches. Soon they were the only sounds he could hear. Then to the left, something snapped. Mark spun and ducked. His gun was up, his ears straining for a direction to aim.

The sound came again, more to the south, level with his position. Mark waited, tracking the unseen person by the sounds. The tracker was almost past him when he

173

heard a whispered, "Dad?"

His heart sank. Crouched, Mark moved with as much caution as he could, closing the distance on his son. Someone was moving behind him now. The posse of soldiers was getting closer.

Like a ghost, Mark came up behind his son, snaked a hand around his face, and slapped his palm over his mouth. Bobby tried to fight until Mark shushed in his ear. He pulled him to the ground shook his shoulders and whispered, "What are you doing here?"

"Two can sound more like a group than one."

Mark's anger and fear for his son's safety faded. He'd have angry words for him later – if there was a later.

More sound behind made his options limited. "Run. Keep me in sight. Do as I do." He jumped up and ran hard. The noise told him Bobby was following.

Someone shouted, "Over here," and the hunt began for real.

Forty-Eight

MARK VEERED SOUTH. The airport was to the right. If they went that way, they'd get trapped in the open. If the chasers flanked him south, they could herd Mark and Bobby toward open ground.

They had to hide somewhere soon. The cover of the woods would not last much longer. If they came to an open area they were in trouble. They might be able to keep a lead on the pursuers, but they couldn't outrun a bullet.

From the right, a scream startled them. At first, Mark thought it might be one of Lincoln's group, but they should've been to the left. Seconds later, the eerie laugh pierced the night. Mark froze. That was the real killer the Army was looking for. If he was alone, Mark would hunt the lunatic down and make a present of him to the Army Brass. For now, he had to think of his son's safety.

He motioned Bobby forward, but slowed his pace. If the hunters caught them now, there was no chance to deny their guilt or explain the truth about the real killer. They would be shot.

With the pursuit's attention drawn to the scream, Mark continued south at a slower, more cautious pace, and made for the road. He adjusted their path as needed.

To keep the pursuit behind them.

Twenty minutes later they reached the road. As feared, the opposite side was an open field. The left offered nothing to use as cover. A quarter mile to the right stood two houses. They didn't offer cover for long, but there weren't any other options.

"Keep low. Cross the road and make for that house."

Bobby nodded and ran across the street while Mark covered him. Bobby dropped below the roadbed out of sight. Mark watched the road and then broke for the other side.

Mark bear-walked for a while to keep hidden from the woods. Stones and twigs dug into his palms, but he kept on. A few grunts came from Bobby; however, Mark continued on without checking on his son. Halfway to the house, he stopped.

His hands were wet. He wiped the blood on his pants and crawled to where he could see the road and the woods. Nothing moved. If someone watched from the woods, he was unable to tell.

He ran in a crouch along the shallow drainage ditch. The house grew bigger. When he reached the front yard he left the small ditch and raced for the rear of the house. There he scanned the road behind them. His body sagged. Two figures ran along the road, heading right for them.

"We've got company." He scanned the yard. Behind them was a large four-bay garage. Well behind that and to the right was a barn. Everywhere beyond the barn was open land. If they ran for the garage, they'd be seen from the road. The house offered cover if they went to the barn. However, the garage had a better chance of holding a vehicle they might to use to escape.

"Bobby, go to the garage and see if you can get in. Look for a vehicle."

He nodded and left. Mark moved to the far side of the

house and waited. Bobby was inside. He was safe as long as Mark could take the pursuers by surprise and stop them from shooting.

Running footsteps announced that the two men had arrived. Mark readied. They came into view. One man made hand signals to the other and they separated, moving toward the garage. One went for the door Bobby had gone through. The other moved toward the opposite side where there was a second door. That man passed within fifteen feet of Mark.

Mark waited until the man had his back squared to him before moving. His first few steps were slow, but he feared being seen any moment, so he broke into a run.

The soldier by the door spotted Mark as he closed on his partner. He spun, aimed his rifle, but didn't shoot. His partner tensed, but was too late to stop Mark's attack.

Mark slapped the gun barrel across the top of the man's head more to stun him than knock him out. "Drop the rifle. Don't make me shoot."

The other soldier advanced on Mark with the rifle at eye level shouting for help as he did.

"Stop or I'll shoot him."

The man kept coming. A blur from behind struck the armed man. He staggered and the rifle fired, sending a round over Mark's head. Bobby and the shooter went down in a rolling mass of legs and arms. The soldier Mark held, turned, grabbed Mark's gun arm, and forced it up. He stepped close to Mark and flipped him over his hip.

Mark was airborne and knew the next move was to snap the gun from his hand. There was not much to do about it so he let the gun go. The man was unprepared for that and juggled the gun trying to grasp it. Mark landed hard on his back, but kicked both legs into the man's knees.

The force of the kicks swept the man's legs backward. He missed the gun and fell toward Mark. Mark sat up and drove a fist into the soldier's chin. His head snapped back and he landed as a dead weight.

Mark rolled him onto his back to deliver another punch, but saw the man was already out. He turned his attention to where Bobby and his opponent were still rolling. Neither man could gain an advantage.

Finding his gun, Mark stepped into the fray and pressed the barrel against the soldier's head. He froze but remained tense. "I'll tell you what I told the other man. I'm not a killer, but if you make me, I will shoot. Roll off him and sit still."

The man complied. Bobby stood wiping his mouth on his sleeve.

"Was there a car inside?" Mark asked.

"Yeah, three."

"Watch them."

Mark went toward the door. Down the road, four more soldiers were in view. Mark estimated he had three or four minutes. He ran inside and looked over the choices. One was a newer pickup truck, one a newer minivan. The last vehicle was an older pickup truck. That one offered the best chance to hot wire.

He jumped in the front seat, forced the column open, and started tearing at the wires. He brushed something out of his face: a lanyard attached to the key in the ignition. With a silent prayer, he started the truck. He ran to the garage door and tried to open it, but it wouldn't budge. Finding the manual release he popped it and shoved the door upward.

"Bobby," he called and drove the truck into the open.

Bobby backed away from his captives. By the time he reached the truck, the four soldiers were taking shots at them. Before Bobby's door closed, Mark had the truck moving.

A thud drew Mark's attention to the truck bed. The captive soldier was not giving up. He jumped into the bed. He stood to reach the cab, but Mark rammed the pedal down and the truck shot forward. The man lost his balance and pitched over the sidewall.

The wheels threw gravel in a shower as they reached the road. A bullet punctured the rear window. Bobby and Mark ducked. More rounds pounded into the body. Mark spun the wheel and sped west.

They had the advantage for a while, but with the two-way radios and assorted vehicles the army had, they were a long way from safe.

Forty-Nine

AT THE FIRST CROSS street, Mark turned south, away from where he wanted to go. No sense drawing pursuit toward the family, even though that was where help was.

He made another quick turn and pulled over. Mark got out, and using the butt of his handgun, smashed the brake lights. Without headlights the going was slower, but it was harder now for anyone to spot them from a distance.

They rode in silence. Mark continued in a one block west, one block south pattern until he had not only lost any pursuit but was lost himself. In the darkness without being able to see any landmarks, he had no idea where they were.

Mark drove west for several more miles, before turning the truck north. When he reached Airport Highway, he stopped. Now he knew their location. Headlights appeared in the far distance to the right. He put the truck into reverse and turned around.

He continued west another two miles and tried the crossing again. This time there was no sign of activity on the road. The truck jumped across Airport Highway, west of the town of Swanton, and down a side road. Mark varied the route until he closed in on the farmhouse.

Mark stopped the truck behind a ranch house and shut down the engine. He popped the bulb out of the dome light and stepped outside. Sitting on the rear bumper he kept vigil on the road. No one followed. Mark was as sure as he could be that they hadn't been spotted, but he wasn't about to take the chance with everyone's safety.

The passenger door opened, and Bobby joined his father. They faced each other in an awkward silence, and then Mark stood, opened his arms, and father and son embraced in a tear-filled emotional moment. After a while, Mark pushed his son back at arm's length to look at him.

"We went to the house," Bobby said.

Mark's throat thickened. Thoughts of his wife and youngest son came to him. On the verge of a massive emotional display, he looked away and breathed in deep. Now wasn't the time. Clearing his throat, he said, "If you ... I thought you might ... You saw the message?"

"Yeah." His voice caught. "On Mom's and Ben's graves." He fought back the sob. "How, how did they ..."

"The disease, or whatever it was, took them." Mark felt control slipping away then. "I thought you and your sister were dead too. I can't believe you're here." He reached for his son and pulled him close. The two hugged again. Mark wiped his eyes and let go to resume watching the road.

"Dad, how did you know Becca and I were there?"

Mark shook his head. "I didn't. I had no idea you two were even alive let alone held hostage. How long were you there?"

"Just a day. But if you didn't know we were there, why *were* you there?"

"I was looking for a member of our community. I

think those men captured him. I guess I was wrong though since he wasn't there with you."

Bobby said, "What did he look like? He wasn't Latino, was he?"

"Yes, his name is Juan. Did you see him?"

"There was a Latino man in the room when we were brought in. I never got his name. The guards took him out after a while. When they brought him back, he was in bad shape. When I got back, the other people told me Becca had escaped and one of the guards had taken Juan to get medical attention."

Mark drew in a long breath. "That means I have to go back to get him. First things first, though. I have to get you to safety and make sure the others arrived." Suddenly very anxious to get home, Mark said, "I think we're safe. Let's get moving."

Fifty

THEY DROVE TO A farmhouse. His dad flashed his headlights twice.

From the garage, a flashlight blinked twice. They drove up the driveway, past the house and parked. By the time Bobby was on the ground, they were swarmed by people racing from every building.

Bobby was surprised at how many there were. Young, old, male, and female, there had to be close to thirty members of the community. Each one carried a weapon of some sort.

A sudden force struck him from behind. Two legs wrapped tightly around his waist.

"Guess, who?" Becca said.

Bobby staggered forward.

"I'm so glad to see you, little brother. I was worried about you, you asshole. You didn't say anything. When we reached the truck and I turned around, you were gone. Myron said he saw you go after daddy. You should've told me. Anyway, I'm glad you're here."

She released him and pushed rudely past everyone talking to her father. Once in the clear she rushed forward and crushed him with her embrace. "I never thought you were dead. I always knew we'd find you."

MARK RETURNED THE HUG. He looked up to see Lynn watching them. She wiped tears from her eyes and gave him a smile. He was a father again. He reached an arm out for his son to join them. He pulled him close too.

The community watched silently. Then Mark saw Juan's wife. Her shoulders slumped forward and her chest heaved as large tears rolled down her face. Two women went to hug and comfort her. Mark's elation evaporated. There were still important things to do.

Releasing his kids seemed to be the signal for everyone to talk at once. He raised his hands to quiet them.

"I'm sorry, Maria. I didn't see Juan. But my kids said he was there. I'm going back tomorrow to find him and bring him home."

Maria's eyes closed and she cried. Several of the women rushed to comfort her. They led her to the house.

Lynn came forward. "Lincoln filled us in on what you found. Are these soldiers going to be a threat like … like before?"

"I don't know, Lynn. I get the feeling there's something else going on here. From what I gathered from Becca and Bobby, the soldiers are looking for someone who killed several of their men." To the group, Mark said, "Did anyone have any run-ins with men dressed in uniforms?"

He looked around, but no one responded.

"I'm not here to judge, but if something happened, it will be helpful knowing about it. These people are angry and want revenge. I'm not so sure we'd be any different."

Still no one offered any comments.

"Okay, for everyone's safety, I think you should all stay here until we can assess the situation. If they're a threat, it's better if we all stand together."

Brandford said, "I have to get my family."

Two others said the same.

Mark frowned and gritted his teeth. *Why hadn't they been smart enough to bring everyone with them? They knew a threat existed. Now others would be at risk to help them.* In a controlled voice, he said, "Okay, we need volunteers to ride shotgun with each of you." Hands shot up without hesitation. "Go now."

Lynn said, "Wait. Caleb, go get the radios."

Caleb ran inside the house. When he returned, he held new two-way radios still in their packs.

"How many of them did you get?" Mark said.

"Six sets. Three sets have a longer range."

"Okay, you three take the long range ones. Leave their mates here. We'll have someone monitoring each one. Report in when you get to your houses and when you're leaving there."

With radios in hand, the three teams drove off.

"Caleb, split the other packs up among the other families. Do you know how they work?"

"I'm pretty sure."

"Okay," Mark said, "help them understand how to use them. Everyone else, get inside. We'll take turns on guard duty until the morning. Lincoln, will you take care of setting a two-hour guard rotation?"

"You got it."

Mark lowered his head and stared at the ground as everyone around him moved. There was so much to do, and if the past was any indication, not nearly enough time.

Fifty-One

"BECCA, YOU, Bobby, and you two," Mark pointed to the other rescued couple, "come with me."

He walked into the garage and toward a workbench. He pulled a stool out and sat. Until then, he hadn't realized how exhausted he was. As the others gathered around, Mark said, "I need some intel on the base. Who was there first?"

Bobby said, "They were there before us," with a nod in the couple's direction.

Mark extended a hand. "I'm Mark. I appreciate you helping my daughter escape."

"I'm Vince. This is Agnes." Agnes looked as though she might faint at any moment. "I'm just glad it all worked out. And thanks for bringing us along."

"You're welcome to stay as long as you want, but just so you understand, we do have some rules, which I can explain later, and everyone is expected to help out. There's always stuff to do."

Vince nodded.

"Now, was Juan there before you?"

"Juan? The little Latino guy?"

Mark nodded.

"Yeah, said he was there about an hour before we were brought in. Your kids came in several hours later."

"What can you tell me about the base?"

"I'm not sure. What do you want to know?"

"How many people are manning the base?"

"Oh, heck, I wouldn't have any idea. From what I saw maybe twenty or thirty people. I'm sure there were more inside the buildings."

"Were you anywhere else other than the room we found you in?"

"First they brought us to a building across from that one. It may have been their command center 'cause that's where the officers were. The guard asked what the man in charge wanted to do with us. They decided to put us in that building because it could be secured and guarded with few people."

"What about trucks and vehicles?"

Vince shrugged. "I saw a bunch, but don't know how many. I did see the two jets though. They seemed to be working on them, like they were trying to get them ready to fly."

Mark turned to Becca and Bobby. "What about you two?"

Bobby said, "The two buildings across from us looked like barracks. People were going in and out steadily. One could have been a mess area. I agree with Vince. The smaller one on the end was their headquarters. Inside the first hangar, a lot of people were working on a jet engine. I didn't see any other jets inside, just the two on the tarmac."

Becca continued, "There were eight trucks lined up near the fence. I also saw four jeeps, one of which had a mounted machine gun. I'm not sure what they're trying to do, but they have some serious firepower."

"Best guess as to numbers."

Becca frowned and looked at Bobby. "I'd say maybe fifty."

Bobby nodded. "Yeah, at least."

"Good. That gives me an idea of what we're dealing with. Anything else?" Head shakes greeted him until he got to Becca. "What?"

"If you're going back to find your friend, I'm going with you."

Bobby added, "Ditto."

"We'll talk about that later."

Fifty-Two

WITH THE FARMHOUSE NOW bursting at the seams and so many preparations to oversee, Mark couldn't find the time to sit with his children and have a reunion. By two a.m. he was exhausted. He gave Becca and Bobby a hug, something he had given up believing would ever happen again, and went to bed.

He didn't remember falling asleep, but a soft knock on the door woke him.

Lynn slipped inside and closed the door. "Are you awake?"

"I am now." He pushed up on his side. "What's up?"

Lynn sat on the edge of the bed. Her face glowed in the slim moonlight that slid through the curtain. She was crying.

He sat up. "What is it?" He touched her shoulder.

She shook her head. "Nothing. I'm just so happy for you. I couldn't imagine the pain you were going through not knowing if they were alive or not, but now ..."

He pulled her close and held her. It wasn't often she allowed any physical contact or emotional display. The ordeal she'd gone through not long ago was still a fresh scar in her memory. Mark had strong feelings for Lynn but understood and respected her distance.

"Thank you," he said.

Lynn placed her head against his chest. He stroked her hair. It was the first time she'd allowed Mark to be this close since he'd recovered from his injuries. He couldn't deny he'd longed to hold her.

She put her hands on his chest and gently pushed free. Her gaze met his. She touched his cheek and then her hand was gone like it had been a light breeze. "I know you have to do whatever you can to protect this family, but we can't afford to lose you. I-I can't afford to lose you. And now that your children have arrived, they don't want to lose their father. Please be careful."

"I will."

Lynn stood and slid to the door.

Mark said, "Lynn."

She hesitated, but didn't turn.

"I need you too."

She nodded and left.

Sleep was a non-starter after that. An hour later, Mark dressed, gathered what he needed, and slid out of the house. Light was the hint of an idea in the eastern sky. He reached the truck, opened the door, and then heard footsteps behind him.

He spun and crouched, a gun in his hand pointed and ready.

The footsteps stopped. "I told you he'd try to sneak away without us," Bobby said.

Becca replied, "You were right, brother."

Mark's heart rate slowed. A breath of relief released. "What do you think you two are doing?"

"Don't be dense, Daddy. We're going with you." Without waiting for Mark to respond, Becca walked around the truck and climbed in.

"Shame on you, Dad. We just found each other and you're trying to duck out on us." Bobby followed his sister inside and closed the door.

Mark stood, mouth open, watching his children. His first reaction was anger. Then the harsh words melted from his mouth and a feeling of pride swept through him. He smiled and got in.

"Okay, but here's the rules. You follow my lead and do what I say with no argument or delay. There is no room for debate. I have a lot of people to look after, and they rely on me to keep them safe. If you have a problem with any of that, get out."

Neither child spoke.

Mark backed out the driveway and drove away from the house. He glanced sideways and saw the smile on Becca's face. "What are you smiling about?"

"This is going to be fun."

Mark shook his head. *I hope this isn't a huge mistake.*

Fifty-Three

MOVEMENT WOKE MYRON. One of the other boys sleeping in the rooms above the garage was getting dressed. Myron couldn't remember the boy's name. So much had happened over the last two days. After being alone for so long, being with all these people overwhelmed him. He'd never had friends before and expected it wouldn't take long for the derogatory comments and bullying to begin.

Not having anyone around to remind him of what a geek he was had been a blessing. But now, amid these people, who so far had been nice to him, Myron couldn't shake the old feelings.

Maybe he should leave. Then the vision of Becca drifted through his mind. He wanted to be near her. Maybe she'd go with him. But why would she? What was he to her? Eventually, she'd see him for the geek he was. No, he'd leave alone. She probably wouldn't even know he was gone.

The other boy looked at him and smiled. "Time to rise and shine, buddy. You can't sleep the day away around here. There's a bathroom downstairs. Breakfast will be served in about thirty minutes. Don't be late." He went over and shook two other boys awake, laughing at them as he did. Then he left, his footsteps pounding down the steps.

Myron sat on the edge of his fold-up bed. His roommates stirred and stretched. They each greeted him. They seemed nice, but Myron remained wary.

In the bathroom, he washed his face and looked at the stranger he saw in the mirror. His face was thinner. His hair was very long and he had a beard. He looked like a wild animal. Becca could never like him. At least not the way he wanted her to.

He walked outside. The sun was just rising. People were moving all around the grounds. He stood, watching, not sure what to do.

"Hey!" The boy from upstairs motioned for him.

Myron walked over.

"Can you give me a hand moving this table? There are so many people here, we'll need the extra seating."

"Ah, sure." Myron latched on to the end and the two boys moved the heavy picnic table in line with the others.

The other boy came toward him. "Thanks. I'm Caleb. Welcome to the madness." He stuck out his hand. His smile looked sincere.

Myron accepted it. "Myron."

"Nice to meet you, Myron. Sounds like you had an exciting day yesterday."

"Yeah, I guess."

"You guess? Dude, the way I hear it, you rescued Mark's kids. You're being modest."

Myron warmed at the praise, but didn't know how to respond.

Caleb walked toward a large fire pit. Myron followed. The taller boy picked up some split logs and Myron bent to help.

"Thanks," Caleb said. "Pitching in around here is important. We all try to help each other."

The two boys deposited the wood in the pit. Caleb arranged it and then grabbed a pile of small, dried twigs and leaves and dumped them under the firewood. Using a long-handled lighter, Caleb lit the twigs and bent to blow on the small flame.

Myron, having built fires when he was a boy scout, picked up a long stick and poked at the flames to move them around under the firewood. Minutes later the larger pieces lit and the fire grew.

"It'll catch logs now. Help me lift the grate."

They lifted a large heavy steel circle that fitted onto four iron legs driven into the ground around the pit. The door to the house opened, and an attractive woman came down the stairs carrying two large bowls. She set them down on a small table next to the fire.

She came forward, smiled at Myron, and gave a hug and kiss to Caleb.

"Mom, this is Myron. He's been helping me."

Caleb's mom turned her smile toward him and shook his hand. "Welcome, Myron. I'm Lynn. Thanks for helping out. Can you two go inside and bring out the pots and pans?"

"Sure, Mom. This way, Myron."

When the meal was ready and everyone was seated, one man stood and said a prayer. Then the food was passed. Myron was suddenly very hungry.

Lynn stood and said, "For the new people, we are happy to have you here. Just remember a lot of people have to be fed with what I have on the table so be courteous. And for the benefit of those new to the group, let's go around the table and introduce yourselves, please. I'm Lynn." She sat down.

Caleb said his name and passed a bowl of biscuits to Myron.

"I'm Myron."

Everyone said hi, and Caleb added, "And he's a good worker."

Myron looked down the line of tables and back up the other side. Becca was not there. A knot formed in his stomach. Her father and brother were gone as well. Maybe they left. He might never see her again. He stopped eating and stared at his plate.

Lynn broke him from his thoughts. "Are you all right, Myron?"

"Huh? Oh, yeah. I'm fine."

But if Becca was gone he was anything but.

Fifty-Four

"I THINK WE'VE seen enough," Mark said. They had been watching the base for three hours from different positions. The inhabitants were genuinely operating as a military base. They lined up for calisthenics, which everyone, including officers, took part in. The only exceptions were the guards. Mark took the opportunity to get a head count. He frowned long and hard as he reached a total of fifty-eight bodies, counting guards and the watcher in the control tower. That didn't include anyone still in a building someplace.

Exercising done, the men and some women went back inside the barracks. Fifteen minutes later, they strolled out in their combat fatigues. They entered another building Mark thought might be the mess hall.

Mark switched to a new location and waited.

With mess over, the troops went about their daily assignments, most of which revolved around the fighter jets.

There were no longer guards in front of the building being used as a prison, so Juan was not being held there. Mark was down to three possible buildings where Juan might be. The hard part would be getting him out of.

The airport stretched a long way to the west. They saw

no sign of anyone guarding the far end of the runways. The tarmac made the entire area too wide open to use as an approach. To cross that much ground without being spotted was impossible.

One of the possible holding places for Juan was the larger building next to the cell. The other two were across the way, next to the barracks and mess buildings. Unable to come up with a plan, they crept back into the woods.

Voices made Mark freeze. He whispered to the kids, "You wait here. Keep alert." From there he crawled forward. Two uniformed men were stringing razor wire along the top of the fence. It would be more difficult getting inside now, but not impossible.

Mark crept farther down the line of fencing. When he reached the spot where the fence turned south, he stopped. *How long would it take them to get this far with the razor wire?* Entry there was too risky.

To his left, past the woodpile, were four fresh mounds of dirt. Graves. They'd lost four comrades. The burials were recent. If the army thought Mark and friends had killed those four comrades, the soldiers would not stop until they found them.

Mark was about to give up when he remembered the promise he made to Maria. He had to find a way. Perhaps the other side of the base offered a solution.

As he was about to rejoin the kids, there was a sudden burst of activity on the base. An officer shouted orders and soldiers moved at a rapid pace. They ran to the trucks and loaded into two of them, eight men in each, plus the officer and two drivers. Nineteen men were moving off on some important mission. *What would cause such urgency?*

Fear surged through him. The officer went into a building and came out dragging Juan by the arm.

Fifty-Five

MAKING MORE NOISE THAN he wanted, Mark reached the kids. "Let's go! Fast!"

If Juan had talked, as Mark feared, the two trucks were on their way to the farmhouse. He increased his speed.

They piled into the truck and raced off. There was no time for caution. He cursed himself for not thinking to bring one of the two-way radios.

Without looking, Mark shot across Airport Highway. There was no time to check for pursuit.

The pickup was flying along the roads at a speed that made its entire body shake. The turn Mark made was so wide, they almost collided with a house. Without slowing, he regained the road and continued at a deadly pace.

One more turn put them on the road that led home. He braked hard at the corner and tore up the driveway, scattering the community doing their post-breakfast cleanup.

Leaving the engine running, Mark jumped out. "Everyone get armed and take cover. Caleb, I want rifles in the windows over the garage. Zac, you handle setting up downstairs in the garage. I need people in the upper portion of the barn. Lynn, organize the house's defense.

And no one fires unless I give the word."

Lincoln raced across the street buckling his pants. "What's going on?"

"Go get Jenny and bring her here. I think the army is on its way."

"Shit!" He took off like he was sprinting for the goal line.

"What do you need us to do?" Bobby asked.

Mark looked at Bobby's rifle. "Are you any good with that thing?"

"You taught me."

"Then I need you in that loft." He pointed toward the barn. "If you see me signal, you take out the officer."

Bobby nodded.

"Becca, go with him."

"Dad, I can fight as good as Bobby."

"And that's why I need you with him. He'll be a target. Snipers will control the ground. They'll try to take him out. He'll need you to protect him."

She studied his face to see the lie for what it was, but ran off anyway.

Mark went inside, poured a cup of cold coffee, and drank it with a shaking hand.

The truck's engines announced their approach a long way off. Mark put on his game face. Once again it was time to face down the devil.

Fifty-Six

"Remember," he shouted, "no one shoot unless they start." Mark gave a last look at Lynn, met her eyes, and walked outside.

He stood with a gun in his hand and waited. The first truck started past the house, braked, and stopped. An arm extended out the window and signaled to the second truck. The officer was smart. He was separating his force and flanking Mark.

Mark waited in the open. Several minutes later, a truck turned up the driveway, moving slowly. The man in charge was giving his troops a chance to get into position. A side glance showed soldiers hiding in the long line of pine trees bordering the road along the side of the house.

The chill up his spine let him know many weapons were now aimed at him.

Mark walked forward, not so much to meet the truck as to put the house between him and the soldiers in the trees. The fewer people with a line-of-sight on him, the better chance he had of surviving.

He waited for the officer to decide it was safe for him to step out of the truck. Instead, he poked his head out the widow and ordered, "Drop your gun or I will order my men to shoot."

Mark stood there. Eight men lined up in front of the truck with their rifles aimed at him.

Mark lifted his left arm over his head. From every window in the three buildings a gun now protruded. The soldiers took note and some shifted their aim toward the house.

The two men whose eyes did not waver from him were the real soldiers. If a gun fight broke out, those would be his first targets. If the others didn't spook and run, Mark was dead.

A very tense standoff had developed. No one moved, but a few soldiers glanced at the truck. The officer stepped out and advanced toward Mark.

He stopped a few feet away and sized Mark up. Mark didn't bother doing the same. He'd been in the Marines. To him, all officers were the same.

"I'm General West. I'm in charge of the combined forces of the 180th Air National Guard and several National Guard divisions and Army Reserve units. We are here to arrest a murderer or group murderers. I am authorized by—"

"You're looking in the wrong place, General. We have not injured your people."

"You broke suspects out of my base. That makes you guilty of violating several federal laws."

"You were holding innocent people against their will. If there *is* a federal government, that's illegal as well."

"I am the federal government in these parts. That makes me the law. You will hand the prisoners over to us and surrender yourself."

"That's not going to happen. These are innocent people. American people, who are struggling to survive just like the rest of the country. We do not kill for no reason. If you had come to us in a more friendly manner, we would've accepted you and treated you like friends."

"Be that as it may, you have suspects that we weren't through questioning."

"Yeah, I saw firsthand your interrogation techniques. You

can't beat confessions out of people. Find evidence and convict them. I know you're upset about losing your men, but that doesn't make everyone else a killer."

"No," West shouted, "but it makes them suspects."

"I'm telling you for the last time, you're looking in the wrong place."

The general paced to the side two steps. "You know I have more than enough firepower to wipe out everyone here."

"Although that may be true, you wouldn't be the first tyrant we've dealt with. I promise, before it ends, you will be down a lot of men."

"You'll die first."

Mark shook his head "By the time you gave the signal, you'll be dead. I have a sniper targeting you."

West's eyes flicked around. When he found the perch, his eyes narrowed.

"It doesn't have to be this way, General. If you're the law here, we're American citizens. We're who you're here to protect. Hasn't there been enough death?"

"I want to talk to the prisoners. If they are innocent, as you claim, I will let them go. However, you have many men here who I will induct into the army. As Americans, it is their duty to protect this land."

"No one is going with you to be interrogated or pressed into service. I can vouch for these people. If someone wants to volunteer to serve, that's up to them. But it should be their choice, not yours."

"Again, I could force you. I have trained soldiers on your women and children. Are you willing to risk their lives?"

"I've seen your men, and I'm not impressed. You have some soldiers, but the others were probably people like us that you forced to join. My people are not trained, which means the longer we stand here, the more likely one of them accidentally pulls the trigger and a war begins. However, it comes out, neither one of us will know."

The general stepped forward, his anger apparent from the

redness of his face. "You have no idea what you're dealing with here. There are things going on beyond your knowledge or understanding. My job is to protect this country and the people who are still alive – but first I have to be able to protect my men – and I can't do that if they get gutted while trying to do their jobs."

"I can't say I know what you're talking about, but I do know we did not kill your men. Unless threatened by your people, mine would not have hurt yours."

The two men stood no more than a foot apart, glaring at each other. The staredown lasted for anxious seconds. Then the rumble of a vehicle broke their connection. An armed jeep pulled up next to the truck. The gunner swung his weapon toward Mark. A wave of fear swept over him, not so much for himself as for those he was trying to protect.

A sneer crept across the General's face. "I think the balance of power was just upended."

"Nothing has changed. You and I will die in the first shots. Your men will die. My people will die. In the end, no one gets what they want, and your army will be severely weakened. Whatever you have been training your soldiers to do will not get done. In fact, I'd guess most of them will disband and go their own ways."

West's jaw worked back and forth with furious movements. "You don't understand the importance of what I do. You will destroy whatever is left of America."

"You're right. I don't understand, but you're the one who will destroy whatever your plan is. Go away and leave us alone."

"I will come back with more men. I will lay siege to your compound and wear you down. Eventually I will get my way."

The words echoed in Mark's head.

Fifty-Seven

MYRON WATCHED THE EXCHANGE from the dining room window. He had a handgun pointed at the ground near the men who stood by the truck. His stomach churned. The others appeared so brave, standing ready to fire on the soldiers. They were willing to protect their community, knowing they may die doing it.

Myron's hand shook at the thought of killing someone. He rested the gun on the windowsill so no one else saw how scared he was.

The words spoken in the driveway drifted to his ears. They were faint, but he could hear most of what was said. Then the officer stepped closer to Mark and started shouting. Things were about to escalate.

He swallowed hard, trying to choke down his fear. His breathing had become rapid and shallow. Myron closed his eyes and tried to find the courage he'd had when rescuing Becca. The thought of her and the image that danced before his eyes calmed him.

That was shattered when he saw the jeep pull up. The bloody corpses by the woods replaced Becca's features. His fear increased to mind-numbing panic. His bladder threatened to release again, but he squeezed tight. Tears seeped out. There was no way of controlling the gun now. It rattled noisily on the wooden sill.

Myron pulled from the window and leaned against the wall. The others in the room turned to look at him. The woman in charge, Lynn, ran to the window and pushed out a rifle. She looked at Myron. Then she reached out with a gentle hand and stroked his arm.

"We'll be all right, Myron. Just take some deep breaths, okay? I'm scared too, but a lot of people are, and they are all counting on everyone else for support and strength. That's how families survive. And you're part of our family now. We're going to need you."

She turned her attention back to the standoff. "Hmm!"

Despite his fear, Myron pivoted and looked out the window.

"What's going on?"

Lynn bit her lip. "I'm not sure, but I don't think I like it."

The voices were more conversational now. Myron could only make out a few words, but what he pieced together sent him stiff with fear.

"That's the deal," Mark said. "You release our friend, and I'll take his place."

Myron yelled, "No!"

A vivid picture of Mark torn apart from a barrage of bullets sent him into action. He bolted for the back door and banged down the steps. His feet carried him toward Mark and the general.

Both men turned toward him.

Mark raised a hand and shouted, "Don't shoot!"

"No," Myron shouted again. "You can't go with them. They'll kill you."

Mark spun in a circle and held his hands high. "No one shoot."

The general held up one hand to his men, but did not speak.

Myron stopped near Mark. "I saw what they do to

203

people who don't want to join them. You can't go."

Mark looked from Myron to the general and then back. "What are you talking about?"

"I saw them." He pointed to the jeep. "They shot down a man and a pregnant woman. They were running from them. The machine gun opened up and then, and … and their bodies …"

Tears streamed down his face, but anger replaced his fear.

Mark said to the general, "Is that true?"

West stiffened in defense. "They were shooting at my men. They had no choice."

"Bullshit!" Myron said. "They were two people running from armed men. They were afraid. The man was trying to protect his family. They never had a chance. The gunner laughed when he was done."

"Maybe the murderer is within your ranks, General," Mark said.

The general turned toward the jeep for a moment and then back to Mark. "It's only this boy's word against my men. They have a right to defend themselves if fired upon."

Mark faced the General. "How much of a threat could a man and his pregnant wife have been?"

"It doesn't change a thing. We have a job to do defending this country."

"No, it changes a lot. You come in here accusing us of murdering your men, and you're the one killing the very people you say you want to protect. And what the hell are you protecting the country against?"

West worked his jaw again. This time, however, his eyes held no anger. He put a hand to his jaw and massaged it as if he'd been punched. "Haven't you wondered what happened to everyone?"

Mark was stunned by the change of tone and topic. His voice softened. "Do you know?"

"Not completely, but we have been in contact with other forces like ours. They say there is an invasion going on. Speculation is that some foreign power, perhaps several, released some form of chemical or biological weapon in our atmosphere. Their troops are now moving across the country, eliminating any opposition."

"What? And you believe that?"

"I don't see that I have any choice in the matter. Isn't it better to be prepared rather than surprised and not be able to stop them?"

"Don't trust him, Mark," Myron said.

Mark rolled the new information around his head. *Could what West said be true?* It explained some things.

Mark made up his mind. "The deal still stands. You release Juan, and I will go with you. I will help you find the person responsible for killing your men. Like I told you, I saw and heard someone in those woods. When we find him, you can deal with him as you see fit, but then we're done. I'm going home. But I will add one more part to the deal.

"There is no reason for us to be enemies, especially if what you say is true. So I will offer this. If at any time you need us to help you fight intruders, you send word and we'll come. That's the best way for both of us to get what we want."

West made no reply. He crossed his arms over his chest.

Mark waited for a moment and then stretched out his hand. "Deal?"

Something hard passed through West's eyes.

"Come on, General. From one American to another, isn't it good to know there are others out there you can call on when needed? It's better and a lot less costly than trying to force us to join you. Just consider us your militia."

"And I'm just supposed to believe you? How do I

know you'll do what you say?"

"Because, as promises were once made in the past, I give you my word."

Mark's hand still hung out there.

West accepted the hand and the deal. "Okay. I'll trust you, American to American."

West walked to the truck and spoke to one of his men. That man opened the door and helped a battered Juan to the ground. Juan stood until Mark called to him. Juan walked slowly toward him, the pain from moving evident with each step. A flash of anger hit Mark. He tried to swallow it.

He walked toward Juan and wrapped an arm around his waist to help him walk. Juan's face was bruised and swollen. One eye was almost closed. "Myron, come here."

Myron ran toward the two men and took Juan around the other side.

"Take him to Lynn and stay in the house until everyone leaves."

"Are you really going with them?"

"I'll be all right. Just stay in the house."

Mark released Juan, and Myron continued guiding the injured man toward the back steps.

West had already motioned his troops back to their trucks. Mark came up behind him. "I'll accept that the damage you did to that man was before our deal. It doesn't excuse it, but I'll let it go. But understand that if any of your men touch another one of my people, I will kill them."

Leaving West with his jaw open, Mark turned toward the house.

"Are you going to honor the deal?" West called after him.

"Yes, I'm going to say goodbye."

Fifty-Eight

IN THE HOUSE, everyone rushed to him and began talking at once. Mark hushed them, his gaze locked on Lynn's. "I'm going with them to help find whoever's been killing their men."

Voices exploded all around, imploring him not to go.

He quieted them again. "I made a deal and I'm going to honor it. You should be all right but keep everyone close to the house for a few days. Set a watch. Send teams two blocks in each direction with the radios."

Outside, one of the trucks pulled away from the property.

"I shouldn't be long. Everyone go back to your windows and make sure all the soldiers leave."

The group moved away. Lynn stepped forward. There was so much Mark wanted to say, but too many eyes and ears were focused on them. He grabbed Lynn's hand and led her to his room. With the door closed, he scooped Lynn into his arms and held tight.

"I won't beg you not to go," she said. "I know you have to. Just please come back to us." Her lips quivered. "Come back to me."

"I will."

Lynn reached behind his head and pulled his face down

to hers. Her lips touched his gently at first, and then pressed harder. She broke the kiss, gave one more firm embrace, and then backed away to let Mark go.

"Lynn, please take care of my kids, and don't let them follow me. Tell them I'll be back and I'm counting on them to protect the camp."

She nodded, and Mark left. He trotted down the back stairs and jogged to the waiting truck. The quicker he got into the truck and off the property the harder it would be for his children to follow.

Mark climbed into the cab and shut the door. As it reversed down the driveway, Becca ran from the barn. "Daddy! Wait!" Her voice screeched with a touch of desperation. She ran harder.

In the distance, Bobby walked, carrying the rifle. He lifted a hand as a wave.

The truck drove off leaving Becca behind. Mark didn't want to watch. He was afraid of how far Becca might chase them on foot. He closed his eyes, but it wasn't enough.

"Stop!" he said.

The driver looked at him. The General narrowed his eyes as if expecting a double cross.

"Please, General, just for a moment."

The General nodded to his driver and Mark jumped to the street. Sure enough, Becca was still following. With a leap she was in his arms.

"Daddy, you can't go. We just found you."

Mark held her tight and then roughly pulled her arms apart and separated from her. He squeezed her arms tight. "Becca, you need to listen to me. I have to go help these men. I am not in danger. I need you to stay and protect the others."

"No! I'm coming with you."

He shook her. "I am your father. You will do what I tell you to do. Go back to your brother. Go now. I do not want you with me. Do you understand?"

Mark climbed back into the truck without another word and without looking back. His daughter was fragile. He had seen that. Mark hoped she survived his rebuke until he returned.

If he returned.

Fifty-Nine

AT THE BASE, Mark stood in a semi-circle of uniformed men giving a briefing. A map was taped to a board behind him. "I first saw this person here." He pointed to the wooded area across the street from the base. "I'm not sure what he looks like. It was just a dark hulking shape. He looked like a moving mound, like he was wearing camouflage. But it wasn't so much the shape that stuck in my memory as the maniacal laugh. I remember the first time I heard it, it sent chills up my spine."

One of the soldiers said, "Yeah, I remember hearing that too."

Mark nodded. "There was a scream too, as if someone was hurt. I wasn't sure what was going on, so I just ran. I heard that same laugh again over here." He pointed to the building Becca and Bobby had been held in.

"We captured one of your men and tied him up. We were going to leave him for you to find. When I returned to the clearing, he was dead. I heard the laugh, but we weren't about to stick around. The killer was in those woods."

The lieutenant said, "So how do you propose we find this invisible killer?"

Clearly he did not believe him. Mark looked around

the faces of the other men. Not many allies here.

"We go out into both sets of woods in groups of two. If the group is too big, the killer may not strike. But we have to stay close enough to help if he does attack and must be alert. The other times he struck, there were other things going on to mask his approach."

"And you're going out there with us, right?" the lieutenant asked.

"Yes."

"But if you're the killer, like I think you are, we'll all be looking for someone else, giving you the chance to kill more of us."

Mark ignored the comment. "I'll be in front of you. You'll be chasing me. That will be the distraction the killer will need. He will attempt to take out the flanks or any stragglers. That's why you have to keep close to your partner."

"I'll be watching you," the lieutenant said, moving two fingers from his eyes toward Mark. "Any sign of you moving toward one of my men and I'll kill you. Also, you are not carrying any weapons. That will keep my men safe."

"And what if the killer tries for me? I'll have nothing to defend myself with."

"Too bad. While he's killing you, I'll kill him. Besides, we all know we'll be chasing the real killer. So if nothing happens out there, we'll bring you back to face a firing squad."

Mark didn't reply. There was nothing he could say. The lieutenant pointed to one of his men. "Take his gun and knife."

Mark didn't move as the weapons were taken from him. If the bait didn't entice the killer, Mark had to somehow disappear. He would not go quietly to a firing squad.

One of the soldiers said, "How will he know we're

there?"

Mark said, "One of you fire a few shots into the woods. That should draw his attention."

The lieutenant laughed. "That won't be a problem. I know right where I'll fire too."

The lieutenant took a bright orange hunter's vest from a table and tossed it to Mark. "Put that on."

"If we don't make it look real, he's not going to take the bait."

"Well, that'll be too bad for you then, won't it?"

Sixty

"Dad said for us to stay. He knows what he's doing."

"Of course he's going to say that, Bobby." Becca paced the barn floor. "He's our dad. Keeping us safe is his priority. But he doesn't know how tough we are or what we're capable of. We make a good team. We can help him."

Bobby shook his head. Becca's eyes flared. Snorting out an angry breath she stopped pacing and closed on her brother. "Bobby, he needs us whether he realizes it or not."

"Even if that's true, we have no idea where he went."

"Yes, we do. They're at the base. That's what Myron told me. He heard them talking. Isn't that right, Myron?"

Myron was sitting on a workbench in the back corner. He jumped down and walked toward them. "I tried to warn him. I saw what they did. They shot down two people. The army guys were looking for a killer, and your dad volunteered to help them."

"You see, Bobby. They're the killers … and Daddy's in danger. I don't know about you, but I didn't come this far to find him only to lose him again. He needs our help."

Bobby looked from his sister to Myron and back again.

"All right, what do you propose we do?"

Becca smiled. "I think we take a vehicle and go after him."

"We need more of a plan than that, Sis. We can't just try a frontal attack. Remember, they think we're escaped prisoners. They'll just recapture us."

"Well, we have to do something."

"We can take back roads, hide the truck and approach through the woods," Myron said. "That's how I did it when I, uh, you know ..."

Becca turned her best smile on Myron. "Rescued me? You are just too sweet."

Becca smiled as Myron blushed beneath the shaggy beard.

Myron added, "We can try that and kinda scout the base out before making any solid plans."

"That's a great idea."

Myron blushed again.

"Come on, Bobby, let's at least try."

Bobby nodded.

The trio left the barn and walked toward the pickup truck. Bobby opened the door. "No keys."

"Let's try the house," Becca said.

Lynn met them coming down the stairs. "What is it you think you're going to do?"

"We're going to help my father," Becca said with attitude.

"Your father doesn't want your help. He told me to watch you and keep you safe. You need to stay here until he comes back."

"I don't think so, lady. We don't need your permission. He needs our help. Now get out of our way." Becca's voice was confrontational.

Bobby moved to intervene. "Sis, be nice. I'm sure ..."

Becca whipped around and glared at her brother. "No, Bobby. Daddy needs our help, and I'm not going to let anyone stop us." She spun on Lynn and took a step closer. "Now, we need the keys to that truck. Either give them to us or get out of our way."

Lynn glared back at Becca with equal determination. "No. I made a promise to your father to keep you safe, and that's what I'm going to do. You stay here."

In a flash, Becca's hand went to the sheath on her thigh. Her rage so consuming, she wanted to gut this bitch, but her hand closed around nothing. She looked down at the empty holder. "What …? Where's …?" Then she remembered. The soldiers had taken it from her when they'd been captured. That was another reason Becca wanted to return to the base. She wanted her knife back, the knife her father had given her.

Bobby stepped between the two women and faced his sister. In a harsh tone he said, "You're out of control, Sis. That's enough."

She moved her hardened glare from her brother to the woman over her shoulder. "If anything happens to my father, I'll be coming for you."

"That's enough," Bobby said, grabbing Becca by her shoulders and shoving her backward. "Myron, grab hold and walk her back to the barn."

"Becca," Myron said in a soft voice, "come with me." He touched her.

She turned on him. Her fury blinded her and she did not recognize the person who stood before her. Myron flinched away from her. Then, as if some magical transformation occurred, the fire left Becca's eyes and the light returned. Her shoulders and jaw relaxed, and her face became less taut. A long exhale released some of her hostility. "Okay, my brave savior, we'll go. For now." And as simple as that they walked away.

LYNN WATCHED THE TWO leave, surprised Becca had gone that

easily. When Myron and Becca were almost to the barn, Bobby turned to Lynn.

"I'm sorry for my sister's behavior. She's afraid of losing our dad, especially after just finding him. The struggles we've had to survive in this new world have been hard on her, but I think the shock of seeing my mother's and brother's graves may have pushed her over the edge."

Lynn responded, "I do understand. It's been hard for all of us."

However, this girl was completely out of control. She had to be watched closely. She could be a danger to the entire community.

"I know you're worried about your father. But this is what he does to protect us. He takes on the burden himself to spare us. I've seen him do some amazing things. He's a survivor. He'll be back." She tried to smile. *I have to believe he's coming back.*

"I don't want to cause any trouble here. And I do respect you as leader here. But he's our father. If he's not back by nightfall, we will go looking for him. Please understand I am not trying to cause trouble or threaten you. It's just the way it is."

Bobby backed away.

"Wait."

Bobby stopped.

Lynn moved toward him. "You have to give your father a chance to do what he set out to do. It may take some time. However, if it gets that late, come to me. I'll give you the keys."

Bobby nodded. "Thanks." He walked back to the barn.

Lynn watched him go inside. Becca's threat replayed in her mind. *If anything happens to my father, I'll be coming for you.* If anything happened to Mark, Becca wouldn't have to come for her. Lynn would die without him.

Sixty-One

MASON CACKLED BUT QUICKLY covered his mouth. His excitement was almost uncontainable. The uniforms were in the woods. They were looking for him. Oh, they were trying to be tricky, chasing the man in the bright orange, but Mason knew they were really hunting him.

Well, he could be tricky too. With so many targets out there, he barely knew where to begin. It would be a long slow process, but he wanted to get them all. He rubbed his hands together vigorously.

A shiver of anticipation raced through Mason. He needed to relax. He flexed his hands and sucked in long breaths. Once he was in control, he set out to hunt. He'd take the soldiers first, and then the orange man.

The uniforms would never take him. *They will not confine me again.* That motivation alone was enough. With a fire burning inside, he moved. Mason Armstrong was hunting again.

SOMETHING WAS WRONG. They had been running through the woods for more than an hour. Mark had done a good job of dodging the pursuit. It wasn't easy to do wearing this ridiculous vest. He dodged behind a tree and rested.

Lieutenant Grayson was more of a sadist than an actual leader. Mark remembered how close the shots had been placed when he started off. The hope was the sound would draw the killer. So far nothing had worked. Other than the soldiers, there was no movement in the woods at all.

If nothing happened in the next hour, he'd suggest moving to the other site where six more soldiers were already patrolling.

Okay, this has to go. Mark peeled off the vest and buried it under some leaves and branches. Grayson hadn't trusted him with a weapon, so Mark was defenseless. Well, that wasn't true. He might be weaponless, but never defenseless.

Peering around the tree, Mark watched and waited. There were six men chasing him, working in pairs. Grayson and his partner were in the middle. Mark pictured where the flanking team nearest him might be. It was time to cheat.

Mark crawled in the direction of the turnpike. To his left, perhaps twenty yards away, someone rustled leaves. Mark froze and focused on the area. A darker shape moved through the dense brush. The figure moved, stopped, and moved again.

Mark scanned to the right of the man. He had to find out if he was the end of the flank or if there was one more pursuer he had to avoid. He waited. When the first form had walked farther away, Mark moved one leg forward.

Dried leaves crunched. Close.

Mark froze again. His heart beat faster. His eyes were the only thing he dared move. He clearly saw the camouflaged legs of a man moving toward him. Within seconds, the soldier would walk right on top of him.

Mark wanted to avoid any conflict with the soldiers. That would only increase their belief that he was the killer. Their pursuit would turn more deadly. But if the soldier continued forward, Mark would be discovered.

The chaser moved closer. He was being very careful, advancing with a great deal of stealth. Mark decided to take the man down without hurting him and then move off in a new direction.

The man stepped nearer. Mark prepared to pounce. He was mere seconds from being discovered. His heart raced with anticipation. He flattened his hands on the ground, ready to spring up. Then, from a distance, the cackling filled the woods with an eeriness so haunting, the entire area went still, as if some supernatural force sucked the life from the woods.

The soldier in front of Mark spun in the direction of the maniacal sound. He paused. The laugh came again, and the soldier ran toward it.

The breath rushed out of Mark. He got up, and in a crouch, moved away from the area. Mark didn't want to be anywhere near when the soldiers found their prey. He wasn't going to get caught in the crossfire. The cackling had saved him. However, if that creepy sound was what he thought it was, another man was dead. The cackle was a sort of victory celebration for the crazed killer. When the soldiers realized one of their number was dead, they'd be shooting anything on sight, which included him.

Mark needed to escape. There would be blood in the soldier's eyes now. They would not care that he had not killed their friend. He'd still be blamed.

Mark broke from the woods and noticed the sun was already setting. He had been in the woods longer than he thought. But he welcomed the night. It made hiding easier.

He slid down the slope toward the roadway below. From there, he sprinted toward the overpass. From now on, he was the hunter. He still had to duck the soldiers, but now he knew the killer was in the woods too. The only way to save his own life was to capture that madman.

As he scooted back up the slope to the very corner of the woods, Mark lay down and scanned the tree line in both directions. The armed jeep was parked down the road at the intersection, guarding against any non-soldier leaving the woods.

He looked to the sky again, at the descending night. Now that he was free, he should run. However, the general would only send a stronger force against the community next time. No, he had to see this through. But the hunt for the killer had to end tonight.

Sixty-Two

BECCA WAS PACING AGAIN. Bobby and Myron had talked her down twice already, but her nervous energy continued to build. Soon they would not be able to stop her from leaving the barn.

Once night fell, Becca became irritated. With each hour that passed, the anxiety increased. Now it was well after midnight. Being forced to rein in Becca had left Bobby tired and irritable. If following their father was inevitable, they might as well go now before further escalation occurred. He no longer had the energy to fight her.

Bobby also wanted to avoid a confrontation with Lynn. Was she serious about giving him the truck keys? He stood, stretched, and casually walked toward the door.

"Where you going, Bobby?" Becca asked.

Without turning, he said, "I'm going to get the keys."

"Now you're talking. Let's go."

"No," he commanded. "You stay here, I'll get them."

"What? I don't understand. Why can't I go?"

He sighed and faced her. "Because I want to avoid a fight between you and Lynn."

"Oh, trust me, there won't be much of a fight."

"See, that's what I want to avoid."

"Why? If she tries to stop us, I'll deck her."

"That's not going to happen. You stay here. I'll get the keys."

"And what if she doesn't want to give them to you?"

"She will."

"Bobby, what's going on?"

Here was the other moment Bobby feared. In fact, had been dreading it for a while now. He hoped that once they found Dad, the old Becca would return.

"Because you don't handle people very well. You're not yourself. You get angry too fast and want to hurt people."

"But only people who try to hurt us, or stand in our way, like that bitch."

"Don't you see, Becca? This is Dad's home. He built it and brought these people together. He put Lynn in charge because he trusts her. When things settle down, we'll live here too. You can't go around threatening everyone. These are Dad's friends. And whether you agree or not, we're going to need as many friends as possible to survive."

"Bobby, I'm still your sister. You make me sound like I'm crazy."

"The truth is, Becca, even though I love you and always will, I can't trust you to make rational decisions. You're too angry. I miss the old Becca. She was kinda prissy at times, but I could count on her. I'm going to get the keys. You stay here."

Bobby didn't wait for a reply.

Sixty-Three

LYNN WAS SITTING AT the dining room table alone, wiping silverware. She looked up as Bobby entered. She sighed and gave him a small smile.

"It's time," he said.

"I know." She sat there without moving for a moment, and then dug the keys out of her pocket and slid them across the table.

Bobby thought there was going to be an argument. He was relieved to see that wasn't to be. Something told him this woman was important to his father. He had seen the way they looked at each other. Bobby didn't want to point it out to his sister. She'd go ballistic.

He nodded his thanks and picked up the keys.

"Bobby, please be careful. Your father is going to be angry with me for letting you go, but I'll be damned if I don't, damned if I do. If I let you go and you get hurt, your father will never forgive me. But if something happens to him, I ... well, let's just say I'd never forgive myself."

Bobby smiled. "I understand. We'll find him and bring him home."

"I hope so."

Back at the barn, he said to Becca, "Let's go."

"Wait, you mean she just gave you the keys?"

"Yep."

"Without a fight or anything?"

"Yep."

"Huh!"

"Yep."

"Myron, you coming?"

"Ah, yeah, sure." He picked up his bow and quiver and followed them out.

Bobby asked, "Are you any good with that thing?"

"Yeah, I guess."

"You ever kill anyone with an arrow?" Becca asked.

"No."

"Well, not yet anyway, huh?" Becca said, excitedly. "Don't worry. This may be your lucky night."

Myron swallowed hard.

Once inside the car, Lynn's son, Caleb, came to the driver's window.

He nodded at Bobby and glared at Becca. "I, uh, I hope you find your father. But if you ever threaten my mother again, I'll put you down like the psycho-bitch you are."

The silence that followed had a life force of its own.

Caleb slapped the truck door, backed away, and said, "Good luck."

Bobby reversed down the driveway and drove away from the house. He expected some wild, angry outburst from his sister. He waited, but nothing came. He glanced her way. Instead, Becca's eyes lowered. Her lower lip quivered. She let out a breath that, for a moment, seemed to deflate her body. Unblinking, she stared out the windshield.

A few minutes later, she said, "Bobby, am I crazy?" Even in the dark, Bobby could see the gleam of tears on her face. He put an arm around her and she placed her head on his chest.

"No, Sis. We're just all going through some tough

times. We'll be all right."

"I'm scared, Bobby. Sometimes I don't think I'm me anymore. I think Daddy feels it too. What if he doesn't want me anymore?"

"Don't be silly, Becca. He loves you no matter what. We just need some time to be normal again without all the violence."

"You think?"

"Uh-huh."

Myron cleared his throat. "I-I don't think you're crazy. I, uh, I think you're beautiful."

Becca lifted her head and looked at Myron. "Aw, Myron, that's so sweet. Thank you." She kissed his cheek, and then wiped her eyes with her sleeve. "I'll be all right. I've got two strong men to lean on. How could I not be all right?"

That was a question Bobby wasn't sure he wanted to know the answer to.

Sixty-Four

MARK ENTERED THE WOODS again. This time, however, he was the hunter, not the prey. A large moon filled the sky, but the trees blocked much of its light. He worked his way toward the opposite end of the trees. Unless something had changed since he exited on the far side he should be coming in behind the soldiers.

Along his journey, the cackle once more chilled the forest. *Down to four.* This time the killer's laugh had come from deep in the woods. He must have circled the soldiers. Pretty soon, the madman would have his targets shooting at each other. As if on cue, automatic fire ripped through the trees. The length of the barrage made Mark think the soldiers were spraying and praying in panic.

"Where are you, you bastard? Show yourself," one of the soldiers shouted.

The voice sounded like Grayson. *Is he calling to the killer or me?* Mark continued until he reached the far tree line. The armed jeep was forty feet to his right. Staying undercover, he moved east. He stopped several times to listen. A little moonlight seeped in, but the rays didn't reach far. Mark wanted to at least locate the soldiers so he wasn't wasting time tracking the wrong person.

A noise to his left froze him. He ducked and peeked

through some branches. Four uniformed men were gathered together. Grayson was giving orders.

"He's in these woods somewhere. Just tell the general we need as many men as possible to surround the area. Go."

One of the men took off running. The rest stayed and fanned out, leaving only about eight feet between them. "Sir, isn't it more logical that he left the woods and is running for safety?"

"I think if he wanted to run, he would've done it before killing Smith. He wants to kill us all. That will be his mistake. He should've run when he had the chance. Let's move toward the far end. When the others come, they may flush that bastard toward us. If you see him don't hesitate, give warning, or announce it. Just fire."

They hadn't moved ten steps when a scream filled the air. Immediately Grayson turned and sprinted toward the sound. The others followed. The cackle made the hairs on Mark's neck stand up. Was the killer a ghost? How did he take down all those men without being seen? With not even a shot fired in defense?

Mark tried to anticipate where the killer moved next to avoid detection from the soldiers crashing toward him. If he moved south, he'd run out of woods. Did he know the jeep was sitting there waiting for him? No, he'd move north where he had room to maneuver.

Mark went straight across the woods. When he judged he had gone a little more than halfway, he stopped. Finding a dense area of branches and undergrowth, Mark set up his watch.

There was scant light now, but just enough to be able to see a man-sized shape move. If the killer came this way, Mark would catch a glimpse. The time slipped by. No sign or sound of the killer or the soldiers.

Then, what looked like a darker shadow passed twenty feet away. Very light sounds scribed a path: a leaf, a twig, the scrape of cloth, moving from left to right. Someone was close. But was the shadow friend or foe? Was there a difference now?

Mark followed the path with his eyes, even though he couldn't see much. Shadows flitted twice, and once a dark shape filled his vision. Mark wanted to move with the shadow, but was afraid to give himself away. Also, he had to consider that the killer was armed and he was not. Still, he couldn't let the image disappear.

Mark moved from cover a few steps still in sight of the dark shape. Then whatever he was tracking stopped. Mark froze and lowered slowly. Neither ghost moved. Movement by someone who didn't care that he was making noise came from the left. The soldiers were coming.

Locking on to the shadow's position, Mark used the cover of the soldiers' advance to move closer. As he crept nearer, the shadow began to take shape. It was not an animal. He circled wider to come up behind his target. His path crossed directly in front of the soldiers unless he hurried.

The thundering steps closed the gap. Suddenly the men were in sight. Mark went flat to the ground. If he tried to shout a warning, he feared they'd shoot him.

Another cry of pain, and a body crashed to the ground right next to Mark. The man rolled and cried, clutching his leg. The other two men looked at their fallen comrade. Then they turned as someone ran in the opposite direction. They fired a long burst.

Grayson took off in pursuit yelling, "Don't let him out of your sight."

With a quick glance at the injured man, the soldier followed his leader.

Sixty-Five

"THE WOODS ACROSS THE street from the base are just past those two houses," Myron said. "If we stop here, we should be able to sneak up on them."

Bobby pulled to the side of the road. They got out and gathered their gear.

"Don't try to take too much. It will get in the way and make noise." Bobby checked his semi-automatic, chambered a round, and holstered it. He carried his rifle and had small binoculars in his pocket, although since they weren't night vision he doubted he'd be able to see much.

He looked around at the darkness surrounding them. Then Bobby shifted his gaze upward at the still climbing moon. It offered some light, although limited once they got into the trees.

Myron carried his bow, a handgun in his belt, and ten hunting arrows in the quiver he wore across his back.

Becca was fingering the empty scabbard tied around her thigh. The missing knife seemed to bother her.

"Here," Myron said, sliding his survival knife out and handing it to her. Her mouth dropped open and a sparkle lit her eyes. "But, won't you need it?"

"It's all right. I think you need it more than I do."

She accepted the gift and hefted it, then slid it into the sheath. "Thank you."

"Let's move," Bobby said. "Spread out a bit. When we get to the woods try not to get separated."

They walked off like they were on a street in an old west gunfight. Past the last house they moved away from the road and entered the woods behind the backyard. It was instantly much darker. Whether it was the night or the woods, Bobby wasn't sure, but a chill closed around him.

Five minutes later, a scream pierced the trees. Gunshots followed. They dived for the ground and whatever cover was close.

Bobby gave the order to advance, but they were much more cautious now. He looked left and right to make sure his team was still assembled, and then checked back and front. The darkness, the scream, and the knowledge a killer may lurk in these woods made for a lot of tension. Bobby couldn't get his muscles to relax. The strain spread across his shoulders.

Twenty yards inside the woods, he motioned for the others to stop and squat. He listened intently and tried to get the knots in his back to release, but they were having no part of his efforts.

The rustling of branches moving off to the left gave them a direction. Bobby signaled and they crept onward. Then someone shouted, and what sounded like a herd of deer went crashing through the trees.

They froze again until Bobby determined the sound was moving away from them. Whatever was out there was not an immediate threat, but how would they know if there was one? And would they be ready for it?

Sixty-Six

MARK CRAWLED TO THE wounded man. The soldier started when he saw Mark. He whimpered and tried to pull his sidearm. Mark clamped a hand over the man's, pulled it free of the gun, and took it out of the holster.

"Please," the soldier begged. "Don't kill me."

"Hush!" he whispered. "I'm not going to hurt you."

Mark took the man's combat knife. "Let me see where you're hurt."

"The back of my foot," the man said. "God, it hurts."

"There's not much I can do for you. I'll try to stop the bleeding." Mark slid the knife inside the man's pant leg.

"Wh-What are you doing?"

"Relax. If I wanted to hurt you, I'd have done it already." He slit the pant leg up about eight inches and cut around it until he had a piece of material. He folded it and tied it as best he could around the foot. The killer had sliced through the man's Achilles tendon. With no doctors around, the soldier would not be walking on that leg again.

"You can either stay here until I can send someone for you, or you can try to crawl toward the base. It's that way. Whatever you do, don't try to walk on it."

"But what if the killer comes back?"

"Oh, now you believe I'm not the killer?"

"I'm sorry. But please don't leave me defenseless."

Mark picked up the rifle and debated between leaving the man the knife or the handgun. He tossed down the knife. "Sorry, you'll just have to hope I find him before he finds you. If you stay still, he won't find you."

Mark left before the soldier could plead further. The man moaned. Mark shut him out. There were more important things to focus on.

Grayson must have stopped. Nothing was moving. Mark went in the direction they had gone. The killer was smart and liked to attack his prey from behind. By now he already flanked the soldiers. With all the noise they made running through the woods, he didn't have to worry about making sound.

Mark changed course toward the tree line at the south end. Grayson should be to his left. If he guessed right, the only person in front of him should be the killer. He wasn't going to take a chance. Whatever he saw he was putting down.

Sixty-Seven

THE THREE OF THEM moved thirty yards deeper. No new sounds came to them. Bobby held up a hand and listened. The complete quiet – absent of man, animal, or even insect noises – was eerie.

He looked at Becca. She shrugged and began moving again. He looked at their new friend, Myron. If trouble started, Bobby hoped he knew how to use that bow, but wished the other boy was holding the gun instead.

Before he moved again, a voice came out of nowhere. Bobby tried to pinpoint the direction. It came from behind him. He ducked and took aim. Taking a quick glance over his shoulder, he no longer saw Myron and Becca.

He didn't dare move or try to signal them. It was his job to protect the rear. He waited, and the whispered voice came closer.

"Please, God, don't let him find me. Please. Just let me find my way back to the base."

The man moved straight for Bobby. What to do? He didn't want to shoot if he didn't have to. The shot might draw others. If he could, Bobby would try to knock the man out. He waited, ready to spring.

The bushes parted in front of Bobby, exposing him.

The man's eyes went wide. He let out a scream and swung his weapon, an AR-15, toward Bobby. In his panic he triggered the gun before it came on target. Bobby leaped at the man, knocking him against a tree with a thud. The gun was still clambering away. Bobby feared the errant bullets might hit Becca and Myron. He had to stop the man from depressing the trigger.

Wrapping his left hand around the gun hand of his opponent, Bobby drove his fist into the man's face twice. The blows stunned him, allowing Bobby to strip away the AR. Bobby took a step back to get some distance and drove the butt of the rifle toward the man's face. However, the soldier ducked and the gun slammed into the tree behind him. From a sitting position, the man lurched for Bobby before he delivered another blow. He wrapped an arm around Bobby's leg and pulled. Bobby fought for balance.

The man had more weight and drove Bobby to the ground. Before his opponent established a superior position, Bobby squeezed out from underneath. He swung a leg over the man's back and tried to slide an arm under his chin. The soldier ducked his head tight to his chest denying entry and reversed Bobby.

Using his speed, Bobby scampered away and regained his feet. His opponent was slower to his feet, and when he stood, held one leg behind him as if wounded. Bobby took advantage of it by landing a kick to his face. The blow sent his opponent backward. He rolled to his hands and knees. Bobby stepped forward to deliver a kick to the ribs, but the man anticipated that and trapped his foot against his chest. He stood in a burst, lifting Bobby's leg.

Bobby tried to hop on one leg to keep his balance, but he was at a severe disadvantage. The larger man hauled Bobby's leg higher. Unable to keep his balance any longer, Bobby spun and dived to the ground. He caught his weight on his hands, cocked his free leg, and snapped it into his attacker's knee. The man yelled and backed a step. Bobby kicked his other leg free.

He got to his feet, and before the other man could raise a defense again, Bobby popped him twice in the face with his fists, and the man went down. He rolled in semi-consciousness. Bobby, breathing heavy, pulled his sidearm. He waited several seconds for the man to try something else. When he didn't, Bobby put a knee on his back and stripped him of any weapons. The injured man was breathing, but not moving. Keeping his handgun trained on the inert form, Bobby backed away to find the rifle. Once he retrieved it, the prone man began to stir. Bobby was about to go back and knock him out for sure when he heard a shot. His lone thought was of Becca.

He turned and moved toward the sound of the gunshot.

Sixty-Eight

WHEN THE SHOT RANG out, Mark dived to the ground. The shot had not been aimed at him, but still he waited. Something thrashed ahead of him.

Grayson's voice boomed, "Show yourself. You gutless bastard, face me like a man."

If Grayson was going to make all that noise, maybe the killer would be drawn to him. Mark was going to use him as bait this time.

Grayson continued to shout and fire a random shot. It was easy to zero in on him. Mark stopped next to a tree. Some undergrowth covered his face. Grayson stood just beyond in a small clearing. The moonlight that dropped through the opening in the canopy above shone on him like a spotlight. He was alone, turning in circles, calling challenges in each direction.

Mark scanned the edges of the clearing for movement. So far they were alone. Grayson screamed as loud as he could. If only he held it together long enough to entice the killer.

"I'm waiting." He fired again. "Come on, you bastard."

On the far side of the clearing, some of the foliage grew denser. Mark used the rifle's scope to look closer.

Grayson kept walking through his sight line. As he stepped to the side, Mark caught a glimpse of the shadow within the shadow. It was large and dark and had a wild hairy face. The killer had arrived.

"BECCA, YOUR BROTHER'S not here."

Becca stopped and looked behind her. *Where had he gone now?* She was in no mood to wait for him. She whispered, "He's probably just watching our backs. He'll catch up."

She started to move.

"Shouldn't we wait for him?"

She turned her gaze on him. "Are you afraid?"

"N-no, I'm not afraid."

Just then, multiple gunshots sounded, sharp and close, behind them where Bobby might be.

"N-now, I'm afraid," he said.

"Yeah, me too."

Becca crept closer to the source of the shot. When the shooting stopped, so did she. She listened. There was the sound of movement in front of them. She moved again.

Then, a shot was fired from the other direction, behind Myron. In a flash, Becca changed course and stopped next to Myron.

A short time later, a third was triggered, and then a fourth. The shots became a beacon guiding them to the shooter.

In a sudden move, Becca dropped to the ground. A large shadow rose in front of them like a demon from hell.

"Oh God." Myron covered his mouth.

Sixty-Nine

THE SHADOW MOVED. The motion was so slow, it could have been branches blown by a soft breeze. Except there was no breeze despite the chill he felt. Mark pushed to his knees and stretched to a standing position behind the tree.

The shadow was working its way behind Grayson. Mark slid the rifle along the trunk. He tried to line up a shot at the shadow, but Grayson kept getting between him and the target.

Grayson stopped. He stood with his head down and rifle hanging at his side pointed at the ground. His hand was on his face, and he looked like he was crying. He had no chance of defending himself if the killer sprang. Mark needed to move to get a better angle.

But it was too late.

The hulking shape burst through the branches directly behind the unsuspecting lieutenant.

Mark stepped into the clearing as well and shouted, "Grayson, behind you."

Grayson, seeing Mark's rifle pointing in his direction, swung his rifle up and fired. Mark froze, his heart threatening to explode through his chest. No bullet came. The fool had emptied his magazine firing at nothing.

Mark breathed again. He quickly refocused. The knife rose above Grayson's head. The arm, or left shoulder, were Mark's only targets. He took the shot at the larger mass.

The shot ripped past Grayson's head and tore through the killer's shoulder. It spun him, the blade hitting the lieutenant's shoulder. He dived to the ground, clutching his arm. The killer howled in pain.

As soon as Grayson was out of the way, Mark lined up the next shot, but the killer hurled his knife at Mark. Mark ducked and rolled in case the wild man followed the knife. When Mark regained his feet, the killer was gone. The knife was embedded in the tree.

Mark ran to Grayson. "You okay?"

Grayson, on one knee, pulled his hand away from his shoulder. It was wet. "Yeah, it's just a slice."

Mark gave it a quick look. "It's not deep." He pulled the handgun from his belt and handed it to him. "Here, in case he comes back."

Grayson took it and grabbed Mark's arm. "I'm sorry."

"We'll worry about that later."

"Get that bastard."

Mark took off in pursuit, not sure where his prey had gone.

Seventy

BECCA HAD BEGUN CRAWLING closer to the shadow.

Myron had no desire to move closer to danger, but he hated having Becca think him incompetent, or worse, a coward. Regardless, he did as she commanded.

He watched as Becca crawled forward, marveling at the courage that drove her into combat. Everything in him screamed to turn and run the other way. In fact, before he met Becca, that's what he would have done, every time. Was it possible for a lifelong coward to find courage? And if he got shot, whose fault was it? Becca's for leading him into danger or his for being dumb enough to follow?

He shook his head. Despite his nature he would not leave her. He sighed. "Don't get me shot, Becca," he whispered.

BECCA SAW THE SHADOW move. The figure was too large to be her father, and it didn't look like he wore a uniform. The way he moved was what set the alarms off in her head. The man was tracking something, or someone, like a predator stalking prey.

She crept closer. She wanted a better view of him. Then he rose to full height and disappeared. He was there one second and then just ... gone. *Had he pounced on his prey? Was that prey my father?* Her heart pounded faster. She advanced with her knife ready.

A shout and a shot froze her. They came from her right. Someone was hit because a howl of pain followed the shot. Becca leaned to her left, trying to see past the trees.

Before she was able dodge away, a monster ripped through the branches and crashed into her. She hit the ground with a thud. The air was knocked from her lungs. Pain shot through her.

The body that hit her rolled over her and lay there just as stunned. She shook the fog from her head and patted the ground for her knife. The hairs on her neck and arms stood. She whipped her head behind her. The monster was crouched and smiling at her.

The crazed laugh he let out drove panic into her soul. She had never known fear this debilitating before. He stood and pulled a knife from someplace. Becca scooted backward as the animal advanced. She whimpered. When she moved, Myron's knife nicked her finger. She grabbed at it, ignoring the pain as the blade sliced her fingers.

The man lifted his knife, took one step, and drove it downward. Becca slashed her knife across the big man's thigh. He screamed and hopped to the side. She slashed again and cut through the calf of the other leg. He fell, but right on top of Becca.

She kicked and screamed, but her arms were pinned beneath the monster's weight. She screamed again. His foul breath blew in her face as he grunted from pain and effort to control her wild thrashing. He put one hand on her chest to push upright and keep her pinned, and then lifted the knife. He lowered it toward her face. Becca continued kicking and screaming, but in the end all she could do was close her eyes.

Seventy-One

MYRON LOST TRACK OF Becca. He was torn between wanting to be with her and doing what she said. Someone fired. In an instant, he was paralyzed again. His breathing was short quick gasps, and the tightness returned to his chest like a vice. But his thoughts were not for his own safety, but for Becca's. He knew she wasn't using her gun. If someone fired, it wasn't her. *Was the shot directed at her?*

Myron had to know. Becca might need his help. The thought of her hurt was enough to evaporate his paralysis. Pushing his fear aside, he crawled forward. He was making too much noise, but time was a factor.

He stopped when someone ran through the woods in front of him. Another howl brought back his fear, but when he heard Becca screaming, Myron broke into a run.

Under the tiny streams of moonlight, Myron saw a massive man sitting on top of his girlfriend. The shock exploded into a rage. The knife descended toward Becca's face. Before he was aware he had done so, the arrow was nocked, the bowstring drawn tight against his cheek. There was no shake in his arm.

"No!" Myron screamed as the point of the blade hovered over Becca's eye. The arrow took the beast through the throat and protruded out the other side. The force pitched the man backward, freeing Becca.

Myron raced toward her, lifted her in his arms, and held her. Becca clung to him and shook. Just then a man burst through the trees and pulled up in front of them with his rifle pointed.

Myron turned his body to protect Becca from this new threat, fumbling to pull the handgun from his belt.

"Oh, dear God! Becca!"

Thank God. "It's all right, Becca, you're safe. It's your dad."

Becca, who had been gently crying on Myron's chest, turned her head. "Daddy?"

Myron set her down and she ran into her father's arms. They hugged while Myron watched. Something disturbed a branch behind him. Myron whirled, ready with another arrow, the bowstring drawn tight, next to his cheek.

Bobby came into sight and pulled up short when he saw the arrow pointed at him. He held up his hands. "Whoa!"

Myron released his breath and slowly slacked the tension in the string. He stared at the bow, not remembering drawing an arrow. Then he looked at the killer.

Bobby walked to the body. The man was writhing on the ground, trying to pull the arrow from his throat. A gurgling sound bubbled from his mouth.

Myron had trouble pulling his gaze from his handiwork.

"Damn, Myron, that's a helluva shot," Bobby said, patting him on the back as if it had been his first deer kill.

Becca moved from her father's side and hugged Myron. "You saved me. Again." She kissed him on the lips this time.

He gasped, blushed, and put both hands to his face.

Mark said, "Come on everyone, let's go. We have some wounded to collect."

Mark led and Bobby followed. Becca took Myron's hand and led him away from the killer. Myron couldn't break eye contact with the man. The trees obscured the sight but not before Myron witnessed his last breath.

Would his forefathers be proud of him now?

Did it matter anymore?

Seventy-Two

"I OWE YOU A massive apology, sir."

Mark smiled. "Yes, you do."

Mark had sent the others back to camp, but he stayed the night on the base. Something was going on and he wanted to know what it was or if it affected the community.

"Lieutenant Grayson said you saved his life."

"We both would've died if he any bullets left."

"Well, thankfully it worked out."

Worked out? You lost four men out there.

As if reading his mind, West said, "We lost a lot of good men out there. With all we face, that's a horrible waste of manpower. They'll be hard to replace."

Mark didn't speak. He knew what was coming.

"We could use a good man like you. I'd make you an officer."

Mark shook his head. "No, General. I appreciate the offer. But there are a lot of people that depend on me. I have to look after them."

West frowned. "You realize you may end up fighting whether you join me or not?"

"I don't understand."

West crossed his arms and looked away, chewing his

lower lip.

Mark said, "General, what are you doing here? As far as I know, there is no government anymore, so who do you serve?"

"I still serve the American people. Whether there's a government or not, we still have a job to do, a mission to complete."

"Mission? What mission?"

"Are you sure you want to know?

"Do you know what killed everyone? Is it worldwide or just in the states?"

"I'm not sure, but the speculation is that it was an attack on the American people."

"Whose speculation?"

"Mark, there are other military bases around the country. We have limited contact with some of them. We are setting up defenses. There is some fact, some rumor, and some speculation."

"Give me some examples."

"You could know it all if you joined up."

"Look, General, I respect what you're trying to do, but it's not for me. However, if there's something going on that may be a danger to my people, I'd like to know about it."

"Walk with me."

The general left his office and Mark followed. They strolled over the grounds. In the distance, a group of men jogged in formation. Others worked on the trucks, while another group was busy hovering over the cockpit of one of the fighter jets.

"What you see are remnants of the air base here, the Army Reserve Center down the road and several other National Guard bases around the state. We've also recruited a few stragglers along the way. And yes, some of them were forced to join, but after they understood what we were doing, they welcomed the opportunity to serve."

To Mark it was all hype, like a recruiter trying to entice a high school grad into enlisting. "And what is it you're doing?"

"Mark, we've had reports that we suffered some sort of chemical attack nationwide. A week ago, reports from several different bases identified what they termed as 'foreign forces boots down in country.' One was on the west coast, another report came out of Texas. We have lost contact with the west coast base."

"So what you're saying is that we've been attacked and invaded. We're at war."

"As far as I know, yes. I have to proceed under the belief that we are. It's better to be prepared than be overrun."

"Have you found other communities like ours?"

"No. That's the sad thing. Whatever agent was used in the attack was very efficient. I've found small pockets of people. Some have joined us, some haven't, and some tried to fight us. I started with sixty-five men. Now I'm down to fifty-two. Without knowing what we're up against, I'm feeling overwhelmed. I wish you'd reconsider. If we are facing an invading army and get wiped out, there's nothing to stop them from rolling over everyone in their path. There will be no noncombatants and this time, no survivors."

Mark rolled what West told him around his brain. If any of it was true, he could understand why West was so determined to build his army. Mark stopped near the jets and asked, "What's the story here?"

"We have two flight-ready jets. However, we have limited fuel and no trained pilots. We're training potential pilots on the ground. We can't train in the air. We can't afford to use up our fuel, and if one of them crashed we'd lose a very valuable asset."

"Although, if no one can fly them there's little value in

the jets at all."

"Well, hopefully we never have to use them, but if we're getting slaughtered, they'll be a nice safety valve for us. Even if we can only use each plane twice."

"There's nowhere you can get more fuel?"

"There may be. I have scouts out looking now."

"Look, General, I don't want to be at odds with you and your troops. We're all Americans here and survivors. There's no reason we can't work together without having to join your army. Let's have a good working relationship. Can we do that?"

West sighed. "Of course."

"If anything happens that we should be aware of, please send a message. If we see anything, we'll get in touch with you. You have my word."

"If that's the best I can get, that will have to do."

"Now, I was wondering if I could trouble you for a ride home."

"I'll see to it."

Part Five

Seventy-Three

"THAT'LL DO IT," Jarrod shouted. He crawled along the roof and climbed down the ladder.

"What was the problem?" Mark asked. Only a portion of the energy created by the solar panels was storing in the batteries.

"One of the wires had come loose. It's patched up good now. It ain't gonna come apart again. Soon you'll be charging up enough electricity to light a football field."

They went inside the house to the front closet converted into the battery room. The small space had been packed with twelve-volt batteries. An electrical panel had been added to control the usage.

"You got lights and electric outlets here, upstairs and down. Here you got the refrigerator? Those are your most important things. If you're generating enough electricity, you can think about whatever else you want hooked up."

"Excellent! Thanks, Jarrod."

"No problem, partner. Hey, since I found that other flock of chickens, I need to expand my yard. I could use a hand sinking some fence posts."

"Just let me know when you want to start."

"I was thinking about tomorrow."

"Okay. I'll see if some of the others will help."

At that moment, an engine announced the approach of a truck. Mark and Jarrod looked out the front door. It had been two weeks since the hunt for the killer. A tentative peace had fallen over the area.

Mark had explained the general's theories to the communities. They decided to take a "wait and see" approach to the news. The family members were all back in their homes but were now always vigilant and prepared to evacuate at a moment's warning. The radios helped keep them in touch. They developed a daily and nightly check-in system. No tension existed between the soldiers and the families. So, when the truck turned up the driveway, neither Mark nor Jarrod went running for safety and weapons.

Several times, Mark's family had West and some of his troops over for dinner. Of course, each time the general was there, he tried to recruit anyone who would listen. Several of the older boys from offsite families to the dismay of their parents, had joined already.

The patrols drove past each of the houses twice a day. The soldiers had become an accepted part of the community. As each group grew more comfortable with the other's presence, a more normal routine returned.

West stepped out of the truck. His troops remained onboard. That and the look on the general's face set off warnings in Mark's head. He nodded. "General. What brings you out here today?"

The General nodded back. "I just wanted to let you know we were pulling out."

Mark lifted his eyebrows. "Oh?"

"We've received some reports that enemy troops have advanced toward the state line. I'd rather meet them there than have to defend our base."

"Where did you get your intel, General?"

251

"A National Guard unit in Indiana. The report told of a large number of troops heading east. The last word I received was that they were moving to meet them. There's been no other contact since."

"Do you have any idea what you're facing?"

"I was told by the general in charge there that it looked like more than a hundred men. He only had twenty. Obviously I fear the worst. I'm leaving a very small force to watch the base. I wanted to let you know that trouble might be coming, and of course, to ask once more for your help."

Mark lowered his head and studied the dirt below him. When he met the general's eyes again he had an answer. "General, we won't march with you, but I'll promise you this. If there is an enemy presence and you find yourself outmatched, send a messenger and I'll bring as many people as are willing to help."

The general frowned. "All right, sir, if that's the best I can get, I'll take it. I'd, ah, appreciate you looking in on the base when you can."

"Sure, General, I can do that." Mark extended his hand and West accepted it. "Good luck, General."

He returned to the truck. As it backed down the driveway, the general saluted.

Mark stopped his hand from returning the gesture and waved instead.

Seventy-Four

AT THE DINNER TABLE that night, there was a lot of anxious talk about the soldiers going off to war. Several times both Lynn and Mark attempted to change the subject, but the topic always returned.

Mark did a slow pan around the ever-increasing family at the table. Although everyone got along, whether the members realized it or not, whenever they sat at the table they were in cliques. The original members, Caleb, Ruth, Alyssa, and Darren were at one end near Lynn. The newbies, Becca, Bobby, and Myron were on the far end by Mark. The members who came in between filled in the middle. Counting Lincoln and Jenny, Mallory and Zac, and the two from the cell, Vince and Agnes, the table now sat fifteen.

It was nice to have a family again, especially when some of it was genuine family. Lynn was watching him. He smiled and winked at her. She returned a rather tentative smile. As nice as it was to have a family, with all the table talk of war, he couldn't stop the nagging sensation building in his gut that they'd eventually be drawn into the conflict. West's words returned to him. *You realize you may end up fighting whether you join me or not.* God, he hoped West's intel was wrong.

Mark looked at his kids. Becca had softened somewhat. She was much more relaxed. She was beautiful, and when she laughed, Mark could see his wife, Sandra, in her features.

She spent a lot of time with Myron. That was understandable since he had saved her life twice. But she was his daughter, so he worried about any attachments that might be forming. The boy had taken to wearing a golden feather in a tiny string of braided hair on the side of his head. Becca said it was to honor his Native American heritage.

Bobby was a real help around the yard. Each morning, he was one of the first up and ready to work. He was silent most of the time, which concerned Mark. What sort of battle was waging within him? Becca and Bobby never talked about the journey, but Mark imagined what the two of them had to deal with on their way home was traumatic. He prayed they all had enough time away from the violence to be able achieve some balance.

After dinner, everyone pitched in to clean, clear, and wash. Mark did his part and was slowly working his way along the length of the tables. As he reached for a dish, his hand covered another. It was the first he was aware of Lynn coming from the other direction.

The contact made him jump and he pulled away. When he realized it was Lynn, he looked away. "I-I'm sorry. I wasn't aware you were there."

She looked at him, a hint of hurt fading from her face. "Are you sure that's all it was?"

"Um, I don't understand. What else would it be?"

Lynn studied Mark's face for an instant and shook her head. "It's nothing."

"Well, it's obviously something, or you wouldn't have said it."

When she bit her lip, Mark knew he was right. Something was bothering her. He looked around at all the busy faces with their rabbit ears. This was no place to talk. He took the dishes from her hands and set them back on the table. Taking her hand, he led her toward the row of pine trees along the side of the house.

BECCA TROTTED DOWN THE stairs from the house. She was happy. For the first time in what felt like an eternity, she felt at peace. When she caught sight of her father leading Lynn by the hand, the smile froze on her face. *What is Daddy doing with that woman? She wasn't their mother. How dare he go off with a stranger?*

A fire built inside her. In seconds, her chest heaved, and she huffed large gulps and blows of air. Her hands clenched into fists that she squeezed tighter and harder until her body began to shake. The past few days of peace and laughter were suddenly lost in the building rage she now felt. A image of her mother passed before her eyes, and tears welled. How could her father be so cold? Her mother hadn't been dead for more than two months, and already he was looking for a replacement. Well, she wasn't going to stand for it.

Seventy-Five

"OKAY, LYNN, talk to me."

They reached the street side of the trees.

"Mark, I don't know what to say."

"How about starting with what's bothering you? And please, don't tell me 'nothing.' I know you well enough to know when there's a problem. Did I do something wrong?"

"No, Mark, it's nothing you did. It's just the way things are."

"And how are they?"

"Your kids are here now. I understand that you want to distance yourself from me. With their mother dead, you don't want me to come between you and them."

"What? Where'd you get that idea?" Had he been treating Lynn any differently? Perhaps not on a conscious level, but he couldn't remember the last time they had talked.

"From you." She held up her hand to stop his objection. "You keep your distance from me now. We hardly talk. You're colder to me than you used to be. Yes, you are. I can feel it. I know I've never given you any real encouragement to pursue me. That's not your fault. I hoped you understood the reasons why. It's not that I don't want to be with you. I'm just damaged goods."

"I've never thought of you that way. And I do want to be with you. I knew it would take some time, and I didn't want to rush you or be too aggressive toward you."

"And believe me, I do appreciate that. But things have changed now. You've changed. Whether you realize it or not, you have a separate family from us now. You spend most of your time with them, as it should be, especially since you thought they were dead. But I think seeing them again has sparked old memories. You want to keep your wife alive for your kids. It's okay. Besides, I've seen the way your daughter looks at me whenever we're close to each other. I think she sees me as a threat."

"Lynn, if I've given you that impression, I apologize. It wasn't intentional. I hope you know that I care about you."

"And I care about you too, but I will not come between you and your children."

From between two pines, a dark blur darted. The figure took Mark by surprise. He turned to defend against whatever the threat, but it veered toward Lynn.

"That's right, you bitch," Becca screamed.

Recognition froze Mark for a split second. The obvious threat toward Lynn unfroze him and forced him to move.

"You'll never come between us and our dad." Becca closed the gap, but Lynn didn't budge. "He loved my mother, and you could never replace her. You stay away from him or I swear — "

"Becca!" Mark shouted over her. "You will stop this now and apologize to Lynn. Whatever we do is none of your concern. No one is trying to replace your mother. But regardless, no one deserves to be treated like that. You apologize now."

"But, Daddy," she almost whimpered.

"Now!"

Becca turned toward Lynn, her hatred barely contained. "I'm sorry for my outburst. Please forgive me." She bowed her head, spun, and ran back through the trees.

"Lynn, I—"

Lynn teared up. She shook her head, held up a hand to stop his words. "No, Mark." She walked away.

Mark stood in disbelief and dismay. His two girls were enemies, and he was caught in the middle. He was at a loss as to which direction to turn first – and then decided in his current state of mind, neither.

He slid his hands into his back pockets and walked along the trees away from the house. As if the threat of war wasn't enough of a problem, now he had to deal with warring females.

Seventy-Six

BY THE TIME MARK returned, it was late and there was no activity in the yard. Everyone had moved inside to either talk or sleep. Mark spent much of his walk deciding what he would say to Becca.

There was enough turmoil in this world. Becca didn't need to create more. What bothered him as well was how he hadn't seen the outburst coming. Lynn was more in tune with what was going on around him than he was.

Mark walked into the house and upstairs. There were four bedrooms on the second floor. He paused at Lynn's door and moved on. Ruth and Alyssa shared one room. One had been given to the new couple. Becca roomed with Mallory.

Ruth, Alyssa, and Mallory were all downstairs around the dining room table, talking in excited young lady tones. When Mark tapped on Becca's door, there was no response. He pushed the door open. His eyes adjusted to the dark enough to see neither bed had a body in it.

Retracing his steps, he stopped at the table. "Have any of you seen my daughter?"

Mallory said, "She looked like she was mad about something. I saw her heading toward the barn."

"Thanks, ladies."

Mark stopped at the bottom of the outside stairs and looked toward the barn. Nothing moved in the area. He steeled himself for the confrontation and paced to the barn.

There was a light on in the garage. It was not yet ten o'clock, which was the lights-out curfew. Lights were a low draw on the stored energy in the batteries, but their use was still limited. He stopped to glance in the window. The boys had hauled a pool table from a bar a few miles away. Each night they gathered around to play.

Becca was not there. He moved on.

At the barn, he slid the door open. He left it open to allow some of the star and moonlight to filter through. It took a moment to find her. Becca was sitting on the hood of a car. He sighed and entered.

"I figured you'd want to yell at me some more, so I waited here."

He sat next to her and put an arm around her. He felt her flinch, but pulled her gently toward him.

"Becca, I can't even begin to tell you how disappointed I am with you right now."

She placed her head on his chest. "I'm sorry, Daddy. I didn't handle that very well."

"No, you didn't."

"When I saw you two going off together, I saw red. I can't explain it."

"Yes, you can."

"I-I miss Mom." She began to cry.

Mark's heart melted. He stroked her hair and let her be for a while. In truth, he was lost in thoughts of his wife. "I miss her too, honey. More than you can ever know."

"Then why are you trying to replace her?"

"Well, first of all, no one can or ever will replace her."

"Got that right."

Mark smiled at that. It faded fast. Now it was time to be hard. "But she is gone. Although her memory goes on in our hearts and minds, she is never coming back. I'm not looking to replace your mother, but that doesn't mean I can't have a relationship, friend or otherwise."

"It was just hard seeing you with … her. I mean, Mom's only been gone for a little while."

"These are different times, Rebecca. I know you've been through a lot over the past few months. You've seen some things and done some things that never would've happened before.

"When your mother and brother died, I was devastated. The only thing that kept me going was the thought that maybe you and Bobby had survived. I felt I failed them, and it was my fault that I couldn't save them.

"When Lynn and her kids came along, they needed my help to survive. Lynn has gone through some very horrible things. Having them with me gave me a chance to have a family again. I've developed a special relationship with all of them and I love them as if they were my own. Please treat them like family, because to me, they are."

"But—"

"No buts, Becca, listen. Lynn deserves your respect. Without her. I wouldn't be here. She is a very strong and caring woman, just like your mother was. I like her. She is special to me. I don't know if we will ever take our relationship past friendship, but that will be our decision and no one else's. Do you understand me?"

"I guess."

"Of course, you may have already taken care of that with your little performance out there. I'll be lucky if she ever talks to me again. But this family needs her. If you give her half a chance, you'll understand her importance here and just why I think she's special.

"Becca, for my sake and sake of everyone here, you have to promise to give her a chance and the respect that she deserves. We cannot survive if we have internal conflict. To the others here, Lynn and I have become the father and mother, if only out of necessity. Our entire existence here is based on the family dynamic. It's how we survive. It's a delicate balance, but we've been able to make it work. Will you give her a chance?"

"I'll try."

"I hope so. After all, would you want me to tell you who to see? Maybe I should forbid you from seeing Myron."

She glanced up.

"I love you, Becca."

"Love you too, Daddy." She squeezed him tight. "I'm sorry. I didn't mean to cause you problems."

"Go to bed. In the morning, I want you to give a sincere apology to Lynn."

Becca moaned.

"I'm serious. Then sit down with her sometime and talk about your concerns and what you're feeling. She's a good listener. And believe me, she'll understand."

"Okay."

"Good. Now go."

Becca slid off the car and gave him a kiss. He followed her out. When he finally got in his bed, he prayed his daughter could control her anger. And although his heart was telling him everything was going to work out, his brain was convinced the hardest talk was yet to come.

Seventy-Seven

WHATEVER HIS NIGHTMARISH DREAMS had been they were nothing to being awakened by screeching tires, honking horns, and a lot of shouting. Mark bolted from his bed, foregoing his pants, but snatching his gun.

He met Lynn coming down the stairs, wearing a nightgown and carrying a gun. "One of the Army trucks just drove up," she said.

"Get everyone up but keep them inside." Mark ran past her for the rear door. A horrible knot formed in his stomach.

He leaped down the back stairs and slowed his pace toward the truck. The passenger door opened and a uniformed man tumbled to the ground. He moaned and rolled. There was blood on his clothes.

Mark ran to him. When he got there, he pointed the gun inside the truck. The driver was slumped over the wheel. Before helping either of them, he had to be sure no one was under the canvass. He went to the opening and peered in. On the floor lay three men who appeared to be badly wounded. *Damn! There must really be an enemy.*

"I need some help out here," Mark bellowed. He ran around to the driver's side as doors opened and people came near. He guided the driver out of the truck and placed him on the ground. He was bleeding too, but conscious.

"Lynn, we need big time medical help here. Caleb, climb in back of the truck and find out how badly they're hurt. But don't move them. Ruth and Alyssa, help Lynn gather what she needs.

"Darren, show Bobby and Myron where the work lights are. Set them up in the barn. You'll need long extension cords. Plug into the garage outlets."

"Daddy, what can I do?"

"Go grab some sheets."

Lincoln sprinted to the truck and dropped by Mark's side. "Aw, shit! How bad?"

"I won't know for sure until I can get them under some light. Can you help Caleb in the back?"

Everyone was in motion. The new girl, Agnes, came forward and knelt next to Mark. He was surprised to see her. She checked the wounded man's body. She looked up at Mark, her eyes wide with fear. "I was a nurse-practitioner. This man has a gunshot wound to his shoulder. I can help."

She didn't seem too sure of her statement, but Mark was glad for any assistance. "Great, I'm setting up triage in the barn. There are three others in the back. If you can see the extent of their injuries, we'll know how to transport them.

Becca came with the sheets. Lynn and the girls were working on the soldier on the other side.

"Fold the sheet in half lengthwise," Mark said.

When she finished, Mark called, "Lincoln."

Lincoln jumped from the truck and came toward him. "Man, I'm pretty sure one of them boys is dead."

"Help me lift this guy onto the sheet."

They picked him up and laid him in the middle. Mark had Lincoln and Caleb carry the unconscious man to the barn.

"What else can I do, Daddy?"

He looked at his daughter. Gone was the hostility. She wanted to help.

"Fold another sheet and take it to Lynn."

Becca blinked at the name.

"Do you think you can lift one of the wounded?"

Becca frowned and put her hands on her hips. "Really?"

"You'll have to carry him with one of the girls."

When she was gone, Mark went to the back of the truck. Agnes was stepping down and Mark guided her. "What've we got?"

Agnes wiped her face. "One's dead. One has a chest wound and will probably die soon. The third one has a leg wound. If the chest wound has any chance of survival, we need to get him out of there now."

"Okay." Mark looked around the truck to the other side. "Hey, you, sorry I forgot your name."

The man came over. "It's Vince."

"Yeah, sorry, look, I need your help getting one of the wounded out of the back."

"Okay, what do you need me to do?"

"Climb in back." He grabbed two sheets. Scaled the bumper and stepped on the bed. While he folded a sheet he said, "Agnes, if you're willing to work on the wounds, go to the barn. When you get there, send two of the boys back. Thanks."

Agnes didn't speak but moved. Mark hoped she wasn't puking on the side of the truck.

They managed to get the chest wound man on the sheet and slide him toward the edge of the truck bed. When the Bobby and Myron arrived they helped lower the man then carried him to the barn. The leg wound soldier was much easier to handle. Agnes had tied a tourniquet around his thigh that the soldier was controlling. They slid him to the end of the truck and Mark lifted him to the ground. With his arms around their shoulders, the two men walked him to the barn.

All the surviving wounded were there. Lynn was working on the chest wound patient while Agnes assisted. The two large wooden work benches had been pulled to the center of the barn. The sheet the man had been carried on was draped over the bench. Halogen lights had been placed around the makeshift operating tables.

"Damn!" Lynn exclaimed. "He's dead. Dammit." She moved away from the workbench the body was on. "Boys, move that body. Put him out back for now. Bring me the next worst wounded."

Caleb and Bobby deposited a gut-shot man on the bench as Myron and Lincoln made room by taking the body.

"Agnes, go ahead and start on the leg wound."

Mark helped the man to a second workbench. Agnes took a pair of scissors and cut away the man's pants. While she worked, Mark grabbed Caleb by the arm.

"Go to the house and use the radio to contact the other families. Tell them we have an emergency and need them all here by sunrise. Call Jarrod first and tell him we need the doc, ASAP."

Caleb nodded and ran.

"I KNOW THIS ISN'T pleasant for anyone," Lynn said, "but if these men are going to have a chance to live, I need help. I need two people holding each man. They're going to be in pain, and other than pain pills, there is no way to put them under. I can't have them moving while I'm digging for bullets."

The family responded and stepped forward to help. Lynn took a probe and poked it into the wound. The man writhed, pulling against those restraining him.

"I'm going to need some help blotting blood so I can see."

A hand reached over with some gauze and pressed it against the hole. For a few seconds the blood was gone. Lynn inserted the probe and touched the bullet. She was going to have to widen the hole to extract the slug.

She picked up a scalpel. "Fold that washcloth and put it in his mouth. Okay, boys, hold him tight. Wipe." The hand shot forward and blotted again. "Be ready to do that a lot." With precision, Lynn scribed the fine blade along the inner wall of the wound. There was no controlling the screams now. They worked as a team.

The process was made more difficult by the man's constant moving. Lynn put her face above the wounded soldier's. "I know this hurts. I wish I could deaden the pain for you. But if I'm going to get that bullet out, I'm going to need you to control the pain for as long as you can. I promise to be quick. Can you do that?"

The injured man nodded and grunted something indecipherable through the towel in his mouth.

"Good man," Lynn stroked his cheek and returned to the wound.

Despite the conditions, Lynn was able to extract the bullet. At that point the man passed out.

She poured antiseptic into the wound and wiped it. Without proper tools there was no way of knowing if the bullet hit anything else. It was quite possible it would have struck the colon, but if that was the case it was beyond Lynn's expertise. She took a flashlight and shone it into the wound. She just couldn't tell. She was a nurse, not a surgeon.

"Thread that needle for me, please," she said to her assistant. "I'm going to close this, but we'll have to watch for signs of more damage," she said to no one in particular. The needle was proffered and she took it. For the first time, she looked at her assistant. Becca looked back. Neither spoke, but Becca nodded to her.

Lynn finished her work and stepped back. Agnes was struggling to get the bullet out of her patient's leg.

Lynn moved to take over. While widening the incision, she said, "Take that man someplace where he can rest and put the next man on the table."

Two hours later she was done. The last man had a clean through and through. "Agnes, make sure there's no life-threatening damage, clean the wound, and sew him up," she said.

The doctor arrived and Lynn gave a detailed account of what she'd done so far. When the last man was moved to the garage, or what was now the recovery room, the doc followed to evaluate the wounded.

Lynn sat down on a bale of hay and could not move. Her head hung and sweat dripped down her nose.

Agnes leaned against the workbench too stunned to even cry. Ruth and Alyssa were washing the benches. Everyone else had gone. Someone sat next to Lynn. She was too tired to look up.

"You were amazing."

Lynn recognized the voice. She turned her head to look at Becca.

"Really, I mean it. What you did, under these conditions, it was incredible."

"It will be incredible if any of them live once the infections set in."

"But none of them would've stood a chance without what you and Agnes did."

"I hope it'll be enough."

Lynn started to rise, but Becca touched her arm.

"I'm sorry for my outburst earlier. My ... mom ... she was great, you know, but she's gone now." Becca choked on the words. "I just wanted you to know I think my dad's lucky to have you in his life."

Lynn stood and looked down at the young woman. There was a smear of blood across her forehead. Lynn used a towel she held to wipe it.

"Thank you," she said to Becca and then turned and dragged her exhausted body to the house.

Seventy-Eight

THE GATHERED COMMUNITY MEMBERS grumbled.

"No. No way, no how," Jerry Martin shouted.

"Why should we risk our lives for them?" Mario Marino yelled.

Adam Brandford said, "Who's going to protect our families if we go?"

"That's right," Tim Grant added. "Our only allegiance is to our families. We've got enough problems without fighting someone else's fight."

Everyone had a comment, and none of them was in support of aiding the Army.

Mark let it go until it started to die out.

"I understand all of your concerns. I do. The last thing any of us wants is a confrontation. I'm not asking any of you to go with me. I'm telling you what's going on. From there it's your decision."

"Damn right!" Szymanski said.

Others murmured their agreement

"But just listen for a minute. Then I'll let you go. I do not want to get into another fight with anyone. Most of you already know what we went through before. I have no interest in doing that again.

"However, I want you to think about this. If this threat

is real, and obviously it is, and heading our way, isn't it better to go face them rather than battle them at our homes, one at a time, with no hope of defending?"

Mark let that hang over the group for a second.

"I'm not going to wait for that to happen. If we fail, at least our families have a chance to escape and stay together. If we let them come to us, we may never be able to mount any kind of defense to stop them.

"I don't know what we face. I can only go by what the wounded soldiers told us. It's up to you. Each one of you must think about what's right. I can't guarantee someone won't get killed. It's war. People die. I can't even say we'll make a big enough difference to drive them away. But I do know that if they reach us, we'll have a lot worse chance and maybe no one survives."

"Why can't we just hole up here?" Sam Nelson asked. "We can defend this place together. Look how we stood down that general."

"That's an option. We can stay here. We could offer some good resistance, but we stood down General West because he didn't want to kill a bunch of American citizens. He was willing to listen and negotiate. The attackers now are enemies. They will not want to talk. They will attack. If that happens, there will be no chance to escape or retreat. We'll be in the open. Our only escape route is through cornfields."

Molly Szymanski offered, "Why don't we all pack up and leave now? We can relocate before they ever get here."

"Again, that's a possibility. But what if they find us again? Will we keep on moving? I happen to like the feeling of having roots. I like having you all around me. Look, if I saw a reasonable way to solve this, I'd take it, but I know what has to be done. I'm not asking any of you to come with me. I'm just giving you the information. The decision rests with you."

A tense silence spread over the group. Then individual conversations broke out between spouses, before spreading to neighbors. The volume increased slowly as Mark watched. His gaze shifted to Lynn. She had been watching him. With a tight smile, she nodded.

"We're going with you," Bobby's voice shouted over the crowd.

Becca and Bobby walked forward and stood next to their father. Jarrod joined them. One of the women who lived at his house, Amanda, followed him.

"I'm in," Lincoln said.

Caleb and Mallory joined the group.

Becca stared at Myron. He raised his head looked into Becca's eyes and stepped forward.

After more debate, four other men joined the small force.

"All right, listen up, everyone. I think all of you should gather what you need and bring it here. Those of you staying will need to build your defenses here. I think you should also have all the vehicles packed and ready in case you need to make a hasty retreat.

"If at all possible, I'll send word if you need to flee. Do not let anyone go off alone."

He turned to his small army of volunteers. How many of them, if any, would return? He pushed the thought from his mind. "We'll need four vehicles. Grab whatever equipment you might need. Caleb, get the binoculars, radios, and extra ammo. Say your goodbyes. We'll meet here in ten minutes."

Seventy-Nine

MARK WALKED INTO THE garage. The inside had changed drastically since the wounded had been brought in. Two of the men lay on fold-up beds. The gut shot man was on a mattress placed on the pool table.

Three women stood over the man with the stomach wound. One, Pam, was a doctor before the Horde had raided the hospital and took her captive. She was living with Jarrod and had arrived when the call went out for the urgent meeting. The other woman standing next to her, Desiree, had been a nurse. She also stayed at Jarrod's. Agnes stood on the opposite side, watching.

Mrs. Brandford and Ruth were seeing to the other wounded men. Mark stopped next to the man with the leg injury. His injuries seemed the least life threatening. He was awake and lucid.

"Hey, boss, what's up?" he asked in a pleasant voice.

Mark smiled. The drugs Pam brought must be working. "I need your help."

The man nodded. "What can I do for you?"

"Just information. Tell me what happened."

"A group of Chinese ambushed us."

"Chinese?"

"Yeah, the sneaky bastards came out of nowhere."

"What makes you sure they were Chinese?"

"Well, 'cause they looked it. Plus that's what General West said they were."

"So you don't know for sure if they were Chinese or Asian. Were they speaking a foreign language?"

The wounded man frowned. "Hey, the only talking I heard came from their guns."

Mark nodded. "Were they in uniform?"

"No, least not that I noticed. I couldn't see all of them. When the bullets started flying, I wasn't trying to look around to see what they were wearing."

"So, we don't know if they were invaders from another country or just a mob."

"I guess not. All I know is if they were shooting at us, they were the enemy."

"Okay, now, tell me again exactly where this attack took place."

"Out past Bryan. We were moving along at a good pace when they came at us from both sides. We were trapped. They had grenades and blew up the vehicles. They took the tracks off the tank. It could fire, but wasn't able to move." A faraway look entered his eyes. His voice softened and cracked. "When we left, I think there were still men inside the tank." He breathed in quickly and continued. "Some of the men went up the hill, some helped the wounded into the truck bed. We lost a lot of men in that initial barrage."

Mark opened a mental map. Bryan was a small town near the Indiana border. "You took the turnpike though."

"Yeah, the general thought we'd move faster, and by staying off the main streets, were less likely to be spotted."

"But most of the road out there is flat and open. How'd you not see the ambush?"

"At certain points the road goes under an overpass, creating slopes on the sides. They were above us just enough that we didn't see them. They must have seen us coming though and set the trap."

"And how'd you get away?"

"The survivors retreated and worked their way up one slope. We drove the truck up the slope. It was slow going. That's when me and Sharkey over there got hit. Those Chinese charged the truck when we reached the top. I was able to accelerate away from them. The others ran across a field and broke into a farmhouse. The general hung onto my door and fired back. It was crazy.

"Before the Chinese caught us, the general ordered us to take the wounded and come for you. Before he jumped off the truck and ran for the house, General West said to say, 'Remember your promise.'"

Mark frowned. The fool had led his troops into an ambush, and now he wanted Mark to risk lives to bail him out.

"North or south slope?"

"South."

"Did you cross a road to get to the house?"

"No, the road was on the other side. We entered the rear."

"Okay, thanks."

"Sir, are you gonna rescue them?"

"We're gonna give it our best effort. Get some rest. If we fail, I'm gonna need you to help get these people to safety somewhere."

"You have my word, sir. Good luck."

Mark patted the man's arm, and then left.

Eighty

THE COURTYARD WAS STILL full of people. Some saying last-minute goodbyes, others just watching. Vince met Mark midway. "I'd go but I don't know how to shoot. I wouldn't want to be a liability."

Mark kept walking. Vince fell in stride.

"Well, you'll learn quick enough. I'll tell you what. Why don't you stay here and help in case we have to evacuate?"

Vince stopped. He looked as though Mark had slapped him.

"I can help. I just need to be taught."

"You need to listen. We're going into battle with some unknown enemy. Some of these people will not be coming back. No one has time to teach you how to shoot. No offense, Vince."

"There has to be something I can do to help."

"There is. I told you what it is. Sorry."

Mark started walking. Five steps later, he stopped and went back. "Now listen, this is what I need from you. You do what I say, nothing more. If you can't do it, stay here. You understand?"

"Yeah."

"I need you to follow us in a separate car. I'll give you a gun, just in case, but you are not to get out of the car. You'll have a radio and binoculars. You stop when we do, keeping back. You do not follow us into the fight. Is that clear?"

"Yeah, but why am I going if not to fight?"

Mark hesitated. "Because if things go south on us, I need you to get word to the house to start packing. You understand the importance of what I'm saying?"

Vince nodded.

"Can I trust you to do that?"

"Yes." His voice was a whisper.

"Good, 'cause these people are counting on you. Get back here and help them. Do not wait for us. You go. I'll keep the enemy busy for as long as I can to give you a head start. If you're coming, get a car."

Mark spun and marched to the waiting vehicles.

He climbed into the passenger seat of a pickup driven by Lincoln.

Caleb was in the back seat. "I've got your rifle and two handguns." He passed them forward.

"You have a radio?"

"Yes."

"Check in with everyone to make sure they work."

When that was done, Mark said, "Give Vince a radio, the extra binoculars, and this handgun." Mark handed one of his guns back. "Tell him to stay well behind us but keep us in sight."

Mark looked out the side window. Lynn stood ten feet away, her face expressionless, but her eyes moist. Mark smiled and gave a quick wave. She flashed a brave smile.

Caleb climbed back in. "All set."

"Okay, let's go."

Lincoln started the truck and backed down the driveway.

"Wait! Stop!" Mark said.

Lincoln jammed his foot on the brakes. Mark hadn't taken his eyes off Lynn. Sudden emotion flooded him. He opened the door, jumped out, and walked toward her. Without a word he swept her into his arms and kissed her. When they broke, he said, "I love you. I just wanted you to know."

Her tears rolled. "I know. You come back."

"I will," he promised.

A minute later they were on the road.

Eighty-One

"SIR, I'M SORRY. I have my orders."

"I understand that, Sergeant, but your people have been ambushed and are under siege in a farmhouse to the west. They need help."

"I've received no orders or message to support that. Why would they send a message to you and not us? We're staying here."

Mark was fast losing patience with the man. "You need to go to our house and talk to the three wounded men who showed up there last night."

"I don't understand. Why would they go there and not come here?"

"Well, at the moment, I'd say it's because they'll get more help from us than you. We're risking our lives to rescue your comrades. The least you can do is send some men with us to help."

"Sir, I have orders from General West to protect this base. That's what I intend to do. For all I know, you're trying to get us to abandon post so you can take it over."

"That's just stupid." Mark poked him in the chest. "Listen, bud, you go look at those wounded men. Then you send half of your men with some heavy weapons to find me. We'll be the ones west of Bryan fighting your fight for you. You do that or, Sergeant, I swear if any of these good people die and you could've prevented it, I'm coming back for you. That's a promise."

The Sergeant did not respond well to the threat. "You need to leave this base now, or I will have you arrested and locked up."

"Not on your best day, soldier boy." Mark turned away. "You better be there."

They drove away from the base. Mark pushed the encounter from his mind. There were more important things to think about now. The drive would take about forty minutes. Mark used the time to issue orders through Caleb and the radio. They had no idea where the farm might be, but drove keeping the turnpike to the right.

It was late morning. A bright sun had climbed overhead. Visibility was good for a long way, increased by the binoculars. As they reached the Bryan limits, Mark stopped. He called everyone to him and spread a map out on the hood of the truck.

"From here, I'm splitting us into two teams. One will proceed to the next main road north of the turnpike", he pointed it out on the map, "and drive a parallel track with us. We'll give you five minutes to get there before we start. Jarrod, you're in charge of that group. If you find them, do not engage. Hide and contact me. We'll join up and form a plan based on what we see."

Jarrod asked, "What if what we see is a hundred armed men?"

"Then the plan will be to retreat to the house, pack up, and leave. I want to help those soldiers if I can, but I'm not sacrificing our lives in a fight we can't win."

"Good to know."

"I'd prefer to find this foreign army without being spotted. So go slow and with caution. If you're not in the driver's seat, you should be scanning the area. Lincoln, you go with the kids. You're in charge of the second vehicle with Jarrod. You listen to him," he said to those driving with Lincoln, "and do what he says." To Lincoln: "Keep about a quarter mile behind him. Bill, you switch and drive for me."

Mark studied the map. "Adam, you're in charge of your car. Follow me, and then break off and stop on the first overpass. Use the glasses to scan both ways. Maybe you can spot the tank. If not, cross the turnpike and scout the other side. Make sure no one can sneak up behind us, and then rejoin us at the next overpass. The radio should reach that far. If you see anything at all, call and get out of there."

He pointed again. "I'm guessing West is holed up somewhere just past Bryan. It will be open ground. We'll have trouble taking them by surprise."

"So, what are we gonna do then?" Lincoln asked.

"One, not get seen. Two, not get shot. Three, I'll know more when I see the layout. Any other questions?"

Jarrod said, "So it's like before … we make it up as we go?"

"Is there a better way?"

"Well, I would hope so, but not that I'd know."

Eighty-Two

ONCE THEY CLEARED BRYAN, Mark ordered a slower speed. They didn't want to rush into another ambush. Mark reviewed what he knew, which wasn't much. *Would anyone still be alive to rescue after all this time?* The initial attack had happened around eight the night before. Fourteen hours had passed.

The majority of the land was now open for long distances. A few copses of trees existed, set back from the road. Farmhouses dotted the roadsides, but not nearly enough to offer cover.

Caleb reported, "Jarrod says nothing yet. Mr. Brandford hasn't made contact."

"Bill, pull up that driveway there and stop next to the house. Caleb, contact Brandford. Before we go any farther, I want to know everyone is still with us."

Mark unfolded his body from the front seat. He took the binoculars and his rifle to the front porch. There he took a long slow scan of the land to the west. It had been nearly fifteen minutes since they left Bryan. They had to be close.

The front door of the farmhouse was open. He went inside and took the stairs two-at-a-time to the second floor. Finding a westward-facing bedroom, he trained the glasses out the window.

In the distance, past the next farm and over a wooded area beyond, rose a slim wisp of smoke. Perhaps it was been nothing more than someone's chimney or the exhaust from a propane heater, except the smoke was black, like something was burning.

How much farther from the woods was the smoke? Only one way to find out. Mark returned to the truck. He looked at Caleb, who shook his head. *Damn! Had they lost a car already? Perhaps the opposing army was bigger than the wounded man had realized.*

"Who?"

"Adam."

That didn't make sense to Mark. Adam's would've been the last car. If something had happened to them, the enemy was behind them.

"Smoke is rising past the next farm. Let's go there. I'll tell you where I want to stop."

The driver turned the truck around and moved down the road. Mark had him stop on the road past the next farmhouse. The woods were still a quarter mile farther. "Pull off the road and head for those trees."

The truck bounced over a low to the ground crop that had grown wild. When they reached the woods, he climbed into the bed and focused the glasses behind him. No one was coming from that direction, friend or foe, nor did he see Vince. He frowned. *Was he missing too?* That meant the enemy was closer than he imagined.

"Turn the truck so it's facing back the way we came. Wait for me here."

"Where you going?" Caleb asked, his voice anxious.

"I'm going to scout the other side of the woods. I'll be back in a few minutes. In the meantime, try to contact Brandford, Lincoln, and Vince."

He looked at the driver. "Bill, if I'm not back in fifteen minutes, leave. But head south for a few miles before going east."

The men locked eyes. Bill nodded.

Mark walked into the woods and made his way to the far side. The distance was not great. He was at the opposite tree line within two minutes. He knelt and aimed the glasses at the horizon.

The smoke rose from a farmhouse a mile straight down the road. There was a large barn and other outbuildings behind the house. One of the smaller outbuildings was burning. There didn't seem to be anyone around.

Mark switched to the scope on the rifle. He made an adjustment, and the farmhouse was right before his eye. A flash caught his peripheral vision to the right. There was a man behind a woodpile. Mark moved the scope up and found more men, many more, taking cover around the other buildings. And they did look Asian, but he couldn't swear they were all Chinese. None wore any sort of uniform.

Mark panned back to the house. The windows in the back were broken. As he watched, a rifle pointed out, spat twice, and disappeared. There were people still alive inside.

He checked the front of the house. No one. The only possible hiding spot out front was the drainage ditch. Mark slid the scope along the top of the slope. A head popped up. Someone from the house shot at it. The bullet kicked up dirt inches from where the head had been.

The house was surrounded. At least two soldiers were alive inside; one covering the front and one in back. With the buildings in the way, and not being able to see inside the ditch, Mark had no way to determine the size of the opposing force.

He lowered the scope. Was the risk to the lives of his friends and children worth the reward of saving however many men were inside that house? The general had left the base with a little more than forty troops. If five had escaped to show up at his door, how many were still alive? The wounded man had said they lost half their numbers in the initial attack.

Mark put his eye to the scope again and looked past the ditch. There was another ditch on the other side of the road. Another small grouping of trees stood fifty yards behind that ditch. If they reached the trees—no, they had to cross a lot of open ground to get to the cover of that far ditch. If the men in the ditch near the house kept their heads down, Mark's group wouldn't be seen. Only the men behind the house had an angle to see them. Did they have a way of contacting those in the ditch? Probably. The only way to get into position was to make a daring dash across fifty yards of open ground.

Mark ran back to the truck. Caleb looked relieved to see him.

Bill said, "Anything?"

"Oh yeah. We found them, and some of the soldiers are still alive. Caleb, contact Jarrod."

Mark pulled out the map again.

"I got him."

"Ask him what the last road was they passed."

Caleb relayed the question and answer.

"Tell him to stop and go back three roads and wait for us there. Bill, drive back to the last intersection and turn left. I'll let you know where to stop." He folded the map and got in.

Mark looked back at Caleb. "Any word?"

"Not from Brandford or Lincoln, but I did find Vince."

"Get Vince on the line and give me the radio."

Caleb handed him the radio.

"Vince, you there?"

"Yeah, I'm here."

"Look, I need you to do something that may put you in harm's way. Are you willing to try?"

A pause, then, "Of course, what do you need?"

"I need you to find the other car that was with us. It was a blue Chevy Impala. Do you remember seeing it?"

"Yeah, it was the car that followed you and then turned right a few miles back."

"That's the one. They're not responding. I need to know what happened to them." The truck turned hard, throwing Mark sideways.

"You think they might have been attacked?"

"It's a possibility. It might also just be that their batteries died. They should have rejoined us by now."

"And the harm's way is I could get attacked too?"

"Yes, so be very careful. Keep on the radio with Caleb. If you find them, I need you to pass them a message."

"What if I find them dead?"

"Then get the hell out of there."

"Ah, what's the message?"

"Tell them to cross the turnpike on foot and come up behind the enemy."

"You found them?"

"Yes. Vince, this is important. Can you do this?"

"I can try. I mean, I'll go look for them, but obviously I may not find them."

"That's all I can ask." He handed the radio back to Caleb as Bill took another turn, pitching Mark across the bench seat again.

"Sorry," Bill said. "You should be wearing your seatbelt."

Eighty-Three

A MILE DOWN, Jarrod and Lincoln were pulling to the side of the road. Bill drove up and parked across the road from them. Mark got out and approached Jarrod's window.

"What's up?" the big farmer asked.

"What happened to Brandford? He's not responding."

"He turned off a mile back and motioned us to continue. We haven't seen or heard from him since."

Mark pointed. "Just beyond those trees is a farmhouse. That's where West is. He's surrounded, but I'm not sure how many of his men are inside. I have an idea."

"You usually do."

Mark smiled. "I hope this one works better than that last one."

Mark gathered everyone around him.

"The farmhouse West and his troops are holed up in is on the other side of those trees. Take both cars all the way around to the opposite side of the farm. Keep your distance so no one sees the car. Then you'll have to hoof it. There's some buildings on the far side of the house that you can use as cover. I saw some enemy troops but there may be more. You'll have to check and clear each building."

What sounded like gunshots echoed across the distance. They all glanced in the direction.

"It'll take some time. We're gonna crawl across the field on the other side of the road and try to get to the drainage ditch in front of the house. Hopefully, it takes about the same time as your approach. There's another group of enemy hiding in the ditch in front of the house on the north side. If we can get unseen into the south ditch, we'll try to take them from behind."

Bobby asked, "What about the other car?"

"We haven't had any contact with them in a while. At this point I have to assume they're no longer available to us. We proceed without them."

More shots were fired. Perhaps a fresh assault was underway. "The defenders may not have much time remaining. So unless there are any questions, let's move."

No one spoke.

"Be smart. Don't take unnecessary risks. It's not worth trying to save them if we lose any of you in the process."

Becca gave her father a big hug. Bobby shook his hand. They went their separate ways.

Mark led his team into the woods. He refused to allow concerns for Bobby and Becca to dwell in his thoughts. Saying a quick prayer for their safety, he focused on the task ahead.

He knelt five feet from the end of the trees. They were not as thick as the ones he had fought the wild man in. There wasn't as much low cover. No one was moving, no one was shooting. *What are they waiting for*? It was as if someone called timeout and stopped the action.

"Caleb, try Vince."

Mark was only vaguely aware of Caleb speaking, his attention full on the scene in front of him. Something didn't feel right. *Could it be a trap*? Maybe his convoy had been spotted, and the enemy troops were using the men in the house to lure his people into the open.

He scanned the area far from the house. If it was a trap, there was no place close to hide extra troops unless they were in the outbuildings. Mark studied the structures. They could hide a lot of men. That was the direction his kids were heading. Alarms flashed in his head. He needed to contact them to warn them.

Caleb shook his head. "I can't get him."

"Damn! We may be in way over our heads here."

A distant motor grew steadily closer. In his scope, Mark watched as small shapes moved across the open field to the west. Surely, Jarrod's team had already begun their approach. The big man was smart enough to turn his radio off to avoid unexpected noises, but Mark had Caleb try anyway. No response.

"Turn that thing off for now. We need to move. We're late. Keep low. Crawling's not an option. We need to get out of the line of sight from the men in the backyard. The closer we get to the house, the harder it will be for them to see us. Stay to my left and right in a V formation. When you see me drop you do it too."

He made eye contact with both men to make sure they understood. "Okay, let's go."

Mark took off at a jog, keeping bent over as low as possible. They had moved about a third of the distance they needed to cover, when a loud motorized sound froze him. He threw himself prone on the ground. Without looking, he knew the others followed him down by the grunts.

The jeep with the mounted machine gun crept from the east. Mark's heart leaped. That .50 caliber gun would lend some serious firepower to the rescue. There were four men inside; two in the front seats, one seated in the back and one standing behind the gun. The engine rattled. A small but steady streak of black smoke trailed behind.

Mark raised the binoculars. "Oh, sweet Jesus."

Eighty-Four

JARROD HELD UP HIS hand for the group to stop. They were halfway across the massive field. He crouched and the others joined him. "There're two buildings in front of us. I want you three," he pointed to Becca, Bobby, and Myron, "to veer off and stay behind that smaller one. We'll go straight ahead. Don't stop again until you get there or if you think someone might see you.

"Try not to get into a fight if you can help it until we're ready. First thing to do is find out if anyone's inside. We don't want to come around the buildings and get attacked from behind. When you get there, signal me what you find. Any questions?"

"What if we do get seen?" Myron asked.

"Cover each other and try to join us. Work as a team. Try to pin them down before they do you."

Gunshots started again.

"Let's go before we get seen out here."

The groups separated and ran all-out. Bobby reached the far outbuilding first. Becca followed. Bobby grabbed Myron before he banged into the wall. The boy was breathing hard. Bobby held a finger to his lips. He moved next to Myron's ear. "Remember, there might be someone inside."

Myron nodded.

Bobby looked at Jarrod and Lincoln and the other two members near the opposite end of the long wooden structure. They had arrived safely as well. Jarrod motioned for them to go around the far side. Bobby waved back. Staying low, they crept to the corner. Bobby peered around.

The rate of fire increased, but Bobby couldn't tell if the shooting was from the house or the attackers or both.

Bobby started around the corner and then jumped back, colliding with Becca. There was a man behind a woodpile off to the left. If they moved, he'd be able to see them. Bobby poked his head around again and took in the yard behind the house. There was a small shed beyond the woodpile and a two-story, two-and-a-half-car garage past that. Each building could hold more enemy.

"There's no way of going this way without being seen. We'll have to go around the entire yard and come up from behind. It's going to take a while." He looked at the other end. Jarrod's group was no longer in sight. If Bobby's group had to detour they might not be in position in time to offer assistance should Jarrod's group get attacked.

"What are we going to do, Bobby? We can't just sit here."

"I know, Becca, give me a minute."

"We don't have extra minutes to spare."

"Becca, stop!"

Bobby glared at her and then peeked around the corner again. The man was an open target for them from the side. But a gunshot would announce their presence. He turned quickly back to face Myron. "How good are you with that thing?"

Myron shrugged. "I don't know."

Becca said, "This is no time to be shy, Golden Feather."

"Let me take a look." Myron crawled forward and sized up the target while Bobby looked over his shoulder.

"See," Bobby whispered. "An easy shot." He hoped his voice offered more confidence than he felt.

Eighty-Five

To Mark, the presence of the machine gun changed the game. However, the men manning the gun and jeep were Asian. They wore no uniforms that identified them as part of an invading army. However, who they were didn't matter. The size of the rounds and rate of fire the machine gun spit would chew up the house in a matter of seconds. *I hope there's a basement.*

On the other hand, if they continued and were spotted out in the open, they didn't stand a prayer. He shivered at the thought of the massive holes the machine gun might rip through their bodies

At the sight of the jeep, some of the attackers in the front ditch began to cheer. Hands raised above the ditch and pumped like someone just scored a touchdown. The slow rate of approach would put the jeep in front of the house within two minutes. But that also put them in range from the house. If they stopped on a diagonal to the house, they might not get complete coverage inside. If they moved up along the side of the house, the line of sight was straight on but they had to cross the drainage ditch. Of course, the Jeep should be able to do that.

But the driver of the jeep didn't choose either

option. When the wheels turned south, Mark swore. They were crossing the ditch in front of the three of them.

"Quick, using as little movement as possible, dig a trench to lie in. Stay low." Mark clawed at the soft ground. Some of the low weeds and browning crops offered cover, but they needed more to keep from being discovered.

He glanced up. The jeep was pointing downward into the ditch. In precious seconds, it would climb and point straight at them.

"Stop moving when I tell you." He slid backward and continued digging out a small ditch. His hands moved frantically. The Jeep began a slow climb up the back of the drainage ditch. The jeep coming straight at Mark. The two men in the back were looking at the house. The driver was looking ahead but was angled upward. The passenger was looking down at the ground over the side of the jeep. They rose steadily.

In seconds, they'd be out of time. "Burrow in and stop moving. Keep your face down. Do not panic. Stay still and wait for me before you do anything."

Mark scooted forward into the depression he had created. It wasn't perfect, but it had to do. He turned his head so his ear was on the ground. He had a view of the jeep. Slowly he reached out and pulled a clump of weeds free from the ground. He placed it on the exposed side of his head.

The jeep leveled off and advanced into the field. The passenger held binoculars to his face. For now, they were aimed at the farmhouse. He motioned with his hand for the driver to keep going. Mark held his breath. As slow as possible, he slid the rifle along the ground so he could track the jeep. If they were spotted, he needed to get off the first shot.

The jeep was halfway across the field before the

driver signaled to turn. All four riders were focused on the house. The jeep moved parallel to the house, broadside and ten yards in front of Mark. The passenger stood on the hood, the binoculars focused on the house. He turned and spoke to the gunner. After a brief discussion, the driver moved forward another ten feet.

The driver stopped and got out. The passenger stood in front of the jeep. A sudden burst of fire from the house launched toward the jeep.

The gunner quickly silenced them by opening up on the house. The bullets tore through the aluminum siding like it was paper. The gunner continued to hammer away, the barrage spraying pieces of the house into the air creating a cloud of debris.

The siege would be over in a flash if Mark didn't do something. He turned to the others. "We need to take them out, or everyone inside will be dead. Can you hit anything from here?"

"I can," Caleb said.

"I think so," Bill said.

"Okay, while the machine gun is covering our shots, Caleb, you take the guy in front of the jeep. You take the driver, Bill. Ready?"

They nodded.

"Come up to one knee, line up your shots, and wait for me to fire. If you miss your shot, don't panic and go crazy wasting bullets. Take a deep breath and shoot again."

Mark looked over the scene to make sure it hadn't changed. All eyes were still focused on the house. Very slowly, Mark lifted to both knees. He planted one foot on the ground and brought his rifle to his shoulder. He sighted on the man sitting in the back. It would be the tougher shot. He wanted to save the gunner for last to allow his fire to mask theirs. He breathed out slowly and pulled the trigger. Two other shots followed. The blasts caused ringing in both ears.

The guy in the jeep fell out. The man with the glasses pitched forward.

The driver ducked behind the jeep, evidently thinking the shots had come from the house. Mark couldn't worry about him. The others had to take him. He had to stop the gunner, who, even though still depressing the trigger, was beginning to look behind him.

He spotted Mark and began swinging the gun toward him just as Mark blew a hole in his head. Two more shots followed, and the driver slumped against the jeep.

"Hurry," Mark called as he scrambled for the jeep.

Heads were poking up from the ditch and looking back at the jeep. It wouldn't take long for them to realize the stoppage wasn't planned. Mark had to reach the jeep before the enemy. He pushed harder.

He knew they'd been spotted when men climbed out of the ditch. Shots fired. He kept running, keeping the jeep between him and the shooters. Some of the attackers sprinted toward the jeep. Whoever reached the machine gun first controled the battle.

It was a race Mark couldn't afford to lose.

Eighty-Six

LOUD CONTINUOUS GUNFIRE ERUPTED.

"Oh God, they've got a heavy machine gun," Bobby said. "We're out of time."

Becca shushed him. "Listen."

Voices came from behind the wall. They were cheering.

Bobby shook his head. "I think we're outmatched here, Sis."

"I know, Bobby, but Daddy and the others are counting on us. We can't just sit it out."

"You're right. But if lover boy can't take the shot, we'll have to go the long way around and may be too late to help them anyway."

"What's the plan if he does take the shot?"

"We move to the woodpile and behind the shed. We take out those in the shed and move behind the garage. I'm betting there's a back or side door we can go through to get inside. From there, we can cover the backyard and pin down the guys in this building."

Becca looked at him with her mouth open.

"What?"

"That's an amazing plan. Daddy would be so proud."

She moved to where Myron sat. She leaned over him

to see around the corner. She purposely pressed her body against his. When she pulled back, Myron was blushing. She smiled.

"Piece of cake shot, Myron. I believe in you." She leaned forward and kissed his cheek. "You can do this." She sat back. "And no pressure or anything, but a lot of lives, including ours, are depending on you." She moved away.

Myron looked at her, his mouth hanging open, his eyes wide and almost bulging.

"Now, Myron," she said with a sweet smile.

Myron turned his attention back to the lone man.

Bobby raised an eyebrow at his sister. She shrugged in reply.

The machine gun continued to chatter loudly. Myron drew an arrow and set it. He stood pressed against the wall.

In one motion, Myron stepped away from the wall, faced his target, and drew back the string. The arrow flew true, driving into the man's chest before the rifle came on bead.

The man staggered backward, the arrow sticking from his chest. The rifle fell as both hands grabbed the shaft.

Bobby understood the problem instantly. If the man didn't go down someone was going to see him.

Pushing his rifle into Myron's hands, Bobby drew his knife and sprinted forward. The man was dancing in circles, trying to pull the head from his chest. He was nearly clear of the woodpile when Bobby reached him. He snagged the man around the neck and pulled him backward at the same time, driving the blade into his back.

He pulled the man to the ground and rolled on top of him. The man was still kicking. The machine gun ceased firing and left a deafening silence over the battlefield. Bobby had to end his prey's screams fast before he drew attention.

Bobby covered the man's mouth and drove the knife in repeatedly until there was no movement. He motioned for Becca and Myron to join him.

When they got there, Bobby was twisting and pulling on the arrow. With a sickening sound, it came free. He handed the bloody arrow to Myron. Myron held it away from him like it was a dirty diaper.

They were about to move behind the shed, when several armed men ran from the side of the garage along the side of the house toward the front. Maybe Jarrod's group had been discovered. If the enemy was running toward the front, controlling the backyard should be easier.

Without a word, he ran to the side of the shed. The machine gun started firing again.

Eighty-Seven

MARK WON THE RACE, but it was too dangerous to jump up and take the machine gun. Mark placed the rifle on the hood, lined up a shot, and fired. The lead runner fell. He switched targets and dropped a second man. The others dropped and tried to hide. Bullets pinged off the jeep. Bill and Caleb arrived and sat behind the jeep, both breathing heavily.

"I need to get up to the machine gun, but I can't do it with all those guns pointed at me. I wouldn't last a second. You two put down continuous cover fire. Can you do that?"

They both nodded with wide-eyed nervous bobs.

"Now!"

Mark fired several rounds and waited for them to get into a rhythm. When the heads in the ditch ducked, Mark leaped up on the back of the jeep and grabbed the gun. He swiveled it and angled the sights downward. The two men still outside the ditch bounced on the ground as the bullets ripped them apart.

Mark walked the rounds to the ditch. At this distance he had no angle to hit anything. He stopped shooting. "Bill, can you drive a stick?"

Bill nodded again.

"Then drive me closer to the road. Stay low in the seat. Caleb, you walk behind the jeep and keep anyone from shooting in our direction."

Bill struggled with the clutch, and the jeep lurched forward, almost throwing Mark to the ground. He grabbed the gun for balance. Bill turned the jeep head on to the road. Shots once again came from the ditch. Men came from around the house to add firepower to the barrage.

They were finding the range. Mark sighted the gun and shouted, "Bill, lie down. Caleb, keep the men in the ditch down." Mark depressed the trigger and quickly sent the new shooters running for cover.

Someone was still alive in the house. Two of the intruders fell from shots fired from inside. "Okay, Bill, closer. Keep your head down. Just put it in gear and give it some gas."

Bill complied, and the jeep jumped forward again. Mark held his fire. He only had limited rounds. A shot came from farther to the right. The enemy was using the ditch to flank them.

A cry of pain brought Mark's attention behind him. Caleb had dropped to the ground. He was holding his leg and howling. Mark swung the gun in the direction of the shooter and let loose a long burst. The man was blown back into the ditch.

"Bill, stop the jeep. We're getting too close. While I cover, you run back and grab Caleb. Hurry!"

Bill ran for Caleb. Mark shot a line across the top of the ditch to keep heads down. Bill dragged Caleb behind the jeep. Just then, two men broke from the ditch to the far right. Mark tracked them. He took down one of them but then the gun ran dry.

He jumped from the jeep and took up his rifle. He sat next to the others and reloaded his lone magazine. There was no telling how many attackers were left. However, they couldn't wait to find out. If they didn't move now, they'd be pinned down. Mark swung his gaze from the ditch to the woods and then to the lone man who had disappeared somewhere between.

With Caleb's wounded leg, reaching the cover of the

woods wasn't possible. Not unless he stayed to give them covering fire. But even then, it was a risky retreat. Mark blew out a long breath. If they didn't get some help, they'd all be dead.

Eighty-Eight

THERE WAS A SMALL window in the side of the shed. Bobby took a quick peek and ducked. Two men were standing by the double doors in front. A riding mower took up much of the space behind them. One man had a rifle pushed between the gap where the doors met. The other had his faced pressed to where there must have been a hole in the wood.

Bobby motioned for the others. They ran to him. He held up two fingers and pointed inside. Becca nodded. Myron still looked stunned.

Bobby put his arm around each one's shoulders and pulled them close in a huddle. "Sis, you go around the shed and stop at the door. I'll go in front from this direction. Myron, you count to ten and then tap on the window to draw their attention. Let them see you."

"Yeah, but don't let them shoot you," Becca added.

"When they come out, we take them with knives."

"What if they don't come out?" Becca asked.

Bobby frowned. "Myron, if they don't open the door within five seconds, you say 'go.' That'll mean we go in. Hopefully, they're still looking at him. You pull the door from your side, and I'll grab the gun that's pointing out."

Becca slid around the building. Bobby ducked below the window and waited at the corner for his sister. When she poked her head around the other side, Bobby moved to the front.

The tapping happened seconds later. They heard movement within, but no one came out.

"Oh geez! Go."

Becca stepped to the front and grabbed the door. Bobby was already moving when she yanked it open. To Bobby's relief, the rifle was no longer aimed outward. He rushed through the door, feeling Becca close behind.

The two men turned as they entered. The man with the rifle spun toward Bobby, who dived at the man, knife held out in front like a spear. The gun went off. A sharp pain exploded in Bobby's side. His momentum carried him forward and he crashed into the man before he could fire again. The blade impaled the shooter. The force of the contact drove him back against the wall.

Bobby turned fast as the body slumped to the floor. Pain shot through him. He grabbed his side and looked for Becca. She was involved in a fight, but all he could do was slide down the wall and watch.

BECCA FOLLOWED BOBBY AND flinched when the gun went off. The delay gave her opponent the chance to pull a handgun and aim it at Bobby. With no alternative but to save her brother, Becca flung her knife at the man. It hit and staggered him but did not penetrate.

Before he could regroup Becca was on him kicking, clawing, and screaming like some wild animal. She clasped both hands around the gun side wrist and sank her teeth in. Her opponent screamed and beat at her head with his free hand.

One of the blows connected solid and dazed her. Becca's grip relaxed enough that the gun was ripped from her grasp. She staggered sideways. Her foe backhanded her on the side of the head with the gun, knocking her down. When she looked up, the gun was aimed at her head.

The first arrow drove her would-be killer two steps back. The second hit him in the eye.

Eighty-Nine

To HER GREAT RELIEF, Myron stepped into the shed with a third arrow ready. The small room was crowded with five people and the riding mower. He reached a hand down and Becca took it.

Bobby stood and gasped, collapsing to his knees.

Ignoring the blood streaming from her face and the pain in her head, Becca rushed to her brother's side. "Bobby!"

He lowered to the floor and rolled onto his back.

Blood-stained shirt. Not the smear of someone else's blood, but the wet and growing spread of his own.

Becca yanked the shirt up to see the blood's source. They both gasped.

"Oh God, Myron, he's been shot."

She wiped at the blood with her hand, trying to see the wound. It covered again. "I have to stop the bleeding."

Myron removed the quiver from around his neck and pulled his shirt over his head. He handed it to Becca. She took the shirt and cut it into strips, leaving one section whole. Using the scraps, Becca wiped away the blood. She turned her brother slightly, remembering what Lynn had done. She was relieved to see there was an exit wound. Folding the extra material, she pressed it to the wound on top.

"Myron, push down on this."

He squatted and held the cloth in place.

Becca did the same on the back and wrapped a cloth strip around it to hold it in place. She used every strip she cut to secure the makeshift bandage in place.

"Becca, we have to move," Bobby said. He sat up and winced. "I'll be all right."

"Bobby, you got shot. You're not all right."

"I'm gonna have to be. Now help me up." He groaned as Becca helped him stand

He walked to the open doors. Becca stood next to him. A gun fight still raged outside, but the machine gun was quiet. No one was in the backyard. "Let's go," he said and ran from the shed before she could stop him. Bobby went around the back of the garage. Becca followed. They stopped at the far corner. A side door near the front stood open.

In front of the house men were firing across the street. She couldn't see their target, but suspected it was her father. She kept watching the men as they advanced toward the door. If any of the shooters turned around, the trio was in the open.

Bobby slid along the wall until he reached the door. He peeked inside. Bobby held up two fingers and prepared to enter. Becca touched his arm. When he looked, she made a gun with her finger and pumped her thumb up and down. Her brother was in no condition to go hand-to-hand. It was time to shoot. He nodded, spun into the doorway, and leveled the rifle. He pulled the trigger as he walked inside. He kept firing until both men were down. Becca followed him in, sweeping her gun arm to the rear of the building to make sure no one else hid inside.

"Here they come," Myron shouted as he jumped through the door following Becca.

Becca looked through the garage door windows and saw six men running toward the garage from the front yard. Bobby looked at her.

She smiled. "Oh well, brother, we came looking for a fight. Now we got it."

Ninety

"CALEB, CAN you still shoot?"

"Hell, yeah."

"They're gonna rush us from the front real soon. You keep watching the guy behind us. If he pops up, you take him down. Lie down and use the scope."

Bill said, "Hey, hey, they're moving up this side."

Mark looked to the left. "They're flanking us. The charge will happen soon. Bill, you take that side, I'll watch the front."

Voices filled the temporary silence. Mark couldn't make out many words, but the ones he heard were English. Mark knelt and sighted across the front seats of the jeep. Six men climbed the slope and charged the jeep.

"Here they come."

The flank opened fire. Bill shot rapidly. He was shouting.

Mark yelled, "Control your shots, Bill. Make them count." He sighted the front man and punctured his chest. As quick as he could, Mark shifted to the next target and took him down.

Bullets were flying from every direction. As Mark switched positions, he noticed Bill was dry firing. He was sobbing, out of ammo, but perhaps too afraid to notice. The flank was pouring fire onto the jeep. It wouldn't be long before a bullet found one of them.

Mark returned a quick shot to the left, and then turned to the front. He fired in rapid succession missing one and wounding another. Four more men were out of the ditch now. They'd be hand-to-hand soon. He set the rifle down and pulled the handgun. It would be faster and better for up close work.

He stood straight up, sighted, and banged out five shots. Bill groaned and slumped to the ground.

"Caleb, cover the flank."

Mark fired again catching more men approaching from the corner of his eye. He fired until the magazine emptied then pulled his knife. The first attacker came around the jeep and Mark drove the knife into his belly, ripping it upward and out.

A second man jumped onto the jeep and launched at Mark. He sidestepped the human missile and slashed down across his back. He landed next to Caleb. The boy turned on his side and shot the man in the face. Mark turned to face the next one. A sudden burst of heavy firing made him duck behind the jeep. With the few seconds' relief from attack, Mark slapped home another magazine and stood ready to fire. To his surprise, there were no longer any targets. He moved left to right and lowered the gun.

Across the street, Jarrod and Lincoln stood. Adam's group had found and joined them.

Jarrod waved and shouted, "You're welcome."

Mark turned and looked behind him. "Caleb, did you get that guy behind us?"

"Yeah, he's down."

Mark checked Bill. He was dead. He pushed the sorrow aside. There would be time for grieving later when he had to tell his wife. "You stay here."

Mark ran across the street to join Jarrod. "What about that building?"

"We took care of that. It's all clear."

There were still gunshots coming from the rear. Since Becca and Bobby weren't with Jarrod, those shots had to be them. He took off at a run.

Ninety-One

BOBBY AND BECCA PUSHED the barrels of their guns through the window frames. "Myron, close the door and don't let anyone inside. Ready, Sis?"

"Let's do this, Bro."

"Now."

They opened fire and cut down two men. The remaining four found places to hide and returned fire. Bullets plunked into the wood door, and some ripped through. "We're not gonna be able to stay here much longer," Bobby said. "Some of those shots are getting through."

"What do you suggest? We can't go out the side door. There's no other way out."

Myron said, "There's stairs leading up. It might give us a better angle."

"Yeah, but if they get inside we're trapped." A bullet tore wood from the frame next to his face. He ducked and swore.

"Bobby, the guys in that building are coming out. There's four more there. I don't know if we can hold them all off."

Bobby fired. "We have to try."

"Bobby, you're the better shot. You go upstairs and

Myron and I will keep them out."

"Okay." Bobby hobbled for the stairs, taking them as best he could fighting back the severe pain. The upstairs was floored and with enough room to stand. There was no window; however, there was a vent in the front peak.

He rushed to the end, sat down, and kicked until the vent fell away to the ground below. By the time he was ready to shoot, some of the attackers below were already directing fire upward.

Bobby took his time, trying to ignore the bullets striking the wood around him. He lined up his first shot and planted it an inch from the head of a guy lying down behind an elevated wooden sandbox. The man panicked and tried to crawl away. Becca shot him in the ass. Bobby finished him.

The shooter standing at the corner of the house made the mistake of stepping into the open to shoot at Bobby. He got the shot away before Bobby hit him. That bullet hit the wood just below Bobby, throwing splinters into his face. He screamed. The shock and initial pain sent him rolling on his back and clutching his face. He fought for breath, but when he pulled his hands away only a small smear of blood showed. Forcing his breathing to a more normal rate he examined the damage with his fingers and winced when he found the small pieces of wood sticking out from his skin.

MYRON WAS GETTING ANTSY. The gun battle raged around him, which was bad enough, but he just stood there doing nothing. He watched Becca line up and take one shot after another. She was amazing. Not only for her skill, but because nothing seemed to phase her as it did him. She never showed fear, while Myron had enough for both of them.

He stood near the door, not sure what to do to help.

"Ha, gotcha," Becca said.

Then the door blasted open, almost knocking Myron over. A man stepped in and leveled a rifle at Becca.

"Ahhh!" Myron screamed and leaped on the man's back. The gun spat out a bullet that hit between Becca's feet. She jumped and let out a squeak.

Myron wrapped his arms around the guy's neck and squeezed tight. His opponent tried to pry Myron loose but couldn't do it with one hand. He lifted the rifle over his head and fired. The bullet ripped the braid and feather from Myron's head.

Shocked by the closeness of the bullet, Myron released his hold and slid to the floor. The man spun on Myron who had no way of defending himself. Myron threw a wild punch landing on the man's cheek. The blow turned his head but was nothing more than a slap.

He pushed Myron backward, but before he could level the gun, his head looked at the ceiling and his mouth dropped open in a silent scream. The rifle fell. He clutched at his back and dropped to his knees. Becca stood behind him, her face alive with color and rage.

She pulled the knife free, placed a handgun against the back of his head, and without pause pulled the trigger. Myron looked from the body to Becca in relief and astonishment.

"I got your back, Myron."

"Yeah, I see that." He accepted her hand and she hauled him to his feet.

Increased fire from out front brought their attention. She scooped up the rifle and aimed it through the window. Myron's heart beat so hard his chest hurt. *Would the killing ever stop?*

"Oh, thank God!" Becca said and lowered the rifle. She looked at Myron and smiled. "It's my father. I think it's over." Wrapping her arms around him, she squeezed tight.

Myron held on, closed his eyes, and whispered, "Yes, thank God."

Ninety-Two

BECCA AND MYRON GUIDED Bobby from the garage. Mark's heart flipped at the sight of the wounded boy with the bloody face. He rushed to him.

They sat him down at a picnic table.

"He's all right, Daddy," Becca said. "The bullet went clear through. He's got a bunch of splinters in his face though. I couldn't do anything about those, and the big baby won't let me touch them."

Mark bent and examined his son's face. Streaks of blood came from a dozen places. The splinters were small and close to his eyes. Some would have to be removed using a magnifying glass.

"Becca, I need you and Myron to go across the street and help Caleb. Bring him over here."

When they went, Mark turned to everyone. "Is anyone else hurt?"

No one spoke up.

Jarrod asked, "Where's Bill?"

Mark shook his head.

The woman with Jarrod had been a nurse. She examined Bobby. When Caleb arrived, she checked him and bandaged the wound.

With the battle over, General West and the remaining eleven soldiers came out of the house. Many had wounds of different degrees.

"You came," West said as he shook Mark's hand.

"I told you I would."

West looked around. "We lost a lot of good people. I'm just glad there was a basement, or none of us would have survived that machine gun. We were lucky. This may only be the beginning of the invasion. We'll never be ready to face another attack."

"I'm not so sure it's an invasion, General."

"What do you mean? It's kind of obvious, don't you think?"

"Look at these men. Other than all being Asian, there's nothing here that suggests they're a foreign army."

"They attacked us en force."

"Oh, I'm not saying they didn't act as a military group but look at them. None of them is in uniform. They're all very young, and most of them have tattoos that to me suggest they're most likely a very organized street gang. They didn't fight as trained soldiers, otherwise they would have overrun you with their numbers. There was little thought to their attack, other than to surround you."

"Why would a street gang travel away from the city and attack armed men? I would think they'd avoid us."

"Unless whoever was in charge so you as a threat. Maybe they attacked you thinking you were going to attack them. Who knows? But this was no army. When they were trying to outflank us, they were speaking English. I'm sorry."

"Well, we'll just have to disagree then."

"I guess so."

"I still have to prepare my men to face this country's enemies. Maybe more will come, maybe not, but someone has to stand up to them."

"As long as you remember who your friends are."

Two vehicles came into view from the west. Everyone pointed weapons until Mark recognized them.

"Wait, they're with us."

An army truck lumbered a short distance behind.

313

Ninety-Three

MARK AND THE GENERAL walked to the street to meet the new arrivals. The vehicles emptied, and a happy reunion began. One of the men was limping. Brandford had a cut on his face.

"It's good to see you. When we couldn't reach you, I thought the worst," Mark said. "What happened?"

"We heard shots, so we stopped and went to explore. The enemy was shooting at the tank, but it was buttoned up tight. They were standing next to it, trying to find a way in.

"We watched, but there were eight of them and only three of us. I told Lewis to contact you, but he dropped the radio down the slope. It rolled all the way to the turnpike. Then he tried to retrieve it but fell. That's when they started shooting. We had no choice but to fight. Lucky we had the higher ground. Unfortunately, none of us is that good a shot.

"It was a standoff. Lewis couldn't get back up the slope without getting shot or we would've just left. Then that crazy son-of-a-bitch over there," he pointed at Vince, "slid down the hill on the opposite side, picked up an automatic rifle, and opened fire from behind. He made the difference.

"The soldiers in the tank poured out and took care of the rest. That was it. We packed everyone up and came here."

Mark looked at Vince with raised eyebrows. Vince saw his look and shrugged.

They sent the wounded back to the house in the truck. The remaining soldiers spent the remaining daylight stripping the bodies of anything useful.

Mark sent everyone but Lincoln and Jarrod home. Then he returned to the general.

"Here's another thing that doesn't make sense, General. What were these men living off? I mean, look. None of them has any food with them. They don't have packs or anything to carry equipment. They have their weapons and basically that's it. How were they supplied? Does that sound like any invading army you've ever heard of?"

"Well, where did they come from? And why attack an army convoy?"

"I don't know. Maybe they came from Chicago. Maybe they wanted your tank. But wasn't one of your trucks filled with supplies?"

"Yeah ... food, water, medical supplies, ammunition, weapons."

"See what I mean? Where are their supplies? Were they just living off the land as they went? That's not how a successful invasion would go. Troops need food. You should send some men to the other side of the turnpike to see if they had a supply truck somewhere."

"I'll do that. We have to go that way anyhow to see if we can salvage any of the vehicles."

"I almost hope you're right, General about it being foreign invaders. It'd be sad to think we just killed a bunch of Americans. There aren't that many of us left."

"Well, there's about a hundred fewer now. But I still say they're foreign. Where else would they find so many

Asian men in one place?"

"I can't argue with that."

"Well, let's say they weren't from China, that they were here on visas or visiting, or something, but they knew the attack was going to happen. Maybe they had an antidote or vaccine for whatever killed everyone. Then after the people died off, their job was to sweep through the country, killing any survivors."

"I think you're seeing conspiracies everywhere. I'll leave that contemplation to you. I'm taking the rest of my people home. You know where to find me if you need anything."

Ninety-Four

THE COMMUNITY BURIED BILL at his family's home. His wife and son moved into a house next door to the Brandfords for security.

The gut-shot soldier died the next day from too much internal damage. The dead soldiers were buried at the base with their other fallen comrades. There were only twenty-five soldiers left.

The community turned out for the soldier's burial. The families prepared food for a wake, cementing the bond between the two groups.

West asked Mark to take another walk while everyone was eating. "You know, I've given what we talked about a lot of thought."

"And?"

"I think you're wrong about the Chinese not being an army. Think about it. With this much death surrounding us, how would that many Chinese people survive in one area? Unless they were somehow immune to the disease or dropped into the country well after the threat was gone."

"Maybe the biological agent was created to be ethnic specific. It does seem strange that so many Asians randomly survived."

"We did find their supply trucks. One was loaded with

food, weapons, and basic supplies. The other held drugs."

"Drugs? What the hell would they do with those? There's no one to sell them to. And what would they get in return? Obviously money isn't a factor anymore."

"It's strange all right, but one entire truck was packed to the roof with bags of powder."

"What'd you do with it?"

"I set it on fire."

Mark laughed.

"I did find a map, however. It had several areas highlighted, but the words were all in Chinese."

"Any ideas?"

"Only guesses. The map could show where they were heading, or it might show areas where other forces were. Maybe that's where the buyer was for the drugs. I don't know. It's all confusing to me. Maybe you are right. The drugs are what's throwing me."

"I guess that means sending out long-range patrols just to make sure no other group is heading this way."

"Already on it. I'm sending a few men to check out the circled area southeast of here. That may tell us a lot."

Mark didn't speak. He waited for what he knew would be coming.

"We're going to need a lot more recruits," West said.

"I understand that. Just don't come for our people. I will not dissuade anyone who wants to join, but neither will I encourage them. Leave them alone, and just as we have, I promise to come to your aid whenever needed. Deal?"

West nodded. "Deal."

They stopped next to one of the jets.

"Any progress with these?"

"If we can find enough fuel, I think we'll have some people ready to fly them. We learned we can use commercial fuel, if necessary. The jets should make a big difference if we determine we're really at war with someone."

"I pray it never comes to that, but it'll be nice to have them just in case."

Mark stared at the machines for a few moments. Too much death. Too many unanswered questions. *The violence had to stop sometime – didn't it?*

Ninety-Five

BACK HOME THE NEXT day, Mark sat down with Doc, as they called Pam, in the barn away from everyone.

"Is there any way for you to determine what caused the mass deaths?"

"Not without a proper lab. Even then, I'm not sure. My experience with biological or chemical weapons is obviously limited."

"I understand but let me ask you this. Could a bug be engineered to only attack certain races?"

"I have no idea how far scientists have gone in that direction. What are you getting at, Mark?"

"The people we fought were one hundred percent Asian. Some looked Korean, most looked Chinese. However, they were not some foreign army like the general thinks. They were American or at least living in this country. There were no other races in their group. You know how hard it was to build our community this much. How did they happen to find that many Asians in any one area? Also, look around. We have a few Hispanic people, and Lincoln is the only African-American. Even the Horde had few ethnicities. What would make them more susceptible than others? Was this a bio-engineered disease designed to eliminate everyone so only certain people were left?"

"You're talking about global genocide."

He shrugged. "I'm talking about a possible massive nationwide terrorist attack. But who is the initiator and who is the target? Is such a thing even possible?"

"I honestly don't know, but I suppose anything is possible."

"Can you do some research on this?"

"I doubt I could find out anything. My knowledge and resources are too limited. What are you hoping to learn?"

"I wish I knew. I guess the more we know, the better we can deal with whatever this is should it happen again."

"Oh God, you don't think ..."

"That's why I want this kept between us. If someone did do this on purpose, when they see how many of us are still alive, they might try again."

LATER, AS THE sun began its slide down the western sky, Mark looked around the dinner table. The other families had returned home. Those remaining he considered *his* family, blood or not. Regardless of what had caused the nationwide deaths, these people had been lucky so far. They were the random few who had survived the deadly event. He wanted to keep it that way.

He stood and waited until he had their attention. "I want to say how proud I am of all of you and how happy I am that we are all together. You're a very caring and special group of people. When someone reaches out for help, you are there to do whatever you can. I hope we never have to deal with a situation like that again, but it's good to know we will be able to if needed. On a much happier note, I want to officially welcome our new friends, Vince and Agnes, who will be staying in the house next to Lincoln and Jenny. Myron, and my daughter and son, Becca and Bobby. I'm pleased to have all you with us." He laughed. "If we grow anymore, we'll have to build a new house."

"That's all you, Mark," Lincoln said.

The others laughed. It was a glorious sound.

"Anyway, I just want to say thanks for being who you are. I consider us all family." He lifted his water bottle in a toast.

BECCA LOOKED AROUND THE table as her father sat down. The voices around the table were loud and happy. For the first time since Bobby and she had started their journey, she felt at peace within her mind. A warm feeling spread inside as she watched her dad talk to Lynn. He laughed loudly at something she said.

Lynn turned and caught Becca's eye. With a smile, she winked at Becca. Becca returned the smile. Lynn would never be her mother, but she was a good person. Becca liked her. Her mother would like her too.

She panned around the table from face to face, at the collection of people her father had drawn around him. They were all good people. She thought about her brother recovering from his wound in the makeshift hospital set up in the barn. Again, the warm feeling passed through her.

Then her gaze settled on Myron. He was kind of geeky and at least three years younger than her. He wasn't very coordinated or athletic, but didn't that make what he'd done for her even more impressive? She smiled again.

Her father looked at her inquisitively. "What?"

She shook her head and smiled.

Becca was finally home.

Acknowledgements

As in all novels there are a lot of people to thank for their support, encouragement, and knowledge. Even in a world outside the norm where I can make up my own rules there is still research that has to be done. I wish to thank Anthony Anderson of Radio Shack for his help with the radios.

To thank Cindy Turner, Electrical Department Manager at Menards for help understanding solar panels.

And, to thank Tech Sgt. Garrett Ebersole with the 180th Fighter Wing for his assistance in understanding jets and jet fuel.

The 180th Fighter Wing of the Ohio Air National Guard has a long and honored history and the people of Northwest Ohio are proud they are part of the community.

Last, I would like to thank EJ, Bill and Jayne of Rebel e Publishers for taking on this project and doing such a great job of making this thriller available for your enjoyment.

About the Author

Having spent 35 years as a teacher and 25 years as the owner/operator of an Italian Restaurant, Ray now spends his time, reading, writing, hiking, cooking, and playing the harmonica.

You can reach him at raywenck.com.

Also by Ray Wenck

Teammates, Teamwork, Home Team, Randon Survival, Warriors of the Court

And for more from Ray Wenck ...

Please turn the page for a preview of the next book in the *Random Survival* series, *The Endless Struggle*

The Endless Struggle

Ray Wenck

One

"Do you see them." Caryn's voice was near panic, again.

"Shh!" Mel said in a hushed tone, but forceful look. "Get down and don't move," she commanded. "And don't make a sound." Her gaze held the tall blonds, until the woman nodded. Mel moved behind a large, old oak, crouched and scanned the long spans of open ground they'd just covered.

Both women fought to control their heavy breathing after the long run. Caryn pulled her knees up tight to her chest, wrapping her arms around them. She lowered her head and leaned against the small birch she hid behind.

Looking through her small binoculars, Mel panned along the woods to the south. Something dark flashed between the trees. She spotted four more dark forms moving away from them and knew they had taken the bait. She relaxed and hoped Tara would be safe. The ache in her heart again made her wonder whether separating had been the right thing to do. But Tara had been adamant and was off before Mel could voice her concern or offer or an alternative plan.

Seeing Mel stiffen Caryn must have thought the men were coming for them. "Oh God!"

Mel heard Caryn's cry. "Relax, she said, more forceful

then intended. "I don't see anyone. We might be okay."

Caryn lifted her head. Tears filled her eyes. Upon seeing the welled eyes Mel rolled hers. *God, the woman was so annoying.* "Come on, girl, after all we've been through you have to be well past tears by now."

"I can't help it. I'm not like you."

Mel bristled. She hated being termed different. "What's that supposed to mean? Because I'm gay, is that what you're saying?"

Caryn wiped a sleeve across her face. "No, that's not what I mean … because you're so strong, and, and brave. I wish I could be more like you. I hate being afraid all the time."

Mel felt a little guilt seep in. For two weeks now, ever since she'd found Caryn cowering in a basement, Mel had been riding her. She was too slow, too weak, too girlie, too wimpy, but Caryn was right, she was not like her. This high-bred suburban princess had probably never had to work for anything in her life. But Mel knew work … work of all kinds. But the work that had been the hardest and meant to most was the fight for acceptance and equality — and to Mel that fight was never ending.

She stood and walked to Caryn. Sighing, she sat in front of her, set her rifle on the ground and reached out, taking Caryn's hands. "Look, Caryn, I'm sorry if it seems like I'm being mean to you, but if we're going to survive we have to all be tough and help each other. If you're afraid all the time and we have to watch out for you, you become a liability and put us in danger. You understand?"

Caryn's tear streaked face lifted from her knees. Her red eyes looked on Mel. "Then what, you kill me?"

Mel dipped her head frustrated. "No, that's never going to happen. What I'm saying is, if you don't conquer your fears you could get somebody else killed.

You don't want that and we don't want that."

"But, how do I conquer them. I've never done the things you and Tara do. I don't want to be a burden, but every time something happens, I freeze up."

"I know it's not easy, but fear can only control you if you let it. You have to force it someplace in your head where you can lock it away. I wish we had extra bullets we could spare to let you practice shooting, but we can't afford to. Besides, the noise might draw unwanted attention."

Mel stood to check the field again. "I think we're safe. They're following Tara. But that might not last. We have to get as far away as possible, before they decide to come looking for us." She reached a hand down and helped Caryn up, the heavy backpack the blond wore made the effort a strain. Since Caryn was always afraid, and not much use for defense, they had her carry the heaviest bag, so Tara and Mel could keep their hands and movements free. The two women stood close. "I promise Melissa, I'll work on it. I don't want to be trouble for you."

Mel nodded and looked away. She didn't believe for an instant Caryn was capable of overcoming her fears, but she was a survivor, and from what they'd seen over the past month's travels precious few of them were left. Mel would not turn her back on Caryn, but she wasn't about to go easy on her.

"Come on, we'll go straight through these woods."

"What about Tara? She could be in trouble."

Mel frowned. She'd been thinking the same thing. Tara had taken off in the hopes of leading their pursuit away from them. Since no one followed Mel and Caryn it must have worked. But was she safe? They'd heard no shots, but that might not mean anything. The men chasing her wouldn't want to shoot, she was too great a prize, but, Tara wouldn't go down with a fight. Mel

332

could only pray Tara was safe and would come back to her, them.

Caryn boosted the pack higher on her back and moved off. After one more look behind Mel slid the glasses in a pocket and followed. She watched Caryn move. The woman had more physical strength than she realized. Mel knew the pack was heavy, yet Caryn walked quite upright, showing no signs of the burden. Nor did she complain about its bulk.

She was right about them being different though. Where Caryn was tall and willowy, Mel was short and stocky. Caryn was pretty and her hair color was obviously natural. Mel was plain, somewhat muscular and wore her hair almost military short. Tara was a combination of them both.

Tara flew helicopters in the Army. She was on leave, waiting for word of her new assignment when the world changed. To Mel, no one was tougher than Tara. A poster child for the female warrior, she had certainly proved herself since the two had met more than a month ago. A lot of raw power was packed in that small, black frame. She was the ultimate butch woman, except, to Mel's great disappointment, she wasn't lesbian. Still, it was hard for Mel to take her eyes off Tara.

Should we leave some sort of trail for Tara?"

"She'll find us." Mel pressed forward, passing Caryn to take the lead.

"How? She has no idea where we are."

"Don't worry, she's trained. If we keep walking straight, she'll catch up to us. She led those animals south. When she loses them she'll double back. Have confidence in her skills. You've seen what she's capable of."

Caryn shuddered. She remembered all right ... every night in her dreams. "I know she's good, but I think I'll throw in a prayer too."

Mel gave a derisive snort. "Knock yourself out. It can't hurt."

They continued on for perhaps an hour. Behind her, a plastic cap clicked open. Caryn had opened a water bottle. "How much water do we have left?" she asked without stopping.

"Eight bottles, I think."

"Man, we're going to have to find a new supply."

Something touched her back. Mel reached over her shoulder taking the bottle. She drank two large gulps, looked at the remains and took a small sip. With a third of the water left she handed the bottle back.

Early September had stayed August hot. The trees still a thick and green canopy making it difficult for anyone to see them. However, the reverse was also true. They might not notice anyone in pursuit until too late. A squirrel darted up a tree. Over head light pierced the green umbrella. Birds chirped, lending the feeling of normalcy. And everything was normal in the world, except for the people—both the lack of and the survivors.

They'd met their share of people along the way. Some were very nice and offered refuge, some, like the band of men they met the night before, had their own agenda. When the three women first came across the encampment they were hopeful, but after looking closer, they noticed the camp was made up of mostly men and a few women. One of them looked to be twelve to fourteen. They all looked haggard and unkempt, their eyes hollow and haunted, expressions blank. But, it was the look of fear and the ever so slight shake of the head of the tall, dark-haired woman that had caught Tara's attention.

They thanked the men, whose eyes wandered freely over the three women, but begged off their invitation to spend the night in the safety of the compound, saying they had to be elsewhere. The men seemed to accept their excuse, but early in the morning, Tara spotted the posse, and the chase began.

"Caryn would you hand me a granola bar, please." To get the bar, Caryn would have to stop and take the bag off her back. That would stop their progress. "Never mind, I'll get it." She went behind Caryn, unzipped a pocket and dug inside. She pulled one out and was about to zip the pocket closed when she stopped. "You want me to get you one?"

"No thanks' I'll have one when we break."

"It might be a while."

"That's all right, I'll survive."

Mel closed up and took the lead. She crunched and tried to remember the last time she'd seen Caryn eat something. Mel rolled that thought around for a while. The pack held two narrow honey and oat bars. Mel finished one and half of the second. She held it behind. "I can't eat no more. Finish this for me."

"No, that's all right. You should eat it."

"Why's that?" She made a sudden stop and turned. Caryn ran into her.

"What?"

"Why should I eat it instead of you?"

Caryn shrugged. "You need it more to keep up your strength."

"And you don't? When was the last time you ate?"

She shrugged again.

"You've been purposely skipping meals haven't you?'

"It's like you said, I'm a burden. You and Tara deserve most of the food."

Mel looked up and muttered, "I can't believe this." When she dropped her eyes they had a hard edge to them. "You think you're a burden now? How much of a burden will you be when we have to carry you? We won't leave you. So you'll just hinder our movements and our defensive capabilities. You think you're doing the right thing, but you're not. That food is for all of us to share. We're a team. Now, eat this before I cram it down your throat."

With a timid hand Caryn took the bar.

"And you'd better eat all of it." She turned and started walking again. Behind, the sound of the crunch was hard to hide. She smiled. A few minutes later, Caryn said, "Thank you."

"No problem."

They walked on until dusk and found a place to make camp, hoping Tara would appear soon.

Made in the USA
Coppell, TX
23 June 2022